Thane

By

Janey Rosen

This book is intended strictly for readers over the age of 18 due to the adult content and themes portrayed. The views expressed and topics within this book are not the opinions nor views of the author. The author does not condone acts of violence in any shape or form against another person unless consensual, safe and sane. The author does not condone nor wish to glorify rape or deprivation of liberty but neither does she believe that such heinous subjects should not be addressed in literature. Literacy, in the author's opinion, is a channel by which to free one's mind and explore topics both pleasurable and uncomfortable, even taboo, just as motion pictures do on a daily basis. This is not advocating that which is wrong, instead it is opening up to discussion and awareness its existence.

ISBN-10: 1539791858

ISBN-13: 978-1539791850

For my husband, my family and friends who have never grumbled when I'd rather write than be sociable. For my loyal readers who are walking this path with me and who have faith in my writing even when I throw them a curve ball such as this book. For my fabulous and dedicated street team: Jane, SJ, Jodie, Emma, Katie, Lindsey. For my Twitter team: Bethy, FC, Becky, Scarlett, all of you - thank you all and much love.

–Janey

Becoming Freya

Betty

With an indignant jut of her chin, Betty tugged down her black faux leather skirt over her ass and breathed through her anger as the dick scurried away, tucking his shirt into his pants. It wasn't the first time a man had slapped her and it wouldn't be the last; it was what it was, went with the territory. No sense dwelling on the bad days, as her mom used to say before the liquor mostly talked for her.

Shoving the fifty bucks in her purse she was grateful that she'd eat today, so a small slap was worth it, right? She needed to toughen up, wear her big girls' panties, apply fresh lip gloss and get the hell out of this alleyway. Still early evening, if she worked hard maybe she'd go wild and take the night off. Heck, maybe she'd check into a motel and pretend she was on vacay like the time Mom took her to Maine way back when. She more than deserved it and besides, she stank like a fucking fish market.

Rubbing the top of her ass, Betty scooped up her purse from the ground. It wasn't the cold hard wall that the prick had taken her against that was making her back hurt like a bitch, it was countless sleeps on hard ground and couch-surfing to blame.

A soft bed. Just one night. Heaven.

Taking a compact mirror from her purse she puckered up and slicked on a dash of hot pink gloss, smacking her lips before pulling them into a practised smile. Dabbing a little powder over her reddening cheek, she thought that she would do; most times they weren't fussy anyways. It was more about the pussy than the pout.

"Ah, there you are."

The mirror clattered to the ground. "Well look at you," she said, bending down to retrieve the cracked mirror, her tits almost tumbling from the scoop of her top. "How are you today?" Curse her luck. Seven years, plus the cost of a new compact.

"I'm well," he replied, his entire frame filling the width of the narrow passage that ran between Dan's Bar and the 24/7 store.

The sun hanging low in the sky had thrown him into silhouette. "Are you looking for some fun, mister?"

"How old are you, girl?"

"Nineteen," replied Betty. "Old enough to know how

to scratch that itch of yours."

"Too young to be leading this life."

Betty scoffed. "Excuse me? There are girls barely out of middle grade doing the same shit as me, so don't judge what you don't know."

The big man stepped closer and reached out both hands, flattening his palms on the wall either side of her head, blocking her exit. Betty could just about make out his face now. Squinting up into his coal-dark eyes she shuddered. She couldn't be this unlucky twice in one day. Taking a deep breath she widened her smile.

"Why aren't you home some place safe?" he asked.

Something didn't feel right about this trick. Pinching her brow in a frown Betty quipped, "Funny you should say that. I was just on my way, so if you'll excuse me…"

"Are those yours?" The man nodded to the small pile of all-sorts in a boarded-up doorway behind her.

Truth was, that shit was all she owned now, it was hers and she wasn't about to have him rifling through it. "No."

He craned his corded neck and threw her a crooked smile. "Are you certain, girl?"

Betty swallowed. Her breathing quickened. Looking for a way out, her eyes darted left to right, over her shoulder to the tall metal grill and garbage cans then back to him. "Please," she whispered. "I've had a shitty day."

The giant widened his stance, biceps bulging like soccer balls from beneath a khaki tee. Gracing a magazine page he would be chiseled black perfection but in person he was menacing, intimidating. The look on his face screamed pure danger.

Betty squeezed her thighs together, she was going to pee herself. "Please, let me be."

Ignoring her plea he asked simply, "What is your name?"

"B…Betty."

"Betty." He rolled her name over his tongue and nodded. On a deep sigh he told her, "I think it's time to say goodbye to Betty."

"What?" Heart thrumming against her ribs, Betty shrank against the wall, the big man closing what little distance there was until his weight pressed into her. Instinctively she jerked her knee, slamming it up between his thighs. On a huffed curse he stumbled back a pace. Seizing the chance to run she pushed to her side, purse slipping from her grip. There wasn't time to scream. Or it didn't enter her mind to do so. Survival. Life or death. She would never, *never,* work this patch again.

A vice clamped around her wrist. Pain ripped through her shoulder, it being almost torn from its socket. Now the urge to scream was instinctive, bubbling in her throat as adrenaline spiked.

I'm gonna die.

Momma!

Her eyes followed the passage of his hand as it travelled in a steady arc from his side as if in slow motion, through the air, punching into her stomach with a sharp sting. He'd stabbed her? Her breath caught. Betty looked down. When he took his hand away she saw a syringe clasped in his fist, the bloody needle protruding between his fingers. Her eyes locked on his and, as darkness pulled at the edges of her vision, those pitch dark eyes creased in a smile. "What have you done?"

"Relax sweet Betty. I'm taking you home."

Orientation

Thanatos

He took her freedom to set her free. No one understood this irony better than Thane himself.

The truth was that Thane already knew so much about her, knew her better than she knew herself. It wasn't arrogance to believe that, it was simply a fact. He'd been watching and waiting for her, you see, for what felt like an eternity but was actually little more than a few days, a week perhaps; he'd lost all track of time. Now, finally, here she was. He could hardly believe it.

Into his large fist, Thane clutched a lock of the girl's hair and marvelled at the starkness of each snow-white strand against the rich ebony of his palm. He'd honestly never encountered a woman as beautiful as her and, up close, she was even more lovely than he'd observed from a distance.

There was only one name befitting. He would call this one 'Freya:' the goddess of love, destiny and fertility. This would be the one from whom he would breed an heir to take on the mantel of power that Thane would teach him. It was honestly all he wanted. His purpose, if you will. The reason for all of this. Why he gave up his privileged life in the first place and escaped the broken world outside of the compound.

Drawing his hand back from between the bars of the cage, he allowed his full lips to tug up in the smallest smile of renewed hope. His fingertips brushed the flare of his nostrils as he inhaled the sweetness of her flesh. Jasmine and moss. Peaty earthiness. Nature and the freshness of a new morning. How apt that she should smell of new beginnings and mother nature. He chose well, very well indeed. He would be careful not to crush this girl like he'd done to Sirona. A muse should be an inspiration, instead Sirona had been a liability whose end had been largely her own fault. Still, he had regrets, lessons learned from mistakes that wouldn't be repeated this time.

Turning to Boy he snapped his fingers and the boy limped to his master's feet with bowed head. Boy didn't speak because he was not a rule breaker. Instead he waited patiently for the honor of serving Thanatos who called himself Thane, and who was good to him for the most part.

"Boy, this is Freya. Take great care of this one. She's special."

***

Boy chanced a glimpse at the tight muscles that rippled beneath the glossy black skin of his master's abdomen, and let his eyes wander to the dark discs of his nipples. He wished, as he always did, that he'd been blessed with a body like Thane's instead of his weedy one.

Nodding his acceptance of the task appointed to him, Boy shuffled over to the cage. He looked down at the new girl and wondered what was special about her, how long she'd cry; it would be easier for her if she stopped sooner rather than later.

"Ensure that she's washed and fed, she's far too thin. Scrawny even." Thane locked his gaze on that of the boy. "Come and find me when you're done." Thane cut the boy a look that dared him to challenge, then strode to the door where he punched in a code. The door slid open, daylight piercing the gloom of the small room, and he was gone.

The young man watched the towering man leave, marvelling at the broad sweep of those shoulders, the vast back that tapered down to a neat V. With Thane gone, the room seemed to grow in space without the big man's presence filling it, even when the door slid closed with a clang as the lock engaged–how empty the place now felt.

The boy gripped the cool iron bars of the cage and dropped to a crouch, wincing as the metal cuff bit into his left ankle as a reminder of his fuck-up. His fingers probed beneath the lip of metal to rub at the smarting flesh over his bone and he wished now that he could do better. He couldn't help his lust and urges, try as he did. And, as much as he wanted Thane's guardianship, every mistake he made seemed to drive a wedge between them.

This was his chance.

This one was special, Thane had said so. He'd be especially careful in the hope that he'd maybe earn some of Thane's time or, better still, Syn's attentions. The thought made his cock lurch. To take his mind off of his predicament, he fixed his gaze on the new girl. She really was scrawny, he was right. Another hooker. Always hookers. Well, hookers or crack heads or both. Her face was blotchy with crying, mascara all smudged up in one heck of a mess. She was pretty though, he could see past all the shit and snot to the bluest eyes he ever did see. The bloodshot whites made her irises pop. He'd stripped her, Thane. She looked as new as if she'd popped straight from her mom's womb. He marvelled at her skin, milk-white contrasted only by the brown rope that wove around her limbs this way and that.

"Hey, I'm Boy. It's best you don't cry, Freya," he whispered with a tip of his head as he watched her slim shoulders heave. "I'm gonna look after you, kind of like a friend if you'll let me be your friend."

Freya

Hearing the softer voice, Betty raised her head and looked up at him through the gritty swell of her eyes. He had to be younger than her. Eighteen. Nineteen at a push. Same age as her but Betty had lived ten lives to this kid's one. She wanted to rub away her tears, hide her fear, but her hands were caught up by something. Her wrists smarted like fire, her arms ached and she wanted so bad to stretch her legs but the fucker had done something to them. The big man had gone and she'd finally felt able to breathe again, to chance a look, to *think* and to clear her head. "Water," she croaked, her lips and tongue as dry as if she'd licked the Sahara. "Please," she added when he didn't move.

Silently the young man called Boy rose to his feet and hobbled away out of sight. He returned and, when he crouched down again, she could see that he held a small tin cup which he passed through the bars with care. Leaning forward he pressed the rim of the cup to her lips and tipped it so that cool water flooded over her tongue. Betty swallowed and drank until the cup couldn't tip up any further without spilling water over her face and onto the soft cushion that she was lying face down on.

Boy sighed and took the cup, setting it down at his feet. "It's always more difficult when he hog ties them," he muttered, perhaps to himself.

Betty didn't know what hog tying meant but knew that it hurt so fucking bad after all this time. How long? Hours, days, she didn't know. Hours. Yes hours, because she was certain that if it was days her stomach would be growling and it wasn't. "Thank you." Boy seemed different to the asshole who took her. Could she trust him? He was eying her tits like a fresh little virgin. Craning her neck up she narrowed her eyes.

"You're welcome," he replied then chewed his lip. "You've gotta have a bath. Eat. I'm allowed to untie you but you have to promise to be good."

The news that she was to be released from this hell hole was music to her ears. Free, she could escape. She had to think clearly but Betty didn't know how strong she would be or even if her legs would hold her up when her feet felt so numb. This kid, this young man who looked younger than her nineteen years, seemed like she could use him. She chanced a weak smile and told him, "I'm Betty. What's your name?" Make it personal. She'd watched enough TV when back home to know how this shit played out. Unable to see his face now, it hurt her neck to crane it up to where she was sure he was watching her still.

"My name's Boy, I told you," he said. "And your name's not Betty, it's Freya now. You'd better get used to it."

Her mind raced. Betty was not gone, she was there and she was shit scared. "I am *Betty*," she affirmed. "You've got a name other than Boy. What is it?"

"Don't matter." The boy stood and Betty heard the jangle of keys. Screwing her eyes shut she tried to control her breathing, the rising panic, waiting as he unlocked the cage she was trapped in like a fucking animal. A loud clank of metal on metal made her jump, she became aware that Boy loomed over her but she didn't look yet. Couldn't look. Her wrists were tugged and pulled until metal bit into skin and the tears pricked her eyes again. She really needed to hold her shit together. It was so tempting to give in to fear, let it consume her, welcome back the foggy bleakness that lingered on the fringes of her consciousness.

Each limb was yanked in such a way that she swore he'd dislocate something. It wasn't the first time she'd felt pain of course, but the pain of her past was anticipated. She'd always felt in control until now. Even the pigs who'd used her had been wrapped around her little finger to a certain extent; oftentimes she'd tease them to a frenzy just because she could. She was that powerful, or so she had thought.

"Sorry if I'm hurting you," said Boy.

The question being: was he saying sorry because he hurt her, or did he hurt her on purpose and sorry was just a meaningless nothing? There was a world of difference, and that difference was trust. Could she trust him? She felt his hands brushing against the bare skin of her hip, her buttocks, thighs and shoulders as he worked loose the bindings. Where were her clothes? The realization that she was stark fucking naked fell like a rock to her stomach. Her hand dropped between her legs, arm over her tits. It was almost laughable how embarrassed, how vulnerable she felt, I mean she was a hooker for crying out loud. A shudder ran down her spine. What was he going to do to her?

"There you go," he said as he gripped her around her waist and pulled her upwards.

As her body unfolded she pressed the balls of her still numb feet into the cushion and rocked back onto her heels. Straightening out the stoop of her shoulders felt like an impossible task but she clenched her jaw, pushed up her chin and stretched her spine with a crunch. Finally opening her eyes, Betty found herself staring into gentle pale brown orbs–kind eyes, her mom would say; you can always see a person's soul through their eyes because they are the windows. She saw in those twinkling irises maybe a vulnerability that matched hers. She didn't flinch when he lifted her by the waist and swung her out of the cage onto cold concrete; anything was better than being confined. Her legs held her with a tremble before her knees buckled. Boy tightened his hold on her and pulled her to his chest, her cheek pressing into the warm curve of his neck and for a moment they stood in an awkward embrace, the fabric of his simple calico shirt and pants course against her skin.

"Sorry." Boy's apology coincided with a hardening that rested between them from groin to a little higher than her belly button.

Betty's eyes widened and when she pulled away he didn't stop her. Reaching out a hand, she grasped the strong frame of the cage to regain her balance and said, "Don't touch me. Where are my fucking clothes?"

The young man appeared to tense, a blush blooming over his cheeks. In the dull light from an overhead bulb, Betty could see a dusting of whiskers over his jaw. The thought struck her from nowhere, that her brother Cody would be shaving properly now if he was alive. She then tried hard to un-think the bad thoughts that seeped in against her will. The preacher had been right, she was the devil's spawn, she was getting what she deserved just as he'd said she would over Cody's casket.

She could actually still hear him spit the words and see his finger wagging and his face redden when he'd spat, "Cursed be he that lieth with his sister, and all the people shall say, Amen. Deuteronomy, Chapter 27, and now your brother lies here. Dead because of you." She'd stood her ground even as he'd continued, "For whosoever shall commit any of these abominations, even the souls that commit them shall be cut off from among their people. Leviticus Chapter 18. You are the devil's spawn and you have no place here amongst us." As she'd walked away from the cemetery that frigid winter's day, the preacher's voice had boomed loud and fearsome over the tombstones. "The Lord will strike you down as he struck this sinner!"

"Freya. Your clothes are gone, I'm sorry."

Her eyes snapped back to the boy's. "I'm not staying stark bollock naked. Get. Me. My. Clothes."

"I can't do that, he's put them away seeing how you don't need them now."

"Put them away? That skirt…You're sorry?" Betty huffed a sardonic laugh.

"Yeah," he said with a shake of his head. "Shit's gonna be hard, you know? I mean, to start with and all. Come with me."

"Over my dead fucking body." Her eyes slid around the room then back to him. "Where am I, anyway?"

"Compound."

"What compound? Where?"

Boy shook his head, eyes darting towards the doorway. "Don't ask questions, I can't tell you anything, it's up to him to."

"I'm fucking scared, okay?" Appeal to whatever shrivelled heart he had. Play. The. Game.

He nodded like she should be scared.

"Will he kill me?"

Silence.

That's a yes, then. Her eyes darted around the room as she weighed up her options. With no idea of the layout of the place, Betty decided her best option was to follow him and see what lay ahead. Hope for a door, a window. Anything.

She hung back a pace or two behind him as he walked through a small archway to the rear of the room, not where the giant black guy had gone but another route that wound low and narrow. As they walked–he with an old man's hobble and she with a shuffle, dizzy and disorientated–artificial light was outshone by a burst of welcomed daylight that turned the stone walls of the tunnel from clay-brown to mellow peach. The odd thing was, the place didn't look as old as it was fashioned to be. Betty didn't know much about houses and all, but it looked to her like a movie set, made to look old. As the tunnel ended they stepped into a room which appeared to have no end, ringed by potted plants and ferns that reached high and wide in a tangle of vibrant greens. In the center of this place, cobalt blue water glistened with soft ripples in a circular pool edged in sparkling quartz tile. Betty looked up at a glass dome above their heads that threw shards of sunlight, sprinkling diamonds over the pool's surface. The rays warmed her skin as she tipped up her chin and closed her eyes. A soft breeze from somewhere rustled leaves and flicked up wispy ends of her hair. A breeze meant an open door or window. A way out.

Boy coughed.

Betty opened her eyes to see that the dude had shed his shirt and pants which now pooled at his feet. She tried not to let her gaze travel down his slim form but found herself staring at the soft thatch of hair that crowned his penis. That he was aroused was apparent and her hand moved to cover the juncture of her thighs as she shifted her weight from foot to foot and wondered what to do. This wasn't happening to her. This…this was so fucked up, her mind scrambling between shutting down and summoning the last bit of fight deep inside of her. Breaths came in short gasps, barely enough to fill her lungs that felt like lead weights in her chest.

She worked the street. Tricks with bad breath and

rotten teeth were who she rolled with. She knew how to deal with that. Fake it and take their money. This. This was something else. Naked, exposed, so fucking vulnerable.

"Take my hand," he said without a hint of threat and she did so because now her mind was a thousand places but here. "Trust me."

As though in a trance, she followed behind the kid as he walked to the edge of the pool and descended a few steps down into the water. Why wouldn't he tell his name? Everyone had a name. Then she remembered that she never used her own given name; the thought made her screw her eyes shut to stem fresh tears. She wouldn't show her fear, never had, never would. You let anyone in close enough to smell your fear, then they have the advantage. You're screwed. Screw or be screwed - that was her mantra.

She would play his fucking game. He wasn't the enemy here, right?

Tightening his grip on her hand he pulled her down another step and another and another. Betty stopped, toes curling around the lip of the cold tiles. "No."

His body twisted until he faced her. The turquoise water rippled its reflection over his pale skin. His eyes implored her.

Again, no.

His tugging was urgent.

"It's not me you should be scared of," he whispered. "We're both here because here is where he brought us."

"Why?" Why didn't he get the hell out of here? Why was he okay with this fucked up shit?

"Why?" His head tipped on the question. His reply

came simply delivered: “Because this is where I’m safe.”

“I don’t understand.”

“You will.” His mouth twisted in a smile, a tuft of mussy hair falling over his forehead. “I know it’s fucked up for you right now but it’ll make sense in time. He’s doing what’s right by us. Always what’s right.”

Betty looked down at her hand in his, her pulse beating fast, irregular. He was so much like her brother, so like him. Same scruffy hair, same eyes that screamed total innocence contrary to his actions. Same twisted mind. Vulnerable yet predatory. Her fingers slipped out of his. She took a step backwards, up the step until water lapped around her calves. His palms opened, lips parted on a sigh. The motion - the water, the situation, her head swam until the gritty Betty - the Betty who would fight until her last breath - was going to pass out and she welcomed that. Bring. It. On.

Taking her hand again, Boy pulled her more determinedly and Betty let him as a fog took hold of her mind. Whatever the fuck the dude had stuck her with was some trippy shit. Soon they were both submerged to their waists, it did not appear that the pool grew deeper than it was right here. So, this was it: she would die of drowning. Of all the deaths she ought to face, this was not one she’d ever imagined. Rape. Strangulation, sure. As a hooker she’d feared it all. Not this. Never this. Her balance was off, the whole place swayed to and fro, to and fro, the drug clawing at her insides, sucking at the last of her control.

Boy reached out and cupped one hand at Betty’s nape, the other on her belly. She found herself eased backwards until her feet rose and Boy supported her across his forearms so that she floated in the warm pool. She could not deny that her aches and pains lessened as she tried to relax, to just allow herself to be, letting Boy and the water take the burden of her weight. She'd play along. Make him think she was docile, submissive. Her long blond hair splayed over the surface, ripples of water lapping over her tightening nipples. It was all so surreal she wondered if this was a dream, a nightmare of some kind. She'd tried dope once and the feeling she'd had then was not dissimilar: kind of out of her body. Maybe the shot in her arm was heroin. There were worse ways to die. She knew that there were trafficking rings where they got you hooked on heroine. Was that what this was?

Drugs crawled deep in her head like spiders. Too tired, Betty closed her eyes, embraced the feeling and let herself be free of this place as the boy began to hum a melody. As he started to rotate, her arms floated away from her sides and she was flying high above Boston, looking down upon a small raggedy girl of nineteen who was leaning into a car and kissing a stranger. She left them behind, way below, and soared upward to the clouds, the sun beating hot over her face, and there he was, framed by a halo of light. Cody. Round and round she spun so slowly as nearer she flew to her brother. His face was perfect again. Gone was the mottled blue around his now pink lips that called to her on a smile, arm outstretched beneath a swathe of golden silk. His fingertips touched hers and she was in his arms, spinning, spinning, floating and she looked up to tell him she loved him but not in the same way as he loved her. She wished she'd told him that for a long time. A scream caught in her throat as his pupils constricted to pin-points then bled out into black circles, a noose tightening about his neck.

"Freya!"

She was thrashing and clawing, water seeping into her nostrils, down her throat until she couldn't breathe. Pain. Desperation as her lungs bunched inside her chest.

"What has happened?"

The boom of a man's voice above her. No no no….

"Went under the water."

"Fool!"

Her body grew lighter and she was floating again but this time her journey ended as she was crashed against something warm and hard yet slick against her cheek. Opening her eyes, Betty blinked until her vision cleared and she saw a wall of ebony brown. Her pulse thrummed in her ears as she lay her hands upon the wall beside her mouth, and let her fingers nestle in amongst black curls of hair. She coughed and spluttered as she was held tight. When she could take a clear breath, she sucked in air laced with a heady musk. Tilting up her head, she saw that she was in the giant man's arms. Fear tainted any feeling of security as he carried her through the water and lay her down on the cool tile.

Towering over her, the man almost blocked out the sun with the breadth of him. Framed by a glass roof, the sun's rays threw a crown around his head. A halo lit the hard edges of his jaw. His chest heaved, muscles popped and nostrils snorted like a wild animal as his coal dark eyes flashed with something deadly. Betty gasped. He was the most manly man she'd ever seen, pure testosterone and danger. A heat spread between her thighs with Betty totally unable to control it. What the hell was wrong with her?

Beside the man was Boy. Boy was crying and shaking

but the giant didn't hit him even though he looked livid, a pulse hammering along a prominent vein cording his neck. The fucker who took her bent low, his voice a deep timber. "You had a panic attack, little one. You could have drowned." He slid his eyes to Boy who stepped back and hugged himself smaller. "I'll take no such risks with you again." Folding over, he scooped Betty up and carried her with little effort, his shovel-like hands of such wide spread as to cover her entire buttocks with his fingers and palms.

Her body trembling with fear, with biting cold, Betty hooked her hands around the man's wide neck and laced her fingers at his nape where his shaved hair bristled against her palms. Glancing up at his strong jawline and firm set of his mouth it crossed her mind that just one bite could end her. More alarming still was the notion that maybe she wanted that.

Heart of Stone

Thanatos

The rage was immeasurable but he bit it back, locked it away until he could deal with Boy later, and deal with him he would. This wasn't the first time the lad had fucking let him down. Now though his primary concern was Freya. His obsession. She held the key to better things. A future. Of all the taken girls in the past who had tried, not even Sirona had been able to unlock his heart of stone and, in the end, her demise had been as inevitable as night following day. Still, he lived with regret for what should have been.

As though her bones were made of glass, Thane gently

laid Betty on the Egyptian cotton sheets where he had once brought Sirona, the only other girl to have ever been in his bed since he built the compound. Bending forward, he adjusted the slight girl until she rested well against a stack of pillows. Tenderly he pulled up a down comforter and rubbed her arms to bring warmth to her still damp skin. He would have Boy bring her food and she would stay in bed until tomorrow morning. Tomorrow would be a caged day as Thane had matters that he must attend to outside of the compound. For now, he drew himself up to every inch of his six-feet-nine and narrowed his eyes at Freya. "Rest. You also need to eat and drink. That's not a request."

The girl offered no resistance and so he strode from the room that contained only the carved four-poster bed and a scattering of rugs strewn over a maple floor. At the entrance he paused to take a languid look at his new girl. He dared not think about what could have happened to her in the pool, but the need to punish Boy was an urgent one. His attention was drawn from Freya by a soft footfall. He turned to greet Syn, his closed confidante, with outstretched arms into which she quietly slipped. Syn was herself a large woman both in stature and personality so for her to be quiet was disconcerting.

"Ah, my dearest Syn," said Thane, looking down at her with genuine affection. "Did Boy send you to guard the girl?"

Syn's crimson lips spread into a smile that rarely graced her face since her friend Sirona had died. With a toss of scarlet hair she pressed her palms to Thane's chest and nodded. "I heard that you have found a Freya and I wanted to come and see for myself," she said.

Thane nodded to the bed where the girl watched them with wide eyes. "She's caused my heart to nearly stop and she's been here just one day," he sighed. "Guard her well," he added, "She's a feisty one."

"Aren't they all," Syn agreed with a frown. "She'll not be leaving this room, trust me."

"Is the boy bringing food?"

"Yes. When he's done moping like a sad little puppy. Honestly, half the time I don't know whether to pet him or slit his throat."

Thane paused a beat and then nodded. "I wonder about him. Perhaps I should just take him back, see how long he lasts out there. It astounds me how soon they forget what they were - the hell I took them from."

"He'd be dead in a heartbeat, don't do that to him. He loves you as we all do. Never doubt that, Thane."

"I don't know." Thane scrubbed a hand over his jaw. "First Sirona, now Boy. It's not how I envisioned it, you know."

"Focus. Remember why you're doing this."

"*Why* am I?"

A small smile reached Syn's mouth. "For the greater good and because you're a good man even if sometimes others don't see it."

Reaching out a hand, Thane rubbed his thumb roughly over Syn's cheek. "Always so loyal, so wise."

Syn leant into his touch as her eyes slid to Freya. "Are you sure this is the one?"

He cut a glare and said, "I'm certain of it. No more mistakes, she's the one."

Knowing better than to question him further, Syn merely smiled a little wider but, when she looked at Freya, she narrowed her eyes and saw the girl wince. "Leave her with me. I'll watch her like a hawk."

Thane left Syn guarding his girl and went to his personal rooms where he would shower and spend quiet time in solitude, praying to the gods that his coupling with Freya would produce the son and heir that had become his primary need for so long. Closing the door, he tugged at the drawstring of his cotton pants and stepped out of the puddle of wet cloth. Clenching his fists at his sides he tensed the muscles in his powerful arms and rolled his shoulders. He knew that tonight he wouldn't sleep. Tomorrow night would be a full moon–he should rest while he could–but it was always the same; the madness took hold of him when the moon shone full and bright in the sky and the night before he feared its arrival. This wasn't some archaic mythology but a scientifically proven phenomena. At least, that's what the shrinks had said; they'd have also sworn the moon was made of Swiss cheese for the money his father paid them. Obscene. Charlatans.

The need to mate burned fierce and uncontrollable in his loins. Taking the weight of his mighty cock in both palms he looked down at it and afforded it a few languid strokes that did nothing more than fuel his edginess. It was no good. He would take her tonight, fuck waiting.

In the bathroom he punched on the faucet and stepped under the scorching jet, pressing his palms and forehead to the tiles as water hammered against his back like driving rain melding with the storm whipping up inside of him. With a low growl, Thane pumped the steel between his legs with a fury that caused as much pain as it did pleasure and he welcomed both equally. As the first wave of release threatened to consume him, he stopped, drew back his hand, balled it into a fist and slammed it into the wall. The first time that he took Freya would not be gentle but so be it. The thought of ripping the petals from that little flower brought to his mind the pressing need for retribution against Boy. Thane would expel some of this frustration through the boy's punishment and just the thought of this slightly lessened his anger as he completed his shower.

When dry, Thane took from a closet a pair of black cotton pants identical to the last and to all the others that he wore while in the compound. Stepping into them, he pulled the drawstring tight, leaving them slung low on his hips. Even such an action as this caused a tender rub on his cock making him hiss out a breath. Thane padded from his room barefoot as always when at home. In search of Boy, he found him in the kitchen talking to his the last of his muses, Luna. Knowing such dialogue was forbidden, Boy stopped immediately he caught sight of his fearsome master. He didn't see much of Luna and no doubt the temptation to speak to her had been too great. The young woman flushed a deep rouge and hurried about her business of folding dish towels. Thane snapped his fingers and Boy followed with a reticence that incited his master to pull him by the ear all the way to the cage room.

Boy went immediately to the far wall beyond the cage where he positioned his feet close to the chains that would undoubtedly be applied. As Thane crouched his sizeable form in front of Boy, it was all Boy could do not to reach out and wrap himself around his master; the urge to be held was more profound than ever. Even when the great

Thanatos snapped a cuff on Boy's ankle to match the first, still Boy loved him.

Taking the boy by his nape, Thane turned him, slamming his chest firmly into the wall. Testing the boy's shackles to ensure they were sufficiently tight, he fixed the chains in place and cupped the boy's angelic face as it twisted to the side. Forcing a strained smile, Thane asked him, "What am I punishing you for, Boy?"

Boy focused not on Thane's face or eyes, even though he wanted to search those deep ink wells for a glimmer of the love that he knew his master held for him. Looking only at his own naked toes he replied, "I spoke to Luna."

With a pained shake of his head Thane sighed. "Yes it's true that you did that, but the reason for my anger wasn't because of your wilful disregard of my rule of silence. What you did was to allow Freya to be in mortal danger. Didn't you, Boy?"

Boy nodded with a heavy heart because deep down he knew he had done this. "Yes, Thane," he said but offered no explanation for how events had transpired for it was wrong to try to justify his incompetence.

"Yet, knowing that she was still under the effects of sedation, instead of washing her as instructed, you took her into the pool." He shook his head. "You must understand," Thane continued, "that I've searched for a very long time for my Freya and she is more precious to me than the air I breathe. You're fortunate that no harm came to her. Had Freya died, the wrath you'd face would make any punishment that you receive now seem like a frolic in fucking meadows in comparison."

Opening his mouth to speak, Boy thought better of it and pressed his lips together. The truth was that if anything had happened to Freya, he would end his own life himself rather than witness his master suffer the pain of her loss and know that he had failed him.

Without another word uttered between them, Thane took down a cat-o-nine-tails from an iron hook and snapped it over his own palm. Boy jumped. The supple tendrils of deer hide tickled down the young man's spine. Boy's eyelids grew heavy, his breathing slowed as he prepared to drift into his special place. The bite of the cat elicited only a small gasp, after three strikes there was no sound at all.

Returning to Freya's room, Thane stopped at the closed door beside which Syn sat curled in a chair like a cat.

"It's time," said Thane simply as Syn rose to her feet.

"Of course," she replied, her brow creasing in a frown.

"Why are you scowling?" Thane growled. "Speak up, little one."

The flame-haired woman pursed her lips. Thane was more lenient with her than he was with the others but she knew not to overstep the boundaries. Still, it was apparent that something was on her mind.

"I'm not sure she's ready, Thane."

Thane matched her scowl with his own. "*I* will decide this," he said, fists flexing at his sides. He was in no mood for bullshit or to be challenged.

Sensing the tension in him, Syn nodded and turned away to return to her room. She knew that darkness in his stare and feared it still, even two years on.

Thane moved quickly to block her path. "Do not turn your back on me nor leave before I've dismissed you."

Syn's eyes widened - Thane rarely had cause to

reprimand her. "Forgive me," she said. "I wrongly assumed that I was dismissed but I now see that I wasn't."

Sucking in a sharp breath, Thane controlled his impatience and allowed his stance to soften enough that Syn knew she wasn't to be punished. "I want you to go to the cage room where Boy's waiting for you," he told her. "Clean his wounds and apply arnica."

"Yes, Thane."

"When you've done so, you're to continue the boy's education in the ways of sex. I'm not blind to the way he views my body. I know that he's young and hormones are rife but he's innocent to the tastes and pleasures of a woman. Use him as you wish, though tonight you really don't deserve such a treat as him."

Dipping her head did not hide from Thane the wry smile that tugged at the corners of her lips. "As you wish," she muttered, no doubt barely believing her good fortune; it was no secret that she'd wanted to take the boy for some months but thus far had only been permitted to school him in the ways of carnal pleasures through words and text books.

"Go."

"Thank you."

Freya

When her captor had gone, Betty had sat on the bed hugging her knees to her chest as the boy entered the room. She wasn't scared of him but, equally, she knew he'd be no help to her in escaping. He was kind but a pussy who was whipped by his boss, of this she was sure. If it was his boss. Fuck. What the hell kind of place was this? Her first thought was that it was some type of high end whore house. Now, with all the weirdness, Betty was pretty certain it was a cult. She'd heard about them, seen them on the news: crazy dude massacres everyone in the name of some fake-assed belief that it was for the greater good. Megalomaniac mass-murdering freaks just like him. Thane. That being the case, it was even more urgent that Betty should get the heck out of there before she was brainwashed or worse.

Boy had glided into the room like he was on wheels, half naked except for low slung white pants. What was it about not wearing fucking clothes in this joint? In his hands he'd carried a fancy gold tray which he'd set down on a fur rug at the foot of the bed. Her nostrils had filled with a rich, gamey aroma that he told her was venison. Ignoring the food, Betty picked up a glass of milk and eyed it suspiciously. "Not poisoned?"

Boy shook his head, his brows pinching together. "I swear."

She gave it a sniff then drained the glass, wiping her mouth with the back of her hand.

Scooting closer to her, Boy speared chunks of venison with a fork then brought the tines to her pursed lips. She shook her head side to side, cried and struck out but he forced the warm, earthy meat between her lips and teeth then held her jaw clamped shut until she'd had no choice but to chew and swallow and dry heave. "Eat," he barked though his face remained too gentle for the harsh instruction. He'd spent too much time around Thane, it seemed.

"I can't."

"I'll be punished. Please. Please eat it," he urged but

she gagged and retched until finally he took it and the tray away. He looked fucking defeated and, as he walked to the door, Betty saw the angry weals webbing over his back in a lattice. *Jesus Christ. The giant is a fucking monster.*

Betty crawled back to the soft bed and cried herself to sleep, in spite of her considerable efforts to stay awake and watch out for the woman called Syn who looked as dangerous as the man who'd taken her. Her dreams were fitful–her brother, Thane: men's hands pawing over her body. When she woke she was bathed in sweat. Unable to judge if it was night or day she'd assumed that it was night, there were no windows in this vast room.

Sitting herself up, Betty threw the comforter back and swung her legs over the side of the bed. Not knowing when the man or woman would return made her edgy. Had she been 'normal,' Betty would have a family worrying about her by now. Her mom would be calling the cops to file a missing person report. There'd be tears, right? Anxiety and calling of friends. There would be CNN news reports and reporters camped outside a nice neat family home while neighbors spoke of a lovely girl who wouldn't hurt a fly. Facebook posts going viral with messages saying, 'We'll help find her. Share share share!'

But Betty wasn't loved. No-one would even know that she was gone. Hell, she wasn't even Betty, she was born Lacey Porter and had been, for the most part, a nice kid until her dad had left and her mom had turned to drink. If her dad hadn't upped and chased after The Whore, Cody wouldn't have dared to touch her at night when he'd crept from his bed in their closet sized room, when she'd pretended to be asleep. She wouldn't have finally let him have her and he wouldn't have died from shame and she wouldn't have had to run away and become no better than the whore her dad shacked up with. She wouldn't have needed to become Betty if she'd been loved in a wholesome way instead of a disgusting way. If her dad had stayed, and mom was normal and her brother just loved her like she loved him. So many 'ifs' would have kept her safe. Truth of it was, her life was a shitty fucked-up mess. Shitty things happen to shitty people every day on the news like a shit-magnet. No one would miss her and why should they? Whores get what they deserve, everyone thought it so don't pretend otherwise.

The door opened and there he stood, filling the space again. Suddenly her throat was dry and knotted, skin crawling, adrenaline pumping blood to her head with a thump thump at her temples. The sick and twisted thing of it was, she couldn't stop looking at the deep V that started at his hips and vanished beneath the waistband of his black pants. Men's bodies were familiar to her; there wasn't a single body type she hadn't licked and sucked for a few bucks. She'd lost her innocence–if ever she'd possessed it–when she was sixteen and there had been hundreds since, but this man reeked of animalistic sex, of control and power and dominance like she'd never encountered before. If her mom had told her as a kid not to take candy from strangers, then this would have been the stranger she meant. Her mom never said that, by the way.

"You're awake."

"Give the man a slow clap. I want to leave."

"I understand, really I do." He took slow, purposeful steps towards her. "Unfortunately I can't allow it. You're mine now, Freya, and the sooner you accept that, the easier this will be on you."

"My name's Betty and you, mister, are fucking loco."

"Watch your mouth." Stopping at the foot of the bed he cupped the wide angle of his jaw in his palm and looked right at her. *Into* her. "My sanity has been the subject of many a studious shrink's research, Freya. I believe though that sanity is subjective, don't you? I mean, look at you. If you were to be analyzed, do you think a psychiatrist would classify you as insane for allowing your brother to commit incest, enjoying it even? To me that makes you a victim, but you see where I'm going with this."

Betty shook her head and stumbled back onto the bed, shuffling back until her shoulders slammed against wood. Any space she'd hoped to put between them was soon invaded by the man called Thane whose deep inhale sucked the air from the room like a vacuum.

"Stop saying shit like that. Stay away from me." She tucked her knees under her chin and hugged herself small. *He knows. He knows everything about me.* His words peeled her skin back, ripped her chest open and tore her fucking heart out. "You know *Jack shit* about me. You shut your mouth!"

"I can't do that." By now Thane had reached the bed side and appeared to grow to an even greater height.

She could be mistaken but it seemed to her that a smirk pulled at his lips. He was enjoying this so what the hell kind of monster did that make him? "Please. Let me go. I won't say a word to anyone, I promise. Just let me go, let me go, let me go." Breaths quickening. Her fingers curled into her palms as the heels of her hands dug into her eye sockets. *Make him go away…*

Thane blew out a sigh. Betty peered over her hands at his orbs that were seven shades of hooded darkness and she knew. She knew that she was doomed.

Then he delivered just three words. “This. Will. Hurt.”

The Mark of Seax

Thanatos

That she physically shook in his presence only served to make Thane's base need of her more urgent. She looked so fucking vulnerable. Fragile. Broken. Fire that had ignited inside of him the first time he'd seen her now seared through his arteries, singeing his heart and licking white hot heat over his skin. He could take her here, right now. He could destroy her or he could save her. That primal power had every muscle bunching including his cock which was now barely restrained by the waistband of his pants.

He needed to regain control of himself or he'd end her

before she'd begun.

In one effortless move he lifted the girl, swinging her over his shoulder. She resisted as he knew she would. Her small fists drummed against his naked back as she bucked and twisted, hissing like a wild cat tossed in a bath. He tightened his grip on her thighs. When she was ready, he would finally take her to his own suite of rooms; that honor had to be earned. Trust. Reward. Revere. These were his watch words.

Traversing the myriad of passages, finally he kicked open the door to a perfectly square room, illuminated by faux flame torches that operated upon the door opening which triggered them to light. There were numerous benches, racks and overhead, in a neat grid formation, an intricate tracking system from which a series of swings, hooks and pulleys were suspended. For the purpose of their visit tonight he set her down on to a long wooden table that afforded her absolutely no comfort whatsoever. Before she could squirm from his grasp, Thane snapped a pair of leather cuffs around each wrist and fastened the buckles to secure her arms above her head. Repeating the action with her ankles, he sustained a hard kick to his right ribs. "Girl, do *not* anger me," he warned, lip curled, as he tugged the last strap tight.

"Let. Me. Go." Her hips bucked, head thrashing side to side, sea of golden curls now a veil over her puce face.

Being a lover of silence–especially at times such as this–Thane stuffed a wad of black silk into her mouth that he kept in a small drawer beneath the table just for this purpose. He would have preferred not to have to do so but the ensuing hush was a welcome respite from the little cat's hissing. At least he hadn't needed to use a ball gag this time. Yet.

On the wall beside the door hung a large brass bell of the type you might see on an old sailing ship. From it was strung a rope with wooden pulley. Taking it in his fist, Thane gave one sharp tug and returned to the table as, far off, a bell tinkled.

Savoring the lull, Thane looked down at the girl who was spread open for his perusal. Her breasts were not as large as he'd thought they'd be but they were pert. He allowed himself one tantalizing touch, rubbing the pad of his thumb in a lazy circle around a soft pink areola then marvelled at how her nipple responded–beading in spite of her own stubborn will. She was exquisite. Just. Beautiful. Blowing out a breath he turned as the door to the cave-like room opened.

"Ah, Luna," he said as she trod reverently to his side. "Prepare Freya for me."

Luna beamed up at Thane, likely disbelieving that such an honor had been granted her. She looked for all the world like she might hug him so it was quite apparent how much this meant to her. She'd envied Boy's closeness to their protector since she'd arrived that fateful day last fall, he'd seen it in her glances, the words unsaid, the looks shared.

Seeing the smile spread over Luna's face brought a chuckle to his throat and a momentary easing of the pain in his loins. "Hurry now little one. My need of her is so fierce that I fear I might die if I don't have her."

The girl furrowed her brow, clearly disturbed at the thought that Thane might literally die at any moment; she really wasn't the brightest candle on the alter. Taking her leave of his side she rushed to a small basin and, taking a large pottery jug from the stone floor, she proceeded to fill it with scorching water. When the jug was full to its brim and steaming, Luna carried it to the table and placed it at Thane's feet. From beneath the table she took an ancient terracotta bowl and put it on the table between Betty's splayed legs.

"Don't let the water cool," Thane warned. His hands were planted on his hips, jaw set firm as he oversaw the proceedings with a keen eye. There was no margin for error.

Luna's hands shook as she raised the jug, transferring the steaming water to the bowl until it touched the edge of an intricate design hand-painted around the inside rim. She didn't dare look up at Thane for fear his scrutiny may cause her to do something clumsy, because she was a clumsy girl. From the drawer she pulled two squares of delicate white muslin. The first she laid on Betty's stomach, the other she folded four times until it was as small as her fist. She was thankful that Betty was keeping still–she'd make a special effort to be nice to her once this was over so as to return the favor.

Freya

Paralyzed with fear she daren't move. She was open, exposed - degraded like never before, even in her line of work and that was saying something.

When he'd loomed large over her in the bedroom– all menacing and fierce–she'd thought for certain that he would rape her. But this man surprized her at every turn so that now she didn't know if his intention was to kill her, fuck her or keep her caged up like a zoo animal. Honestly, she preferred death.

Betty knew that she had wound the man up with her wriggling and demands to leave; she needed to think clearly–to play the game. She'd have her chance to escape but right now survival itself seemed an insurmountable task. The entrance of the woman had again astounded her. How many were here? If they'd all been taken like Betty why the hell hadn't they escaped and why did this one look so calm, so happy to do whatever the fuck the man asked? Younger than Syn, the one she'd met earlier, this woman was dressed differently. Natural. No fancy clothes, just a plain white shift. Who are you, she wondered fleetingly, and then: would she help get her out of there? The fact was that there was no one there she could trust, who wasn't totally mind-fucked and controlled by this bastard. This. Was. Batshit. Crazy.

She bit down on the wet balled silk and screwed her eyes tightly shut, tears squeezing out of the corners. Breathing rapidly through her nose, she knew she was on the verge of hyperventilating. *Slow. In and out. In and out. Shut it all out…*

The only sounds were of sloshing water and her own pulse hammering in her ears. Unable to close her legs all she could do was wait for whatever.

Agh! Heat swept over her clitoris as her folds were prized open by gentle fingers. The girl's fingers. His would be bigger, rougher. She couldn't look, wouldn't look; her head snapped to the side.

Wet heat again: slow, deliberate wipes from top to bottom, clit to ass. Water sloshing. Betty bit down harder; the heat verged on burning her sensitive flesh. She could do this. *Breathe.* The cheeks of her bottom were parted, the puckered entrance tingling as light flicks of the hot cloth cleansed her there. She felt her face flush with embarrassment. Her breathing became more rapid still when something pushed inside her vagina then withdrew. It felt like a coiled cloth. In and out. The shame she felt melded with other, more worrying feelings that she tried to shove from her mind. Fingertips stroked the inside of her thighs now at the same time as a hot trickle struck her bud and ran a course down to her ass. Betty heard moaning, shocked to realize it was her own voice. Cursing her body's wilful disobedience, she had no choice but to feel her hips start to rise and fall in a rhythm that matched the continual assault between her legs. She was building to a climax when she would rather die than orgasm.

As quickly as it had begun, it stopped. Opening her eyes, Betty blinked as her vision adjusted to the dappled light. Her respirations slowed. Tipping up her head, she watched the woman carry the bowl away, pouring water somewhere in the shadows. Chancing a quick glance at the man she saw that he had his face tilted to the roof, his mouth working silently though no sound passed his full lips. Transfixed, she noticed that his mouth seemed to form the same words again and again, seemingly oblivious to her, nor did he seem aware of the other woman's movements. Betty watched the woman return. Her gaze dropped to the her right hand which held…a knife. Betty's eyes widened, her head thrashed left to right, hips bucked. *No!*

"Calm down," said Thane.

Her head snapped up to him. She implored him with her eyes not to hurt her–not to allow the girl to stick her with the knife. The scream that she felt inside translated only to a muffled cry behind the gag.

"I warned that I would hurt you and I will," he continued, "but I hurt you not with malice but with love."

"Ugh. Ugh!" Again she shook her head.

"The dagger, girl…."

The woman dropped to her knees. Craning her neck Betty could see the woman offer the knife towards the man. He accepted it into his open palm, wrapping his sizeable fist around its wooden handle. Luna remained at his feet as he raised the blade above his head with his powerful right arm–bicep popping as he did so.

Tears leaked from Betty's eyes. She'd known that he would kill her but not when. Not how. This was too soon, she wasn't ready. Not here. Not like this. A kaleidoscope of images flashed through her mind: her brother, parents, and all those men who had fucked her, abused her–the pittance she'd earned and the penance she'd paid. Even then, was her life worth so little for it to end like this? Her body pressed down onto the table, arms pulled and twisted, held firm by the cuffs that bit into her wrists. There was pain. There was also the stench of death, of fear. Hope was a fickle friend walking away.

"Breathe, Freya."

She tried to do as he said. She tried to breathe as much as she tried to be brave, failing miserably at both. She was going to pee herself.

Thane stepped to the table's end and locked eyes on hers. "There will be pain," he stated as matter-of-fact as if she were at the dentist, "but it will soon pass. If you embrace it–welcome it–then it'll carry you to a place where you'll feel peace and tranquility."

So this was it. She wanted to ask him why he'd cared

when he'd thought she was drowning. Why he hadn't killed her when he'd taken her from the alley as she'd tugged her skirt down, thighs still wet from her latest trick. But she couldn't talk. The gag was forcing her tongue to the back of her throat. She was going to be sick.

Thanatos

He had taken the dagger and held it up skyward; the carbon steel like an extension of his mighty forearm. Since he'd turned his back on his familial Baptist faith and created this Norse-like blend of beliefs, he'd discovered an enrichment beyond anything he'd experienced before. A freedom, if you will. That he'd teased out the parts that suited him was not something Thane cared to dwell on. The religion he'd created had formed a foundation on which he'd rooted his little compound community. It gave him leadership direction and a set of ethics and rules that grounded them all. Some might think it bizarre, but if you believed then you were rewarded, it really was as simple and uncomplicated as that.

She was an absolutely exquisite sight spread out before him, fully at his behest. When Freya's slim but curvaceous body began to heave he'd lowered the dagger, forced his fingers into her mouth and retrieved the sodden silk gag in case she choked. It was just one of the kindnesses he intended to show her during their future years together. Sirona had called him a beast–cruel, tyrannic–and he didn't deny that he was, but he could counter those with empathy. He wasn't a goddamn sociopath. He took what he wanted and made no apology for doing so but he cherished and protected those whom he possessed, almost to the point of obsession. Such was his Achilles heel. He really should care less, perhaps then he would not be subject to disappointments and sadness when people continually failed him.

Thane began to chant, the words indiscernible, melody little more than a growled hum. The girl at his feet swayed back and forth. Betty had grown quiet. Thane wondered if she really believed that he intended to stab her with the dagger - a ludicrous notion yet he didn't dispel it if so. Truth be known, he was a little sadistic that way. When his chanting ceased, Thane bent at the waist and clutched one of Freya's thighs. The enormous spread of his hand nearly encircled her limb. The tip of the dagger, which he'd named Seax (because a dagger like his deserved a name), pressed into the milk-white flesh of her right inner thigh. He held still when Freya twitched in response to the sharp sting.

"Drift away," he soothed.

"Please. Don't hurt me." She was sucking in gasped breaths. The tears had stopped as they do when you reach the point of absolute dread. A part of him needed her tears, craved them even; he wanted to extract every emotion from her until he owned them all.

"It will soon be done." A crimson bead formed on the blade's tip, followed by a fine rivulet trickling down to stain the wood. With precision and concentration, Thane carved the initial T into her thigh by way of branding what was his. Freya had screamed as the first cut traced like fire, quietening only with the final crafting of the letter's stem. He knew it hurt like a bitch because he bore a mark too. Now he stood back and brought the blade to his tongue, dragging it down with caution as he savored

Freya's blood. Having licked the blade clean he handed Seax to the girl at his side and said, "Take it. Clean it."

The girl jumped to her feet and hurried out with the dagger to do as he'd asked.

Turning back to Betty, he took the dry muslin square from her stomach and pressed it to her thigh to stem the bleeding. His heavy brow creased in a frown. "You're trembling. Stop, you'll bleed more." His gaze rose to meet hers, his eyes creasing in a smile. "I'm honestly so impressed with you, Freya, that I want to reward you in some way. I hadn't planned on this yet but, now I've marked you, you can come to my rooms where we'll finish this together." Never had he felt so close to a taken girl as he did to this new one. The bond that they'd share when he took her for the first time would be so monumental that even his stone heart clattered harder against his ribs at the thought of entering her.

The girl started to cry again as he released each of her four limbs and carried her in his arms, still as a rag doll, back through the passageways to his private rooms. This was perfect. *She* was perfect. On reaching his expansive bed he threw her down. The fall appeared to stun her; a loud gasp was followed by a frenzied scramble away from him to the top of the bed where she attempted to thwart his advances with a large pillow. He couldn't help himself. Throwing back his head, he let out a roar of laughter which rapidly dissolved into a narrow-eyed glare when she cursed at him.

"Leave me the fuck alone!"

"Freya. I won't warn you again about your dirty mouth."

"Fuck. You!"

Thane's fingernails dug into his palms. She was really pushing his fucking buttons. "I'll tell you one more time. Watch your mouth."

After only a brief pause of reflection, Betty rose onto her knees and hurled the pillow, striking Thane's stomach with a soft thwack. With a sharp inhalation, his fist uncurled as his arm rose to backhand her and teach her some fucking respect.

"Thane!"

His head snapped to the left. He flashed a warning glare at Syn. "What the hell do you think you're doing entering my room without permission?"

With a rustle of red taffeta only one shade brighter than her long flame-red hair, Syn closed the distance between herself and Thane. "Calm down," she said more softly now. "If you beat the girl half to death you completely lose the entire point of her being here."

Thane tipped his head at Syn and narrowed his eyes, his back to Betty. "I will not tolerate disrespect." He jutted up his strong jaw.

Syn reached out a hand and stroked it over the man's pectoral muscles, marvelling at the firm ripple beneath her palm. She held little fear of Thane, well, not like the others anyway. She knew how to play him like a fiddle.

Covering her tiny hand with his own, Thane blew out a slow breath and nodded his agreement. "Okay. I'll control my anger, you're right. Tomorrow is–"

"A full moon. Yes I know, and we'll deal with that as we always do" she cut in. "But tonight is about you and Freya. Don't let her sass spoil what you want to do, Thane." Drawing back her hand she leaned up and whispered, "Tame her. Crush that spirit of hers and dominate her. Make her earn that mark of yours."

A gentle tapping on the open door drew both their attention. "Enter," Thane called, barely containing his exasperation by this point. Why didn't the whole damn world just step right on in?

Luna walked lightly on her bare feet and placed a simple enamel dish on a nightstand beside the bed. Thane narrowed his eyes and watched her as she walked backwards out of the room, scurrying away when she reached the door. That girl was adorable but required a great deal more training before she would be to Boy's standard of servitude. He fleetingly wondered if her twin sister might not have been a better option but couldn't deny that her help around the compound was useful enough to keep her. For now.

"Thane."

Drawing his attention back to Syn he leaned down and pressed a chaste kiss to her forehead. "You've made your point. Leave us."

"As you wish, or I could stay and hold the girl while you take her. One can't be too sure what she may try to do to you." Her grin widened as her tongue flicked over her teeth.

Thane chuckled. "Always the protector. Look at the size of me and the size of her." His face straightened. "Who do you think would win a fight to the death?"

Syn arched a brow and pinched her lips together. "I just thought that maybe I could stay?"

"Ah. I see now, little one." His full lips tugged into a rare smile. He tipped her chin up with a single digit. "You see something you like there?" Thane nodded over to Betty who was hiding behind the remaining stack of pillows which were now stained with the girl's blood.

He'd read her mind. Syn lowered her eyes and mumbled, "You know me too well, Thane."

"That I do." He nodded. "Not tonight but you can have her tomorrow," he said. "Tonight she's mine. Now leave."

Syn rustled from the room knowing better than to argue the point. Tomorrow the new girl would be entirely at her mercy with Thane gone. Who would protect Freya from the protector? She laughed at the irony, the shrill warble echoing around the compound.

Claimed

Freya

If she could make herself really small or even hide, she stood a chance of surviving whatever terrible plan Thane had for her.

Thane. Her mind had given the monster a name. What the fuck was with that?

Betty's eyes darted around the room for a place to duck into while he was busy with the slut in red talking about her like she wasn't even in the room. She'd met enough whores in her time to know that this one was pure liquid trouble. She was practically creaming her panties over Thane, honestly it was laughable. The way she looked at

Betty was with cruel, violent eyes. It was as if Syn wanted Thane to fuck Betty knowing that if she did, she would have a reason to claw her eyes out or slit her throat.

It was a masculine room with most everything–bed, nightstands, drapes–as black as night, the only color in the room right now apart from white bed linen was the flash of Syn's red dress as she left them. Now alone with Thane, Betty clawed at the pillows to form a barrier between herself and the beast watching her from the foot of the bed. The cuts on her thigh were smarting like a bitch as she drew her knees up to her chest; blood smears on the white linen were shocking. She wanted not to cry but dammit, tears streamed over her cheeks and her nose ran a river. There were at least windows; she couldn't tell how many or how big because long closed drapes stretched the entire length of the wall to her right.

"What are you going to do to me?" Her voice was small, no more sass. Shit got real.

Thane stepped to her side of the bed, his expression was dark, menacing. Saying nothing, his fingers pulled at the cords of his pants. Her eyes widened as the garment began to slide down over his narrow hips revealing first a trail of dark matted hair, sharply defined V and then…*oh dear God! No!* As his pants pooled at his feet, so the most enormous cock that Betty had ever seen sprung free. She was transfixed. It was as though she was rubber-necking a car crash. Like a deer caught in headlights she was too panicked to actually move though her brain screamed at her to run for her fucking life. It would split her in two. She'd never survive if he stuck it in her. Heat pulsed between her thighs which she squeezed together, her body again doing totally it's own thing for fuck's sake.

"Come," he commanded, hand outstretched.

She shook her head and hugged a pillow harder.

"Don't be scared. Come here."

Again, no.

Thane hissed through his teeth and cast his eyes down at the bowl beside the bed. The lighting was low, all Betty could see was dark liquid. Thane reached down and scooped a hand into it. Cupping some liquid he brought it to his chest and smeared it over his pectoral muscles, smoothed his palm over his abs and coated his shaft. Betty gasped.

"Don't be alarmed," he said. "It's just goat's blood. You'll find I have some strange ways but everything I do is for a reason, even if that reason isn't clear to you yet."

She wanted to ask what the fuck goat's blood would do for him but was equally afraid of his answer. She watched him as he repeated the action, this time taking longer to work the blood over the growing length of him. That he could get bigger was beyond her. She couldn't tear her eyes away from his hands as they stroked and rolled and dipped in the bowl and stroked some more. Up and down his cock until his back arched, his eyes rolling upwards into their sockets, a low growl coming from his parted lips. It was mesmerizing as it was terrifying.

Thane stopped. His eyes snapped open, head dropped and he glared at her beneath hooded lids, his hands still wrapped around his erect shaft. "Come. Here." This time it was not a request.

Betty's chest rose and fell, her heart clanged in her chest and thumped in her ears but she didn't move. Couldn't move.

With a near deafening roar, Thane tore the pillows from

her naked chest and one vast hand gripped a fistful of her hair. "*I said, come here,*" he boomed. Her scalp burned. She tried to lean into his hand to stop him from pulling out a clump of her hair but his grip was so strong that she was dragged from the bed, stumbling off the edge as her feet found purchase on the hard floor.

"Get *off* me!" She screamed, hands flailing at his chest, nails raking over the solid frame. She struggled and hit and kicked but her wrists were grabbed and held firm in just one of his mighty hands. "*No!* Don't. Fucking get away from–"

Slam! Her back smacked against the wall, arms wrenched above her head. Pinned. Her breathing came in sharp ragged gasps. She bared her teeth. Snarled.

Thane's eyes flashed with something wicked - feral like a wolf. The broad sweep of his nostrils flared, his teeth biting into his bottom lip, breath hot over her face. Averting his gaze for a second, he increased the pressure on her wrists, bent to the side and grabbed the bowl bringing it between them. His face close to hers again, she felt a wet warmth wash over her breasts, her stomach, between her parted thighs. Betty looked down and saw that she too was awash with blood.

"You sick fuck!" She thrust her chin up and locked her eyes on his. It didn't matter now. She was dead, it was just a matter of the how and when. If she was going down, she was going down fighting.

"Watch. Your. Mouth."

Betty laughed a hysterical manic laugh.

Thane let the bowl drop to the floor with a clatter. His empty hand shot out and cupped her pussy, his gaze never wavering from hers as he massaged blood over her lips, invading her cunt with forceful thrusts of his slick fingers. As hard as she tried to clamp her thighs together, to block his entry, he was stronger.

"Now," he snarled, "now you're ready to be mine." With that, Thane released her wrists, his hand dropping to her hip before sweeping around to spread over her backside.

Her hand trembling so bad, she drew it back and slapped his face hard enough to pop his head to the side, palm stinging like a motherfucker. He didn't even flinch though his mouth set in a hard line, his other hand joining the first.

"That. Is the one and only time you ever hit me, understand?"

Before she could hit him again Thane lifted her by her spreading buttocks and adjusted himself beneath her. She cried out, struggled at the realization of what was about to happen, but to no avail. The crown of that shocking penis was felt first as pressure against her perineum before she felt him at her entrance. It was too big. She would tear wide open. Thrashing harder in his grip she was unable to rise up away from the spear, and with a guttural growl Thane lowered her onto it. Crying with pain and the helplessness of it all, Betty's head fell forward. Her teeth sank into the taught muscle of his shoulder as she felt her insides stretch and fill. She waited for the tear, the pain, darkness - longed for darkness. He paused. The air thick with tension, her pulse rising to a thud thud thud in her ears.

"So fucking beautiful and all mine."

Squeezing her eyes shut, Betty didn't dare move. The feeling of fullness was like nothing she had ever experienced, and she'd fucked a lot of men. This was insane. She'd always known in her 'career' that she risked being raped or worse but this…never did she think it would be this way. Drool dampened Thane's shoulder, melding with a sheen of sweat. Her face moved to the crook of his neck where she rapidly breathed him in on a pant. His scent was animalistic, musky, pure testosterone. Her fingers were curled around his biceps, nails digging into unyielding muscle.

Thane grazed his jaw along the swan-like curve of her neck then tilted his head to draw her earlobe between his teeth, rasping in her ear, "My sweet Freya."

She waited. Seconds, minutes, who knew? Caught in the beat between hope he'd stop and the certainty that he wouldn't.

His mouth pressed to her ear, he rasped, "I warned you that I'd hurt you," as he thrust up and slammed her down, his cock striking her very end.

She hadn't torn. Or maybe she had, she had no idea. So many dark and desperate thoughts flooded her mind as he began a punishing rhythm. Again and again the fierce rub hurt so bad until the pain lessened, morphing into something else: the first waves of pleasure deep inside of her. Cursing her body she cried harder, soaking his skin with bitter tears. She was lost. Out of control. Her teeth bit down into his shoulder to quell her screams as she jerked and tightened and shattered around him.

"So wet," he growled before she even realized that she was.

When Thane turned them both and eased her down onto the bed she didn't protest. Even when he covered her body and half the bed with his giant frame and pulled her knees up, driving deeper still…she didn't fight him because it ripped through her again then. Her body shook as rippling waves grew to a mighty crescendo that lashed over her body with a ferocity that had her screaming and clawing and cursing some more.

Like a piston he drilled deep until, when he climaxed, it was with growled empty words of *love* and *devotion* that would stay imprinted on her memory forever, however long forever may be for her. His weight pressed down, his forearm across her windpipe. She fought to breathe as her throat closed under the pressure. Feeling herself slipping off the edge of consciousness, he rolled to the side and there they both lay. Gasping lungfuls of air.

When her breathing settled, Betty rolled away from him, drawing her knees to her chest in a foetal ball. She couldn't be brave any more, sobbing into a pillow. She'd been raped certainly but what was infinitely worse was that she hadn't wanted him to stop when the pain went. She'd chased her own fucking sick release instead of fighting him. And worse still–she cried harder–she knew that even though she'd been so brutally claimed by this man, that she couldn't say hand on heart that she didn't want him to take her this way again. And again. His possession of her was all consuming; she'd never felt anything as powerful as what he just did to her. She was ruined. Death would be better than this. Anything to quiet the battle raging in her mind. All she'd ever wanted as she grew up was to be loved. How wrong her old friend, Kelsey, had been about love. If she ever saw her again she'd kill her. Love was fucking selfish and love was fucking sordid.

* * *

Thanatos

Thane knew that it would be like that. Incredible. Momentous, even. What he hadn't mapped out in his greater plan was this curious feeling that had him craving the softness of her lips on his, or the need to see her smile to see if it lit up her eyes to the color of cornflowers as he suspected it would. When he'd spat his sentiments of love and devotion as he'd exploded inside of her he'd meant them with his whole stone heart, it hadn't been a case of him speaking on behalf of his dick like countless of her customers had likely done before him. *Damn!* The thought of any other man touching her powered him with a very real need to kill. For now, he shoved this inner conflict to the dark corners of his mind. For now, he was sated and the madness that had threatened to consume him earlier was, for the time being, locked away too. Turning onto his side, Thane lifted onto an elbow, head resting on his hand and studied Betty, taking in the scattering of freckles over her nose and apples of her cheeks and the finest of lines threaded delicately across a forehead that frowned too often.

He could make her happy, he knew he could with no shadow of doubt. They were branded in blood, sweat, juices; united together by the ceremonies that would appease his own personal beliefs. Her eyes leaked tears and whereas he had thought that he wanted to own her tears it bothered him, unnerved him even. Thane furrowed his brow and thought about this odd emotion inside of him. Tears were not uncommon to him; he savored his muses' misery at times because it served to remind them that all of the power was his and every facet of them belonged in his ownership. This was different. Without thinking, Thane's hand moved to rest on the full curve of her hip. She shuddered at his touch and shrank away from him. He withdrew his hand and ran it instead over his shaved head. "It won't hurt that way next time," he mumbled as much to himself as to her.

"Leave me alone," she sobbed.

This was too much; these thoughts in his head were fucking with his ordered mind. Shoving off the bed he paced along the draped wall. Stopping half way along he took the edges of the fabric in his fists and tore them apart. Turning a key he threw open a pair of doors and stepped out into a courtyard beyond, inhaling the cleansing night air. Feeling the coldness of a spring breeze over his damp skin he was thankful for it. Another sign that the gods were kind, that they would always meet his needs. Tipping his face up to the night sky he looked at the constellations and thanked them for Freya, even if she seemed broken right then.

Don't let me destroy this one.

He loved Syn and Luna. Hell, he'd loved Sirona and he adored Boy in his own way, but this one was making him feel things he didn't believe he could feel. He'd wept private tears for Sirona at the back of the chapel and felt sorrow for her family's loss as he'd clutched a hymn book and sung his heart out. Before the funeral, even after he'd put her lifeless body back in her apartment and set the place alight, he'd felt remorse so he knew he was capable of loving and of the pain of loss. Knowing a thing and experiencing it were two separate entities though. The caring love he'd felt so far was just a cinder compared to the flame he felt for the new girl. Trouble was, the flame threatened a fire that would likely get him burned. Or her.

Thane let the cool breeze temper the wet heat fizzing over his skin. This was why he'd never allowed himself to fall for a woman before. Men who loved beyond reason were weak fools. If there was one thing he'd inherited from the suffering of his enslaved forefathers, it was the belief that you rely only on yourself, that you dig deep inside of yourself for freedom and power. Man is only caged by his own mind or by the heart of a woman; he'd read that written inside the cover of a family bible that he kept hidden, the only reminder from his past brought to the compound.

The scrawled handwriting of his great grandfather was as clear to him now as was the memory of his own homestead. His mom dressed in her finest, his dad upright in pressed suit and he as a boy–real name John–hiding behind a church pew as his parents discussed their mutual disappointment in their son. That feeling of not wanting to go home, of being the last out of church…the memory of begging the preacher to let him stay and the preacher calling him an ungrateful delinquent because his mom and dad were fine pillars of the community. He'd wanted to tell that preacher who stank of incense that his mother used to brag about his father's donations and how she said the church would shut its doors if it weren't for their generosity. The word on the street was the preacher beat kids with a cane and Thane figured that would hurt more than his dad's belt so he kept quiet.

Thane punched a fist into a wall and stormed back inside. If she thought he was finished with her, she was wrong. So very wrong.

Dark Dawn

Freya

Betty screwed her eyes shut. It was too damn bright… *turn off the fucking lights.* Her tongue licked over her lips. Eyes opened a crack then blinked wide. Sunlight! It was the first time she'd seen natural light since when? The pool. When was that, yesterday? She couldn't remember. He wasn't there but she was in his bed. Stretching out in the vast mattress Betty winced, the soreness inside of her proving a stark reminder of what he did. Memories of last night flooded back in a rush of shame. Rape. There was no flowery way to dress it up into some fancy love affair, it was rape plain and simple. He hadn't used protection. Fuck! She was on birth control, she'd taken her pill yesterday or the day before. It would still be in her system, wouldn't it? She almost felt like laughing because she had no idea if she'd even make it out of here alive so pregnancy or the pox were the least of her worries right now.

At the end of a long painful stretch Betty swung her legs over the edge of the bed and looked down at the dried up brown mess that coated most of her front. Her fingertips traced over the encrusted wound of a large letter T on the inside of her right thigh. She was branded by him forever. Her shoulders heaved on a deep sigh. Days ago, before she was taken, she could have cared less about her life. The odd thing about reaching rock bottom is that you can't imagine life getting any worse, but then it does. Life's a bitch. Her mother was a bitch. The bitch wouldn't even know she was missing. If Cody had been gone with no word she'd have had the entire state of Massachusetts scouring the streets. Betty? Hell, her mom was probably raising a glass of bourbon, wondering how long the bottle would last. It wasn't always that way. She'd been a good girl once in spite of everything, mostly for her dad. His princess. She'd wanted that inscribed on his tombstone but her mom had said that it was all kinds of fucked up to plan his grave when the man wasn't dead. He was dead to Betty. The day he walked out on her for The Whore who'd been the family's therapist after Cody took his life, that was the day the piece of her heart died that had belonged to her dad.

A key disengaged a lock with a clunk. The door opened. Betty hid her nakedness with a sheet as best she could, fear pricking her skin, the fine hairs sprung up on her arms and nape. She held her breath and pursed her lips.

"The little chosen one is awake I see." Syn. She stepped into the room clad only in a black string dress of sorts; most everything was on show. Even hookers like Betty showed more modesty than this tramp.

"Don't people ever wear real clothes around here?"

Syn narrowed her eyes, her lips pinching together. "Real clothes like the stylish ensemble you rocked up in?" She huffed a laugh, her eyes sliding over the dishevelled bed, the mess on the floor. "So, he let you sleep here. You do know he'll tire of you soon, poor lamb." It was a statement.

Betty curled her lip on a growl.

"Cat got your tongue?" she smirked. "Oh fine, be all moody and sorry for yourself or alternatively come and eat something."

Silence.

Syn glared, keys swinging from her hand. "Venison. Lucky you. Five minutes. Put this on and you can bathe after you've eaten."

Betty looked at a ball of bunched up white lace as the woman threw it in her direction, missing the bed it fell in a heap near her feet. The woman didn't seem to like her very much; so far only Luna had shown her any kindness at all. Boy, she wasn't sure of. She needed an ally here if she was to stand a hope of getting out alive, yet she trusted no-one. "Tell me something."

With a quirk of her brow Syn smiled. "Sure. Should we start with an A-Z of your STDs?"

"I'm clean, you bitch."

"A clean whore. Well there's an anomaly."

Betty glared. How difficult would it be to take the bitch down? She stood a foot taller than Betty's small frame. Still, height didn't necessarily give Syn the advantage. Betty was fast. Usually.

"Don't even think about it my dear." Syn wagged a finger. "I'll snap that pretty neck of yours before you even cross the room. Now, what did you want to ask?"

Oh, she'd get her. "I was going to ask why you stay here but I can see why."

"Really? And why is that, Freya dear?"

"Because you're a sick fuck. As twisted as that bastard Thane."

With a shrill peal of laughter, Syn spun on her heel and walked to the door. Flashing Betty a grin over her shoulder, she quipped, "Be careful. I eat little girls like you for supper. Remember, I can make your life here hell or I can be your friend. Five minutes, snap snap."

The door shut, Betty slid off the bed and scooped up the white garment, slipping it over her head. It was only when she tugged the lace slip down over her hips that it hit her. Doors. Her head had been so full of last night's events and her sore body that she hadn't even registered that the sunlight was flooding in through parted drapes. Rushing over to the double doors she turned the key, barely able to believe that Thane had been dumb enough to leave it in the lock, stupid bastard. She was all fingers and thumbs but the lock yielded. Throwing the doors wide open, Betty glanced over her shoulder at the bedroom door and walked out into what looked like a small yard. There was even a square patch of emerald grass in the center. Four or five pots containing herbs scattered around, and walls. Four stone walls boxed the yard in on all sides. There had to be a way out of there. Something moved in her peripheral vision. Her head pivoted in its direction. Three goats were chewing on a pile of what looked like hay. She wondered, not for the first time, where the hell this place was. It smelt familiar with feint undertones of cloying gasoline.

Betty listened. Bird chatter and beyond that was a distant rumble. She knew these smells and sounds. Traffic. Impossible. She'd been sure he'd taken her some place far away - Arizona desert maybe. Mexico. Being drugged up to her eyeballs, disorientated, when she'd gotten there and with there being so few windows…could it be true that all this time she was in fact right where she'd always been?

Could this still be Boston?

An urgency rushed through her. *"Help!"* She yelled then yelled some more. Someone had to hear her. Please, please, anyone, she silently begged. Her eyes darted around the courtyard. Sprinting over the soft grass, white lace billowing behind her, Betty reached a small doorway right ahead. Without hesitation she turned the handle. The door swung toward her. Pushing her hair from her eyes, she leapt through. The pool. *Shit!* There had to be another way.

Back into the courtyard, eyes frantically searching for another door. There had to be one. Wait. Behind where the herb planters stood was a wooden door partly hidden behind a tall fern; she ran to it, the goats bleating in protest as she lunged for the handle. Locked. She turned the handle again and pulled and pushed and rattled the door. Bringing her knee up she kicked at it hard with the sole of her bare foot, splinters stabbing between her toes.

A sharp sting on the side of her neck.

A bee?

Her hand rose to the throb. Her head swam, knees buckled but she couldn't stop herself from falling… something caught her. Lifted her. Dark eyes. Thane.

Thanatos

"Damn you girl," he snarled as Betty collapsed into his arms. As if she weighed no more than a feather, Thane carried her back into his room, hesitating near the bed. No. He would take no more fucking chances with this one.

Sensing his reticence, Luna at his side chanced a soft touch of her hand on his strong arm. "Thane?" In her hand she still held the syringe, being careful not to stab her own thumb.

"Cage," he barked.

Luna fidgeted foot to foot. "She could stay in my room?"

Thane inhaled. She was really testing the last shred of patience he had left. "Cage."

"I'll go and get it ready," she replied, evidently finally exercising a little common sense.

Ensuring the cage was secure and that Freya was safe, Thane stood back and frowned. That she had required sedation was beyond frustrating but not altogether unexpected. What troubled him more was how close she had come to leaving him and that could not be permitted to happen again. Though the door was locked, it did in fact exit onto a street, albeit there was no sidewalk and her cry would have likely been drowned out by traffic noise. Still, the fact that merely a piece of wood had separated her from a future with him and a return to her old ways was troubling indeed. He cursed himself for allowing her to stay in his private room overnight. Never before had he bestowed such an honor upon a taken girl so soon. Special or not, Freya had not earned such a privilege and evidently could not yet be trusted. He was weakening, curse it. Tonight he would rectify that under a burgeoning full moon. Thane shuddered in anticipation.

Though he wanted nothing more than to sit and watch Freya sleep, time was pressing on. Once showered and dressed in outside clothes of suit pants and white dress shirt that strained over his muscular chest, Thane gave concise instructions to Boy and to Syn. He'd be away until the early hours of tomorrow morning when he would return once it was safe to do so. This was a lie because he rarely held such willpower to deny himself the taking and beating of Luna, sweet pitiful masochistic girl that she was, but his intention was always to resist his urges when the madness struck him.

Thane stepped out onto the street, shoving his hands in his pockets. With every pace away from the compound his shoulders stooped a little more as the weight of the real world bore down. As always, he was becoming the man he abhorred. He kept these excursions to a minimum these days but he had responsibilities. The outside world always made him feel this way even though he should harbor a sense of freedom away from the constraints of his compound. Conversely, he felt like a caged animal; only at home did he really feel free. To be confined by the suffocating constrictions of society was a very great burden that Thane bore with contempt. He was not ignorant to the wrongfulness of his deeds if his actions were gauged by social norms, by the laws and conformity created by suited leaders for the world's oppression. He knew without doubt that his lifestyle was different. Some might say that it was a heinous sin to take the women he'd stolen. To those accusers he would say this if he had the chance: the women he took had no life. He gave them an alternative based on protection, removal of stress and that he loved each of them was unquestionable. He loved Boy too and he loved that Boy chose to come to him and to stay by his side. Boy was near death when Thane had given him salvation. A street dweller. Beaten, abused, as they all were.

So many thoughts ricocheted around in his head during the brisk walk, that he barely registered his arrival at Milk Street. Throwing a cursory glance over at Franklin's birth place, Thane climbed the steps and pressed an intercom. This would be a quick in-out meeting. Necessary but far from enjoyable. As long as his affairs were being taken care of, all was good.

The familiar scent of bees wax and dusty books took Thane back to the reading of his father's will right here in this very building not too many years ago. He pushed the memory away.

"Good to see you," said the lawyer as he released his hand from his client's death grip. "Take a seat. Coffee?"

"Bingham, good to see you too. Thank you, no."

"So, how've you been?" The willowy man sat behind his desk.

"I've been well. Yourself?"

"Oh you know. Everyone needs a lawyer, right?"

"I should increase the rental on this building if business is booming."

Bingham raised his hands and laughed. "Now, I didn't say we were rich."

"Uh huh. So…any issues?"

The lawyer rocked back in his chair with a tight smile. In front of him was his wealthiest client. The client who could destroy him. The client who was a cash cow. "Nope, as always everything's just fine. You pay the best team in Massachusetts, John. It's our job to make sure that when you sit there, there are no problems that haven't already been resolved."

The use of his real name, his given name, always felt like a punch to the solar plexus. Thane's jaw ticked. It was a reminder of everything he'd walked away from. "Good to hear. My mother?" Thane inhaled as her name knotted his throat.

"Is doing okay by all accounts. Since they changed her meds she's been calmer. The clinic sends through its monthly report and, as always, I have the files here if you ever have need of them."

Thane shook his head, scrubbing a hand over his face. "All I need to know is that she's being well taken care of," he said, expression dour. "Things change with her, you let me know."

"Of course. I'd call you right away. And you? You seem well."

Thane knew what he was referring to and cut him a reproachful glare.

"My apologies," said Bingham. "You know I care about you as a friend as well as your attorney." Not strictly true.

Thane nodded. "Thank you. The Nathaniel Foundation?"

"Doing fine too," replied Bingham, reaching for a file which he drummed with his fingers. "Very fine indeed - your great, great grandfather would be very proud of you. I have all the stats here if you'd care to have sight of them."

Thane reached out a hand and took the file from Bingham. Long-gone Nathaniel lived a life of slavery. He would not be proud of him. The thought made his heart heavy as lead. He was trying. In his own screwed up way he was trying. Taking a good long time to ingest the information, when he'd read enough, he passed it back. "So the refuge expanded as we discussed?"

"Yes sir," he beamed. "Solicitation arrests are down too and I think it's fair to say the Foundation had a hand to play in that."

Chewing his lip, Thane considered what his lawyer had said. "But the sex trade continues. Homelessness continues."

Bingham nodded with a wry smile. "My friend, you'll never eradicate the city of its sex trade, much as you may want to. It's just a fact, same as litter and dog dirt. Laws will never stop folk from doing what they want to do."

This was not what Thane wanted to hear. Most of his family's money was invested in achieving that very goal. "Then I'll release more funds."

"You can't. Most every cent you have is already being eaten up by the Foundation, John. Unless you sell some of your real estate, I mean that's an option."

Thane needed only a small chunk of income to fund

the compound. He had no care for the millions remaining. "Do it. Sell my portfolio over in Quincy and get the best price you can."

"John…"

"I said do it."

"Fine, I'll do it." Bingham stood and paced. "We should talk about the Remond building though."

Silence.

"John."

"Don't."

"C'mon John. You're burying your head in the goddamn sand. How long do you think you can do this?"

"The Remond building is none of your fucking business."

"Oh really, none of my business? You expect me to turn a blind eye? Risk my career? And it's none of my business?"

"How's the new house out on the Cape? Your discretion comes with a big price tag. Don't forget that."

Bingham rubbed at his temples. "It has to stop."

"It stops when I say it does."

"Yeah, well don't count me in for the long-haul is all I'm saying."

Thane stood. "Then don't count on a pension."

"You're unreal. Your father was a decent man."

"My father's in his grave and this meeting is over. Send me the papers on Quincy."

"John, please. Okay, the compound, or whatever the hell you call it, is a taboo topic from now on, I swear. Hell, we'll both pretend Remond's just another piece of real estate you own."

"Good day."

Extending his hand, Thane gave a brief shake of the frustrated man's hand and left the office.

The rage was gnawing at him, eyes already misted with red fog. This was not good. He was ticking inside like a bomb. Tick, tick, tick. Truth was, Thane didn't know how long he had before the madness ate his brain like his mom's. Maybe it already had. As he walked home, shoving aside any fucker who got in his way, he imagined tiny crazy worms chewing on each cerebral lobe until all that was left was a drooling mad man, sedated, vacant. By the time he reached the polished door into which was carved 'The Remond Building–Private,' it was his own head that he banged against the wood. He should turn around now, not risk the safety of those inside. Not take the chance that he could destroy everything. Even as he thought it he knew deep inside that there was no turning back. The darkness was all around him, oppressive, cloying. There was only one beacon of light. His 'one'. His Freya. Thane knew that the selfish pursuit of his own salvation could destroy the one thing he'd searched for, his most precious jewel. The decision was made. So be it.

Madness Within

Freya

He loved her enough to lock her up, Boy had said when she woke. What kind of fucked up love was this? Love was only for fairytales, for movies, Betty knew this, but this was a whole barrel full of fucked up.

The boy sat cross-legged on the cold stone until his butt was numb but he didn't mind. He watched Betty through the gaps in the bars and chewed on his lip. "If you wore a feather dress, you'd look like a song bird in a gilded cage. I saw one once. She was in the window of an antique store. Fancy place in Nobscot Road. I named her Lucky, and once I snuck in and fed her a whole chunk of rye bread and I was starving so it was a big deal. Next time I passed by, the cage was gone so I went inside and asked the mister, did you sell the bird? Know what he said?"

"What?" Betty rolled her eyes, her reply pure sarcasm.

"The cage was sold for export so he'd drowned the bird in a pail out back. I guess she wasn't so lucky after all."

Betty cut him a glare.

Boy chuckled. "Sing little bird, sing a song of suffering."

"You're as batshit crazy as him."

Boy flapped his arms like a bird and chirped a tune through his teeth, eyes dancing with mischief.

If she could hit him, she would have. The horror of waking to find herself in the cage was tempered only by the fact that she wasn't tied up with rope this time - small mercies. If only she could punch the smile off his face. "Get me the hell out of here."

"Can't do that, sorry."

"Yes, you can and you will."

"Nope."

"Let. Me. Out." Betty took a few calming breaths. Confined spaces freaked her out, always had since she and her brother had been crammed in the apartment, up close and personal in more ways than one. Her fingertips prodded at her neck where the sting had happened. She felt no lump or bump. Had the fucker stuck her again? It would explain why she felt so weird, so spaced out.

"Nu uh. You have to eat."

"Not hungry." Her stomach countered the lie with a growl.

"He'll be pissed and I'll be the one in trouble." Boy reached through the bars and pushed a plate of meat chunks in gravy closer to where she lay. "Have a bite and I'll hide the rest."

Not wanting the boy to get into trouble again on her account, though she had no idea why she gave a damn, Betty pulled herself up, yanked the crumpled lace dress over her ass and took the smallest piece of meat. It was chewy, cold, disgusting. She forced it down, her mouth dry as a bone. "Where is he?"

"Thane?"

"No. Santa Claus."

Boy chuckled. "Outside. Had stuff to do." He watched her take a second mouthful. "Likes to keep himself busy when it's a full moon so he goes off and gets done all he needs to get done. Takes his mind off it I guess."

She cocked her head, swallowed the meat and frowned. "When it's a full moon? He a werewolf or something?"

Boy snorted on a laugh. "Owwww," he howled. "Not a wolf no. He just gets kinda freaked out."

"Hmm. And what kind of stuff? I mean, does he work? Does he have a life outside of here?"

Boy shrugged. "Not for me to say." He toyed with the cord of his pants then raised his eyes to meet her stare. "It'll get easier you know."

"Never," Betty hissed. "And if he's not here, then why the fuck aren't you all escaping?"

Boy laughed caustically. "There was a time we all felt like you do now," he said, face straightening, eyes darkening. "But to be honest, none of us would likely be alive if Thane hadn't taken us."

"What do you mean?"

Boy bit down on his lip.

"What do you mean?"

He sighed and looked for all the world like he might cry. "I mean, he chooses. He takes the ones he knows have shitty lives and he brings them here."

"What is *wrong* with you? He fucking kidnaps. Rapes!" Betty's hands gripped the bars, her forehead pressed to the cold iron. "Has he brainwashed you all? Gotten you all drugged up and shit like he did to me?"

Boy shook his head. "That's bullshit."

"Excuse me? Bullshit? Are you for fucking real?"

"Ok, to start, sure. We all get doped up in the beginning or we'd never stay long enough to learn from him, to see what it's really like here. Heck, we're all a mess to start with though, you need to give it time."

"Time. I have no words."

He shuffled closer on his knees so that his face was separated from hers only by two bars. Boy's knuckles brushed over her fingertips until she recoiled and rocked back on her heels. A flash of hurt crossed his face. His voice little louder than a whisper, he added, "We could leave. Any time we wanted we could go now."

This revelation had her reeling. This couldn't be true. "You mean…you all stay here through *choice?*"

He nodded, the edges of his lips lifting in a smile. "Yeah, we do. And you're luckier than all of us. He chose you as his Freya so you're like his queen. The queen bee of the hive. Buzz buzz."

"I need to go," she croaked. "This is nuts. Help me, please. I'm begging you."

"Go where? You were a hooker, right?"

Her eyes narrowed. "That's none of your damn business."

Boy shrugged and shuffled back. "Suit yourself. I'm only saying you're no better than the rest of us were. Your life wasn't so awesome."

Her heart bunched. She covered it with a hand, eyes stinging with hot tears. "That's not fucking true. I had a life. A good life." She wasn't about to admit that he was right. "I had choice." Curling her hand into a fist she banged it over her heart. "I chose. I chose what the hell I did. Who I saw. What I ate. Who I fucked."

"You're kidding yourself." Boy shook his head on a frown.

"No!"

His face softening, because he really did get it, Boy told her, "You can make a good life here. He takes care of us. I mean, he really loves us, you know?"

"This isn't love. This is control. This is just plain fucking sick."

"You say that now but you don't know him yet." The boy pushed up to his feet. "You know nothing about him so don't you run your mouth, you hear me?"

"It's a freakin' cult," she whispered, "that's all this is. A cult and you believe anything that fucker tells you."

"You're wrong. You'll see."

Betty blinked through gritty eyes at his gullible, stupid face and asked herself what it was about Thane that had them all caught under his spell. She would not succumb to his will. Never. Over her dead body. His words echoed around inside her mind though: she was nothing but a hooker, it was true. She wiped away her tears, inhaled. "So, what makes you so much better than me?"

"Nothing at all. I'd still be thieving, you see. I'd still be the pathetic, spineless little rent boy waiting for a fat pig to get home and beat the crap outa me for not having brought enough bills home for him to buy his goddamned liquor. I'd still be sleeping with my back to the wall and one eye open waiting for the pig to drag me to his bed and use me 'til I couldn't walk next day. I'm no better than you 'cept I know which life is better. This. This is where I'm safest."

Her heart ached for him right then. "I'm sorry."

"Sure."

Betty was lost for words. She got it, she really did, but their lives before didn't justify what Thane had done, what he'd likely carry on doing. If she could change things for Boy she would but right now she needed out. And she also needed the bathroom real bad.

"Can I go pee?"

Boy pursed his lips. "You're not allowed out of there. Pee in the cage."

"Are you shitting me? I'm not peeing in here. Please. I don't have a whole lot of dignity left, don't make me do it in the cage. I'll be good. Hell, you can even come in and make sure I don't try anything, not that there's a damn door in sight that leads anywhere."

He hesitated, looked around and nodded. "Okay but I'll be right outside the bathroom. Don't try anything."

"I swear."

He took a bunch of keys from a hook on the wall and unlocked a padlock. The top bars fell back with a now familiar clang.

Grasping his hand, Betty climbed out. "Thank you," she said, nudging her side into his.

"If he finds out about this I'm in a shit load of trouble." Although obviously scared shitless, he pulled his lips into a smile for her.

"Then we'd better not let him find out."

Thanatos

Somewhat relieved that his monthly visit with his lawyer was now behind him, Thane couldn't shake fresh concerns about his mother. He paced a while outside the compound, going nowhere in particular, just using the time to restore a semblance of order to his cluttered mind. That she was insane was indisputable; that he'd inherited her madness was a probability. At least, that's what the psychiatrists had told him way back in another lifetime, before he'd walked away from it all. If he let the rotten memories in, he could see the thready bald man in a white overcoat staring down at him as if he were a lab rat. The man was talking to his mom and dad about 'lunar madness,' saying it was uncharted territory: might be faking, might be psychotic. Narcissistic Personality Disorder perhaps.

His mom had sent in a letter to his teacher: *'Johnny suffers terribly on a full moon, please make allowances for him because he can break things when the rage hits and his doctors confirmed it's a genuine phenomena an' all.'* A bunch of kids at school had gotten wind of it and called him a werewolf, a freak. His mom had totally bought into it, revelled in it almost to the point of obsession. She'd kept him home according to the moon's cycle but now, after years of seeing her own fight with sanity, he wondered if it was more than a correlation to the moon and if he hadn't simply inherited her crazy gene.

His jaw ticked. He was edgy as fuck. There was

nothing outside the compound that held his interest yet it was safer to be outside than in. Trouble was, Thane wanted in Freya with a fire that was hard to temper. He'd always used Luna when the madness gripped him. Could he risk being near Freya tonight? He wanted to keep his promise to himself that he wouldn't put her at risk, that he would resist temptation by staying away until tomorrow, but fuck! With a roll of his shoulders and clenched fists, he unlocked the door.

"Where is she?"

Syn was at a loss to answer him. The last she'd seen of the girl was when she'd taken in a plate of food. Boy had agreed to watch her, to make sure she ate and she told Thane this since it wasn't the first time the boy had messed up.

Thane tried to breathe through the rage that fisted his gut, fingers rubbing small circles at his throbbing temples. "Is it too much to fucking ask that, between you all, you watch over Freya while I'm gone?"

"I'll go and look for her." She bowed her head.

He knew it hurt Syn's heart to fail him but fail him she had. They all had. Ripping his jacket off he hurled it against the empty cage, his shirt sticking to his heated flesh like a second skin. "Where's Boy?"

Syn shrugged.

Thane cracked his knuckles. "If she's gone, may the gods strike him down before I get to him. You take the east wing, I'll take west. Meet by the pool."

As Syn scurried off like a scolded puppy, Thane marched down the passageway. Doors that were locked were kicked or punched open, his eyes darting around closets, larders, a cold storage room, pantry and kitchen. Nothing. Onwards he strode to the bedroom wing, first the rooms of Boy and Syn - each yielding nothing but neatly made beds. Luna's door was ajar, he kicked it open with a crash of wood on plaster. Luna cowered on the bed. "Where's Freya and Boy?" he growled.

"I don't know Thane," she whispered, trembling and mindful no doubt of events of the last full moon.

"If you see them, send them to the pool."

"Certainly. Thane?"

Thane ignored her, not about to waste precious time on conversation. Onwards he strode to three vacant rooms, yet to be assigned to future muses if and when he took them. One was Sirona's old room that he planned to use for Freya when she'd passed the stage of confinement in the cage. When she could be trusted. What a fucking joke that was now.

Where the hell was she?

He paused and listened. He could have sworn that he heard ragged breaths emanating from somewhere. "Come out little one," he called. Silence. *"Freya!"* Almost blinded by panic, his control ebbing, Thane's footsteps thundered over polished flooring around the pool. He had to remain calm or…he didn't care to think about what he would do to Boy when he found Freya. If he found Boy. Maybe Boy had fled too. If he knew what was good for him, Boy would do just that as it would be an iron fist that punished him for this.

"Thane!" Syn appeared breathless, shaking from the passage that led from the east wing.

"You've found her?"

"I've found Boy," she panted. "Come and see. Please.

Hurry."

Never Let Go

Freya

If she could have one wish. Just. One. Last. Wish. Betty would be that ant. She'd carry away a crumb of food the size of a car into a hole in the dirt and live in darkness for the rest of her life…just her and the forever-meal. Just because the little fucker was free, she crushed the ant with her bare heel and peeped out, pressing against the wall until she was invisible as Thane stalked past. Only when his back vanished through a doorway did she venture out from behind the tall potted tree. Her heart thumped hard against her ribs. She felt sick, clammy. Every turn she had taken so far had led back here to the pool; the place was a maze with no exit. There had to be one. They'd gotten her inside, she had to be able to get out, but where? She wouldn't cry. Think. Where haven't you been?

When she heard Thane roar she knew he'd found Boy. Screwing her eyes shut didn't help block out the image of his face or the panic in his eyes but she needed to not think about him right now. She'd done what she'd had to do to survive and Boy of all people would understand that.

Footsteps. Thunderous claps of shoe soles coming back her way. Betty ran. Weaving through ferns and palms, she ducked around a corner and into the first open door she came to.

"Freya!"

Betty gasped and stared at the woman.

Luna sprang off the bed and pulled Betty into a tight hug. "Thank God," she beamed, releasing Betty. "Thane was so worried about you. Where have you been?"

Betty took the woman's hands in hers, sucked in a deep breath and locked her eyes on Luna's. "Please, I'm begging you, help me. I've got to get out of here. Where's the exit?"

Luna's eyes grew large, she shook her head. "You can't. He'll never let you go."

Their heads turned in unison to the loudening footsteps outside. Thunder claps in the storm that was Thane. Luna quickly shut the door and hissed with urgency, "Come with me."

"Freya?"

Thane's voice boomed. He was close, so close. It was just a matter of time before he found them. The two women looked at each other, each acutely aware that this would be very bad for them both if Thane found them.

"The bathroom," Luna whispered.

Betty followed quickly behind the young woman who ran in a cloud of blue chiffon into the adjoining room. Shutting the door, Betty leaned against it, chest heaving. They waited in silence, hands clapped over their mouths. Her eyes fixed firmly on those of Luna, Betty could see the conflict there; the girl was indoctrinated by Thane - utterly controlled by him. She wanted so bad to help her, to take her with her and escape together but, truth was, she wasn't sure that Luna would leave this place or leave Thane.

A loud bang preceded the sound of heavier footfall on the other side of the bathroom door.

"Luna?"

Betty put her finger to her lips and shook her head.

"Luna. Come out."

Silence.

Luna's expression was fearful. She wavered, shoved a shaking hand through her hair then called out, "In here, Thane."

Betty closed her eyes, her shoulders sagged. She was done for. It was over.

As a great weight pushed against Betty's back, Luna mouthed 'sorry' and stepped forward to take Betty's hand. "Please, Freya," she urged, "let him in."

The pressure increased until Betty's bare feet slid along the tile floor, and there he stood.

Filling the entire doorway was Thane: vast and dangerous, eyes burning into hers, then Luna's. "Here you both are." His voice was ice cold. He looked at Luna.

"Leave us, little one. I'll meet you on the bench shortly. Go and wait for me there."

Without a word, Luna scurried from the room.

"Ah, Freya." Thane closed the bathroom door. The air grew thick.

Jutting up her chin in a last vestige of defiance, Betty pursed her lips and glared up at the man, her heart clattering against her ribs. "You can do what you want to me, but you'll never own me. I fucking *hate* you." She thought she saw a flash of something resembling pain flick over his eyes as he inhaled sharply and drew back his shoulders. She noticed a small tick in his jaw and temple.

"You hurt Boy," he rasped.

She regretted hurting the boy. She was a survivor on the streets, had to be, but she wasn't cruel. "Is…is he okay?"

Thane narrowed his eyes, fists clenching and unclenching at his sides as he replied. "He's concussed I think. It's quite a gash you gave his head."

Betty blew out a slow, shaky breath. When she'd grabbed Boy's hair and slammed his head into the wall, he'd dropped like a stone, she'd been sure she'd killed him. "I'm glad he's alive," she whispered. "I didn't mean to hurt him badly, I just wanted to leave. I panicked. I just…I can't be locked in a cage, Thane." Her eyes fixed on his. "You have to see, this isn't right."

Thane shook his head, his mouth set in a line. "I lock you in the cage to keep you from harm," he said quietly.

It was hopeless. He was never going to let her go. She wondered if anyone in the world was looking for her yet. Who? Betty swiped at tears that wound their way over her cheeks. She was exhausted, mentally and physically; any fight she'd had in her just oozed away through the soles of her bare feet. Her shoulders sagged and, like a house of cards, she folded up as her legs gave way. She crumpled to the cold tile and rested back against a plastic bath panel, head in hands.

"Stop this."

Betty glanced up from beneath a curtain of hair and saw him looking at the scab on her inner thigh, lace dress ridden up. She didn't care. He'd take what he wanted anyway, just like last night. "What do you want from me?"

Thane tugged up his suit pant legs, lowered his substantial frame to the floor and sat beside her, legs outstretched so that they spanned the small space. He laced his hands in his lap, tilted his head toward her and said plainly, "I want you to love me."

That was not what she'd expected him to say. Tears and snot streaked her face as she scooted around to look at him, incredulous. "To love you? Are you for fucking real?"

His wide brow furrowed as he nodded.

She laughed. "You seriously think that by raping me and keeping me here against my will…that I'll *love* you?"

"In time, yes," he replied, deep caramel eyes searching hers.

"Unfuckingbelievable!"

Unlacing his fingers, Thane brought a hand to her face and smudged away her tears with the heel of his hand. "I'll overlook your colorful choice of words for now. Listen, I want you to understand about me. About here."

This man was confusing - a mix of double standards and contradictions. Betty was so far out of her depth that she didn't even know if she should be more afraid of his anger or his affection. At least in her line of work she'd known exactly what the men had wanted from her. A hundred bucks–fifty on a quiet night–and all she'd had to do was wear her mask and fake it and that was enough for those guys. They didn't want any more from her than their dollars would buy. But this man, this big, beautiful, ugly man, he was batshit crazy. He went from drugging and imprisoning her to raping her, to demanding her *love?*

She could feel a blind fury building inside of her. Narrowing her eyes, she spat, "You need some serious relationship lessons mister cos, let me tell you, no girl is gonna love a guy who treats her like he's gonna kill her." Her voice rose an octave. "Flowers, you know? Take her out on a date or two, dinner, a movie. What never ever works is sticking them in the neck to knock them out, raping them and keeping them prisoner. Don't you see that?"

Thanatos

Thane sat in silence as she continued, the corners of his lips tugging up into a smile he couldn't fight and that only seemed to fuel this tantrum of hers. She had no idea how beautiful she looked when she was pissed. He almost wanted to capture the moment in a screenshot and savor that fire to enjoy at his leisure. That she possessed immeasurable passion was undeniable. It would be his duty to harness the passion and direct it in a more constructive manner.

When she'd blown herself out like a tornado, Thane closed the space between them and pinned her to the bathtub with a firm grip to both of her slim shoulders. He would make her understand. "You think I'm a monster, and you're right, I am. However, be warned. You haven't seen me at my worst yet." His expression as tempestuous as a squally sea in a storm.

Betty sat dejected, forlorn, chin dropped to her chest.

He shook her. "Look at me."

She didn't. She was starting to get on his last nerve, humor fizzing out along with his smile.

His fingers wove through her hair, finding purchase at her nape. Twisting it into his fist he pulled her face to his until their foreheads pressed together. "I said, look at me."

Her fearful eyes tipped up to his on a gasp.

He studied those beautiful iridescent blues and thought that he had never seen so clearly into another's soul. Vulnerable. Terrified. Dejected. Threading his fingers back through her hair he cupped her cheeks and softened his expression. "You're scared of me, I know, but I'm the one person in the world who would die to protect you. There's nothing I won't give you. Nothing I wouldn't do for you. I want to fucking worship you, Freya."

Her lips parted on a sigh. "Then let me go."

Closing his eyes, Thane bit down on his bottom lip. "I can't. I've waited for you my whole life. How can you ask me to give you up when to do so would be to cut out my own heart?"

Betty's hands gripped his strong forearms as she narrowed her eyes and replied, "You kidnapped me. You're nothing more than some two-bit cult leader who has no real understanding of love." She couldn't stop herself. "The only reason the others stay here is through fear…or brainwashing or something, but not love. You're incapable of love. You're just a fucking hypocritical crazy guy, and when they find me you'll be locked away. See how you like being in a damn cage."

On a sharp inhalation his eyes widened. They say truth hurts. It did. "That's how you see me?"

Betty nodded, crying hysterically now, her palms slapping against his chest.

Thane maintained his grip of her and chewed over her words, tasting their bitterness before swallowing them down on a gulp. If she would give him the chance to get to know him as the others had done, she'd see that he wasn't so evil. Or perhaps he was, after all it wasn't the first time he'd been told that. When he'd failed at school and been beaten by his father, it was allegedly because Satan himself needed to be caned out of his ass. The goodness of his forefathers skipped his generation but he'd make damn sure his own son grew up a better man than he was when he was blessed with one.

"Let *go* of me," hissed Betty, trying to free her wrists.

Thane released his grip and scooted back against the opposite wall, his face twisted in a tortured scowl. "You have no idea what you're talking about," he growled, eyes fixed on hers. "This is no cult. I don't expect you to agree with the manner in which I bring my chosen ones here. I know. I *know* the depth of my love for Luna, Syn, you. Hell, even Boy. And those who have gone before you all. I've protected. I've been respected!" True, he had failed one or two but largely he provided the majority with a far better life than they themselves had managed to build without his intervention.

Betty sat, head in hands as he continued.

"And yes, I know it's hard to start with. I'm under no illusion that I am loved when I've tilted your world on its axis, but in time…in time you'll see that this compound is a safe harbor. Never will you be more loved and cherished than you are in my arms." Levering himself on the washbasin, Thane rose to his feet. "And as for being crazy? Yes. Perhaps I am insane, if insanity is to turn my back on the wrongs that have been executed against me. If insanity is to want something better in this world then yes, I'm a lunatic." Crouching down in front of her. "But I make a solemn vow to you now. Tonight you'll see me at my worst. A full moon. If after tonight you wish to leave, then I will allow it."

Her breath caught, heart thumping a little faster as she looked up at him searching his eyes for truth or trick. She saw only sincerity. "How can I trust you to keep your promise?"

Taking her hand, he brought it to his face and pressed her palm to his course stubbled cheek. "I make this vow to you." he said. "May the gods strike me down if I break my word."

"Why?" she gasped. "Why would you let me go tomorrow, after everything you've said and done?"

A wry smile played over his lips. "It's simple. If you truly are my Freya then you'll stay by my side. This will be a test."

As he stood again he pulled Betty to her feet and towered over her, intimidating and volatile. That he was taking a risk was without question, in fact if this backfired he knew that it would destroy him. She would undoubtedly be terrified by his transformation over the ensuing hours but if she accepted him after this then she was his forever. He'd never before granted such a favor as this. He'd mourned the loss of Sirona. That she'd died at his hand still haunted his dreams. Now he fleetingly wondered if perhaps he should have given her this opportunity. Had he done so, would she have stayed? He'd never know. Right now he needed to focus. Twilight was fast approaching.

Thane guided Betty from the bathroom, through the bedroom and out to the pool. Past the potted trees he strode, Betty trying to match his pace, his grip a vice around her hand. Glancing up at the glass domed ceiling, Thane frowned at the violet blackness above where charcoal clouds skittered, chased by a dying sun.

Fine hairs at his nape rose, each muscle in his body contracted and pulled taught. This was going to be violent, of this he was certain.

Blood Moon

Freya

Betty didn't know where he was taking her or, worse still, what he would do; her mind was a cacophony of emotions and thoughts. Would he free her tomorrow or was that bullshit? Ducking into the tunnel-like corridor, Thane tightened his grip on her hand, crushing her fingers to the point of pain, as if sensing her reticence. She wanted to run as far away from this place and his dark intentions as she could. There was no escape. The realization hit her anew - a rock in the pit of her stomach. She tried to control her breathing, on the verge of hyperventilating. Stay calm. One more night and you'll be safe. He had no reason to promise it if he didn't mean it. Or was this another mind fuck?

Thane kicked open the heavy wooden door, old iron hinges creaking in protest. She didn't want to be back in this room where she'd been cut. Of all the dark and godforsaken hell-holes she'd been in her life, this room took her right back to her mom's apartment. Ironic. It was nothing like her mom's apartment decoratively or in any tangible way; it was a feeling deeply rooted in her. A feeling she got right before something bad happened. The gnawing tightness that had her thinking the walls were closing in and it's cozy and terrifying all at the same time. A womb-like place that ought to be safe, because your mom's womb is the only place you're ever really safe before you die, right? And when you're born, then your mom's home becomes an extension of her womb…now imagine you're violated there. That one safe place. How do you ever feel safe again when the one place in the world that should've given you life, instead caused you to die inside? This room where she'd been cut, yeah…same vibe.

The scab on her thigh pulled and smarted, reminding her of what he'd done. The fake flames flickered on the wall sconces casting a dull orange glow - no windows, no moonlight. Betty's eyes settled on Luna. Spread open and bare on a low wooden bench, she looked like a rag doll, still and silent, face like porcelain. Her instinct was to cover the woman up with the slip which lay in a puddle on the floor nearby.

As if reading her thoughts Thane let go of her hand and glanced over his shoulder. "Go to her," he said. His voice was cold, brittle as glass.

With tentative steps, Betty trod over to the bench and forced a tight smile for Luna. Her eyes were open, her chest rose with slow measured breaths. Eyes darting from Luna back to Thane, Betty hesitated then dropped to her knees. Her voice barely audible, she whispered, "What can I do to help you?"

Luna's plump lips curved in a smile. "Help me?" she replied. "I don't need your help. This is why I'm here. For him. I want this, for heaven's sake."

Betty checked that Thane couldn't hear them and brought her mouth close to Luna's ear. "Bullshit! I could try and knock him out," she said. "Is there anything I can use? If I have to kill him I will, I mean it."

Luna's eyes grew wide and alarmed. "Stop! Don't even talk like that." Glancing over to Thane, who was unbuttoning his shirt to expose broad planes of sculpted chest, she added urgently, "I want to do this, don't you see? I take the pain and it heals me. Heals him."

"Heal him how?" asked Betty. Her hand hovered over Luna's.

Luna's fingers curled around Betty's, lacing tight in a handhold that connected the two women in a way that was unfamiliar to Betty. It felt strange. Sisterhood.

Thane's shirt flew in a waft of white silk to the center of the room, settling like a blanket of snow over a three-legged stool. Both women watched as he walked into the shadows, and listened to the metallic clangs of implements they couldn't see.

Luna spoke again as Betty tried to focus on her. "Every day he takes care of us. When the moon is full we take care of him, you see. It's really as simple as that."

"How?" asked Betty, her skin prickling in response to

new sounds behind her. "What does he want?"

Luna smiled and squeezed Betty's hand. "To expel his demons," she said simply.

"He's crazy."

"No. His mom's crazy. Thane thinks he's insane too but he's just damaged, not mad." Her eyes creased then flicked to Thane as he strode towards them.

Just one night. She had this.

He was as beautiful as he was evil.

A satanic angel.

Every edge of him, from the thick cords of muscle straining under ink-black skin to the squareness of his jaw and sculpted lips, was so defined as to be chiselled from stone. Betty's fearful gaze travelled down over Thane's chest in a hurried path leading to a trail of black hair which disappeared beneath the waistband of his low slung pants. When she noticed directly below the elastic the sharp edge of a staggering erection, she gasped. Her hand flew to her mouth. She pushed up to her feet as the hairs at her nape bristled and moisture pooled at the juncture of her thighs. Mentally cursing her body, Betty gave Luna's hand a final squeeze; whatever was about to happen, the two women were united in facing it together.

"Freya. Come here." His voice was the low rumble of a train vibrating through her core.

"Please don't hurt me," Betty whispered.

In his hand hung a length of rope, the other hand extended toward her. Taking two steps forward, Betty lifted her hand to lay it gently in his palm. Long fingers curled around hers and caught her in a vice-like grip, pulling her close enough to feel the heat of his breath waft over her face. She stared at his chest, not daring to lift her eyes up to his and give him the satisfaction of witnessing the liquid heat and terror in her soul. Instead she focused on the dusting of black hair over his chest and the dark discs of his nipples, even when he took both of her hands and slipped the rope around her wrists.

"Breathe, Freya," Thane commanded.

Betty did as she was told and tried to breathe but the air was thick with the animalistic scent of him, of her own terror melded with lust that she didn't understand or want.

With skill and precision, Thane bound her in intricate knots and loops until all four limbs were webbed with rope. Further twists and tugs and she felt the bite of hemp between her legs with steady pressure on her clitoris. She bit down on her bottom lip, closed her eyes and battled so hard against the rising panic. Just one night. If she survived whatever it was he planned for her, then she'd be free. What would freedom bring? She couldn't answer this question that her subconscious mind kept screaming at her when her instincts were base and yelled louder that she needed to run.

"So beautiful," he sighed as he ran the rope underneath her breasts, forcing them upwards and her nipples to tighten. Betty felt a finger and thumb tug at her right nipple sending sharp waves of unwanted pleasure right to her core. She couldn't help the soft moan that ensued, hoping Thane hadn't heard it.

"Feels good, Freya?"

Fuck! "No," she hissed through her teeth.

Still not opening her eyes, she bit even harder on her lip as he thrust his hand between her legs, a finger sweeping down between her folds. The way he had tied her down there meant, she was sure, that her lower lips were parted, exposing her. With ease he slipped one then two solid fingers up into her entrance and crooked them until they rubbed against her pleasure spot.

Thane growled deep in his throat. "Dear God you're drenched. So responsive…"

As his hand pulled away she cried out as he caught hold of the rope that ran up her stomach and gave it a sharp tug. Pain bit into her groin and her vagina contracted. A sheen of sweat coated her top lip. *Jesus!*

"This is NOT about your pleasure," snapped Thane. Cruel sadistic bastard.

Somewhere behind her, Betty heard Luna say, "No it's not. Freya, this is for Thane, remember your place." And Betty wanted to rip her a new one right then.

"Silence, Luna," Thane snapped.

The girl fell silent. Needing but not wanting to know what was happening, Betty opened her eyes to see Thane grabbing hold of an overhead pulley with a grating groan of old metal. The broad girth of his arms swelled further as he exerted strength to pull it towards her. On the end of the pulley was a large iron ring; when it was directly above her Thane took the loose ends of rope and pulled them up. Her arms rose as any slack in the rope was lost. He worked swiftly to tie the rope to the ring. With a final tug, her feet were barely touching the ground, her weight supported only by her toes. It hurt, oh did it hurt as every muscle was stretched to its limit. Betty whimpered. "I can't do this."

"You can and you will," he bit back. "But this will be very much more painful for you unless you relax into it."

Betty shook her head and choked out a sob.

Thane moved behind her out of her line of sight. She felt his fingers working on the rope that tied her ankles. Suddenly each leg in turn was lifted from the ground. She felt herself falling forward and let out a scream.

"I have you. Go with it."

"No, no!" The rope caught, she didn't fall. Betty's legs were bent so that each heel was forced back to touch her ass and there the rope was looped to bind them in place. She could feel Thane attaching her legs to the pulley system. With more metallic grating, her folded legs were forced apart. She felt as though she were floating - suspended now entirely by the tracking overhead. Another adjustment and her ass was pulled up higher than her head and shoulders. Blood rushed to her head, misting her eyes, pulse thrumming in her ears. A tear dripped onto the ground below.

"Perfect. Give me your beautiful bitter tears my love." Thane ran a palm over her ass, then *thwack!* he slapped her hard, setting her rocketing forwards and back, forwards and back.

"Agh!"

"Shh little one."

As she swung slightly to the side, Betty could see Luna; she was watching Betty apparently in awe, with a faraway smile playing over her lips. Luna's hand was rooted between her own thighs, her fingers rubbing in steady circles, her eyes hooded as they met Betty's. Betty found that she couldn't look away; in spite of her predicament and the sharp sting to her buttock, it was the most erotic thing she'd ever seen. The look of bliss–the total lack of care of being watched. Sinful and decadent. Betty didn't think she could ever be as carefree or untroubled; she'd felt the way she did for as long as she could remember and it was polar opposite to the girl staring back at her.

"Oh…," the sound escaped Betty's lips.

"I think I'll withdraw the benefit of speech, my dear muse." With that, he produced from somewhere a gag, slipping it over her head and forcing a small ball between her teeth. Her tongue pressed and poked against it but it was lodged tight.

All Betty could do was watch and wait for whatever came next. As it transpired, Thane turned his attention to Luna whose hips were bucking off the bench as the rhythm of her own touch intensified. Betty's breathing quickened as Thane towered over Luna. She watched as the woman's hand stilled in his presence. Reaching down, Thane took Luna's hand and brought it to his tented pants. Luna spun around as she sat up, her hands tugging down his pants which slipped over his hips to the floor.

From her vantage point Betty could see him side on - enormous, erect, glistening in the flickering light. Leaning forward, Luna took the vast swollen crown of him into her mouth as he fisted her hair and began to fuck her there, his buttocks clenched and firm. She watched too as Luna gagged and struggled to take more of him than her reflexes allowed. When she retched, Thane bowed forward, slipped from her lips, drew back his hand and slapped her face. Betty struggled and twisted, sending herself into a slow spin. She wanted to make him stop. So many emotions flashed over her mind that she couldn't begin to make sense of them and, deepest of all, was a bitter envy. Jealousy. Seeing him with her was…what was it? Jesus fucking Christ. She wanted it to be her mouth, her throat, her that he needed, not Luna.

She couldn't damn well get loose of the ropes and now she faced the wall so that she couldn't see them. The clatter of a latch and creak of a door. Betty craned her neck, catching sight of Syn and the boy. Boy was dragging in a goat by a makeshift collar of green twine about it's neck. Syn was naked except for a mask. Made of silver card or perhaps fabric–difficult to tell from where Betty hung–it was shaped in the curve of a half crescent moon, small spheres cut for her eyes to see through. Betty was transfixed not on Syn or Boy, but on the goat as it struggled against its cord leash as if sensing the mortal danger it was undoubtedly in. Neither of the two spoke. Boy led the goat out of Betty's line of vision whilst Syn stood in front of her with a dour expression. Her narrow frame looked almost elfin in the poor light but then everything looked smaller in Thane's giant shadow.

Thane let out a feral roar just as Syn spun Betty around to face him. It was into her eyes that Thane looked as he spurted his seed down Luna's throat, the girl struggling to swallow at the pace with which he ejaculated.

Panting, Thane snapped his head toward Syn and withdrew from the girl's mouth. "The knife!" he bellowed. "Give it to me, Syn."

Betty screamed against the ball gag. He couldn't…he wouldn't kill Luna.

Fire and Ice

Thanatos

As always he was only part-way sated, for whilst physical release was welcome, it did not purge his angst in its entirety. Thane was not deluded enough to think that it would be any different this time, even with his Freya just a breath away from where he stood. In fact, it was because his girl was so close and that it wasn't her mouth he'd fucked that he'd had to almost choke out a release at all. For the first time, it felt wrong to be with Luna. What the fuck was that all about? He took what he wanted, who he wanted. Only the ritual would be the chattel by which he could once again morph into the Thanatos who was safe.

The Thane who was in control.

"The dagger, Sir."

Opening his palm, Thane received the handle of the ceremonial knife he'd named Seax, the knife that he had used to brand his woman with his own carved initial. That single act had given a new reverence to the weapon now gripped in his fist as it still bore smears of her now dried blood. One day–he reflected without morose–it would be crusted with his own blood in a final act to rid the world of his madness. One day he'd slit his own throat with his trusty dagger. Now, he held it high so that its tip pointed directly at the gods whom Thane hoped beyond hope were observing. He couldn't pinpoint exactly when the gods had become the focus of his life but then a great deal of his past was purposefully scrubbed from his memory. It was safer that way, you see, not to dwell on the past, just be guided by a greater good. What Thane did know was that this room–though sparse and comfortless–was the beating heart of his compound. Every monumental thing that had happened to Thane had been witnessed by these very walls. Here he was cocooned yet free. Here he had been reborn. Here too his life would end one day, he was sure of it.

As all of his muses watched on and inspired him, as was their reason to be, Thane dropped to his knees and pried the goat from Boy. It put up a brave and spirited fight until the serrations of Seax's blade scoured down and through its narrow throat as he slit it. Warm blood spurted, a little of it splashing over Thane's jaw; his tongue licked around his lips, savoring the droplets found there. It was a rich and sacred life-force. As the small goat thrashed about on the hard stone ground, everyone watched as Thane ended its life with a violent slash that severed the goat's head from its body.

Behind him Thane heard his Freya crying, as best she could considering she was gagged. He was sorry for her shock but the end justified the means. Sacrifice like this was a necessary evil and she'd do well to learn that for it wouldn't be the last she witnessed. If she stayed. He tried not to allow his mind to dwell on the possibility that she might leave, instead he placed the knife down and coated his hands in a puddle of blood before standing once more. Turning to Boy, Thane said, "Bring me a torch and ice."

The boy scurried away to do Thane's bidding. Thane threw a glare at Syn through narrowed eyes. "Why are you standing there, little one? You know what needs to be done."

As though her trance were broken by his words, Syn dropped her chin and whispered an apology. Syn had spent her whole fucking life apologizing for every bruise to her skin and to her mind, inflicted by her husband in her past life, so now it genuinely pained him to see her anything less than happy. He'd address it with her later but, for now, Freya was suspended before him at his utter mercy. It was time to focus. If he was to expel this fire that licked at his soul, he needed to do this right. He wouldn't hold back–after all, he'd cast no false hope of this night being anything less than intense and terrifying.

Behind him, Luna stretched back on the bench, while Betty observed his every movement. Syn walked over to a tall mahogany closet that was simple in its design. It wasn't wide but it stretched upwards from ground to ceiling. The slight woman pressed her shoulder and hip to the side of it, shoving with a loud grunt until it shifted along the ground. When she'd moved it perhaps a foot, a slither of moonlight pierced the small cavernous room through a previously hidden square window set high in the wall. The pale blue light illuminated the still twitching carcass of the goat where it lay sodden in its own exsanguination.

When the boy returned, Thane took the flaming torch from him with a curt nod, a smell of fuel melded with the metallic stench of blood. Looking past the boy, his master called to Syn, "Hold her steady."

"Freya?" she clarified.

Thane nodded.

Betty shook her head, eyes like saucers as they followed the flame that sizzled and spat on the end of the rod. He stepped beside her as Syn held his girl's face in her hands, crouching until her mouth was a single breath from Betty's.

"Look at me," whispered Syn and Betty did so, scared eyes pleading with the woman to help her. Futile yet rather endearing. Syn glanced at Thane and back to Betty. "Focus on me and not on the pain, okay?"

Thane glared at Syn. "Did I give you permission to speak to Freya?"

"No. Forgive me Thane, you didn't, but may I please?"

He considered her request and granted it, "You may, but do so quietly."

"Thank you." Syn returned her attention to Betty who she could feel was trembling in her hands. "The pain needn't be bad," she purred. "If you don't fight it, you'll go to a place you've never been before. It's peaceful there, you'll see."

Thane listened to the girl. He suspected that Betty

wanted to be some place peaceful away from there, and that the thought of enduring pain was abhorrent to her. There was, however, no physical escape, only a mental fleeing of the mind should she empower herself to let it happen.

Tipping his head up skyward, Thane blew out a deep breath and raised the torch. "The first offering was the fluid of life which I pray you take in exchange for a new life. A son."

Syn continued to mutter but Thane was no longer listening.

"Next, I offer you fire and beg that you take the fire from my veins that fuels the madness in my mind." Slowly he lowered the flame and held it six inches above Betty's shoulder blade. She was trying to writhe but was held firm by the rope. Tracing the torch from shoulder to shoulder and down her spine, Thane took great care not to allow the flame to touch her skin for more than a fleeting second.

Betty chewed hard on the ball between her teeth while Syn stroked her hair, her face, kissed her lips around the ball - urging her on as well she should.

The flame licked over Betty's genitalia. Her hips bucked as high as they could considering her bondage and she continued to writhe as the flame followed a path down each thigh, each leg and finally each foot. Waiting for a nod from his master, the boy then took the torch from Thane who acknowledged the young man's own arousal with an arched brow and a growl.

"Syn. Take Boy and do something about his problem."

"As you wish." She smirked and snapped her fingers.

He watched his muse relieve Boy of the torch which she

tossed into a pail of sand, then lead Boy to the table where he'd carved his Freya's thigh. Within moments she had him supine, vulnerable, and was riding him hard. He wouldn't last more than a couple of minutes, pathetic really.

Syn's absence left Betty without moral support so he called to Luna to replace her. Luna leapt up like a zealous kitten, nuzzling her face in the crook of Betty's neck.

Looking down at Betty's naked back he could see that her skin bore only a pale redness from the flame. She'd be sore but not blistered; he'd done well to show such restraint when the anguish inside was barely contained inside the shell of him. A bundle wrapped in muslin sat at his feet where Boy had left it. Bending down, he picked it up, peeling back the cloth to reveal a handful of ice cubes. Offering them skywards, Thane said, "And ice that you counter that with warmth in my heart so that I can love Freya as she should be loved and cherished, and to love the son that she bears me."

Setting the bundle of ice on the ground, Thane took out one small cube and traced it along the same path that the flaming torch had taken, cooling and soothing Betty's skin.

He then retrieved two further items from a wall rack. His skin was alight as surely as if he'd used the torch on himself; beads of sweat trickled down his back, winding their way into the crevice of his taught buttocks.

"Luna, remove the gag."

"Yes, Thane."

"I want to hear the girl scream."

With a sharp 'snap!' Thane introduced the suspended girl to a whip.

Freya

With a gasp Betty sucked in a lungful of air as the gag was finally torn off. She couldn't take any more, her whole body shaking uncontrollably. Before she could beg him to get her down, a snap followed by a sharp sting on her bottom took the pain to a whole new level. Straining against the ropes, Betty let out a scream. It was a strange noise that she didn't recognize. At first she thought perhaps it was Luna screaming but as the sound repeated and she struggled to breathe between lashes, she was aware that it came from herself.

"Good girl," he growled with the eighth strike.

Luna kissed away the tears as they leaked over Betty's cheeks. She stroked her face and kissed her hair and told her how proud she was of her, told her to 'let go' which Betty didn't understand. It hurt so goddamned bad. During a short pause between lashes she felt something pressing between the still smarting skin of her thighs. The velvet steel of Thane's cock grazed her vulva before a steady pressure entered her vagina. A rhythmic pounding struck her core as he pistoned inside of her.

"Agh!"

"Shh," Luna soothed, "drift away. I promise it's the most magical feeling if you'd only let go." She swallowed Betty's next scream with her own mouth amid gentle lashings of her tongue until the two women's tears merged and Betty didn't struggle any more.

Betty's eyes misted over, her mind ran scenarios and wild visions until it all melded into something different.

Tranquility. Peace. The bite of the whip didn't hurt as much, or perhaps it did and she wasn't aware of it, even as it ripped at her flesh in perfect symphony with the force of Thane entering her. She was almost euphoric as waves of pleasure emanated from her apex and dampened the pain until she was lost to a crescendo of pure, spine twisting, core-clenching ecstasy, as vile as it was incredible, as hated as it was craved. Wave after wave rippled through her body until finally she settled. Spent and confused, Betty hung limp and let darkness swallow her.

It was night still, or was it day? Her swollen eyes failed to see properly until she blinked away crusted tears. It took several minutes, or maybe hours, to focus on the face just inches from hers. She wasn't caged, for this she was grateful to the beast that lay beside her, his arm draped over her hip. Betty ran her tongue over parched lips.

"Thirsty? Here." Thane reached across her, his weight pressing down but she didn't move. Daren't move. With care, he touched the rim of a glass to her lips. "Drink," he ordered. When she stayed as still as a statue, he repeated his command more firmly.

Betty tucked her elbows behind her and pushed up as he tipped cool water in a steady stream down her throat. She swallowed, relieved to quench her thirst. "Is it over?"

Thane reached down and set the glass on the floor then tucked an errant curl behind her ear. His face looked different…deep troubled crevices were relaxed into a sleepy smile over lips that before had cut a stern line. "You slept for a straight nine hours."

Nine hours? Betty groaned. Everywhere ached. Stretching out her arms, she glanced down at a lattice of marks that criss-crossed her skin. Peering down beneath the sheet, she saw that her legs were the same and so, she assumed, was her back. Rubbing her eyes with balled fists, Betty looked around Thane's private bedroom and noticed the drapes were drawn shut, a little dappled sunlight sneaking through a narrow parting, enough to add warmth to the otherwise stark space. "What time is it?"

Thane ran his palm down her arm. "A little after eleven."

"In the morning?"

"Yes, the morning after the night before." He huffed out a laugh of sorts.

Betty couldn't remember hearing him laugh before; he was always so serious, so sinister. Turning to face him, she pulled the tousled white sheet up and tucked it under her armpits. "I remember," she said with a frown.

His jaw clenched as Thane nodded. "And?"

"And…I don't know what you want me to say." Betty chewed at the inside of her mouth and chanced a glance at him. His cheeks and jaw were peppered with black stubble, he looked tired, dark shadows circling his rich hazel eyes. Thane moved on the bed to rest his cheek on his crooked arm as he watched her. A sunbeam that had snook in danced over his irises making them turn from hazel to spun gold.

"That's the first time you've looked at me that way," he said, barely audible.

Self-conscious, Betty looked away.

Thane reached over to tip her face back to him, his thumb rubbing over her cheek. "Tell me, what do you see when you look at me, little one?"

With a tip of her head Betty studied his face, unsure how frank she should be with the man who had scared her half to death not ten hours ago. "A man who is seriously fucked up in the head," she chanced.

If her reply angered the man he didn't show it, his expression unreadable. "So intuitive, Freya."

"Betty," she corrected. "My name's Betty."

"But it's not is it?"

"What do you mean?"

"You were born Lacey Porter, were you not?"

Betty's eyes widened, her jaw grew slack. "How?"

"How do I know this?" He smirked. "Ah, Freya, there's so much you don't know about me but one thing I can tell you is that I'm a wealthy man and money buys information."

"You had me investigated?" she asked, incredulous.

Thane nodded with a wry smile. "Of course. I have an excellent lawyer who looks after all of my interests."

"When? After you took me?" She raked fingers through her dishevelled hair, tugging at the knotted ends.

"No. I'd been watching you for some time."

"Wait…you've been following me?" Her hands dropped into her lap and curled into tight fists. "Like, properly stalking me?"

"Semantics."

Betty shook her head. Scowling at him she quipped, "Whatever. You said I could leave today, I'm assuming that was a fucking lie."

"Mouth." Thane shot her a glare and ran a palm over his shaved head. "I never lie. Not ever. My word is my bond. I said you could go today if you still wanted to after last night, and I meant it." Sitting himself up, Thane looked at Betty with great sincerity. "I'd hoped that you'd want to stay. That you'd see me at my worst but that you'd get it."

"Get what? That you're a sadistic animal? Sure, I get it alright."

He sighed deeply. "That the life I can offer you here could give you a new freedom -constrained yet liberated. Don't you see that, don't you get me at all?"

Betty scoffed. She didn't want to wind him up, make him change his mind, but she had to laugh at the irony of his damn words. "No I don't get it, Thane. What I see is a sick and twisted man who manipulates and controls to get what he wants, so forgive me if I'm not more enthusiastic about extending this vacation."

"I see."

"Do you?" Was he for real? "Do you really see what it's like to be locked in a cage and told to pee there? Or to be gagged and tied up and scared shitless by a freakin' giant?"

"This is how you see me…this place?" Hurt cut across his eyes.

Betty nodded. He was beyond anyone she'd ever encountered before and she'd had the misfortune to come across some arrogant pricks before.

"Then you're right," he said. "I'll have Luna bring your clothes and I'll take you back to where I found you."

"To the alley?"

"To the gutter," he said.

Finding Betty

Thanatos

His word was his bond. He was a principled man. It did not mean that he was weak in keeping his promise. If she was destined to be his then she would have wanted to stay as the others had, or she'd come back to him. If it was meant to be, it would be, he really believed that with his whole heart. Still daring to believe that she'd pass this final test, that his faith in her wasn't misplaced, Thane's hand was forced, the arrangements made. Destiny decided and fuck, it was a bitch.

The car was returned from the parking garage and lined up curb-side in front of the compound. Usually when he took someone he'd drive himself. He trusted no-one, dared not, but needs must and the lesser risk was his lawyer, Bingham Suffolk. The scowl that Bingham threw at him was nothing more than Thane had expected. You wouldn't exactly call them adversaries although they'd never formed a bond of friendship. Thane's dad had called him 'a safe pair of hands.' The relationship between Bingham and Thane was a more grounded one: money bought the lawyer's silence in return for a nice fat pay check and rosy retirement. It just worked. Over time, Bingham's greed had led him to overlook his client's increasingly bizarre behavior and now he'd likely be in as deep as Thane if ever he had the notion to betray him. Both men knew this. Both accepted.

Thane handed the man a folded square of notepaper.

"This the address?"

Thane nodded.

Bingham sighed and waited on the sidewalk for whoever needed a ride. He'd laugh at how he'd turned his hand to chauffeuring after studying so damned hard for his bar exams but he didn't find it funny. There hadn't been many visits to the Remond building, those few times had been just like this. He was never invited inside.

Deep inside the belly of the compound, dressed casually in pants and sweater, Thane embraced a pensive Syn and Boy who both looked desolate in response to his darkening mood.

"Can I come with you, Thane?" asked Boy, looking up at Thane beneath a scruff of hair and sorrowful doe eyes.

"Not this time," replied Thane. "I need to do this alone with Freya."

Boy chewed at his stumpy fingernails. He didn't like to

see Thane look so sad and wished he could make it better; in all his years he'd never wanted anything more. He'd happily lock Freya in the cage and keep watch until he was a hundred years old if it pleased his mentor, but he knew better than to push. A no was a no.

"She'll come back," said Syn. Taking Thane's powerful hand in hers she brought it to her rouge lips and pressed a kiss into his palm. "I prayed this morning and I feel sure that this isn't the last we'll see of her."

Thane rolled his neck and managed a lopsided smile. "If it's the will of the gods then so be it," he said quietly. It was a tender moment between Thane and Syn. It took a while to notice Betty hovering in the doorway clutching her purse.

"I'm ready," she said on a frown.

"Ah, here you are." Uttering the very same words he'd first said to her in the alleyway, Thane drank in the sight of his Freya. He wished he'd burned her fucking clothes. Hips swathed in cheap black skirt, tight as her fucking skin, it took all of his self control not to tear it from her, to rid her of the stigma of her tainted past so that it did not contaminate her future. Instead he drew his hand from Syn's and offered it to Betty. "Let's go."

There was of course the risk that she'd bolt as soon as she set foot on the sidewalk. For this reason he'd pinned her to his side beneath the strong sweep of his arm for the few paces it took to reach the open rear door to the imported Jaguar. In truth, she'd hesitated momentarily–a fleeting glance up the street, big scared eyes–but by the time she'd decided what to do, he'd helped her onto the backseat with a shove. Thane thought of himself as a gentleman for the most part, an animal too of course. His father had raised him to open doors for the gentler sex, not to then shove them into cars. There were a great number of things Thane did that folk from generations before him would turn in their graves over and so be it - he'd spent his entire damn life in their shadow.

He held her hand throughout the drive and she let him. Traffic was heavy, the journey interminably long, punctuated by her silence. Thane knew what was going through her mind: she didn't trust him, he'd most likely kill her…or would he really let her go? It was bitterly disappointing that she'd not met his expectations but there was still time. One more test, the greatest challenge for her yet, perhaps.

"We're here," he said, leaning down to peer out at the sign that read 'Dan's Bar.'

"Right, I'll be off then." Betty held her purse tight to her chest.

"Not yet," replied Thane.

Betty looked at the lock on her door which was still engaged. She turned to Thane. "Please. I won't call the cops, I swear."

Thane tilted his head and smiled down at her. "I'm pleased to hear it. Things would be very bad for you if you did."

"I won't, cross my heart and hope to die." She etched a cross over her heart with her finger and added, "I'm sure you'll be watching me anyway so you'd know if I had, right?"

Thane shook his head. "No, little one. In setting you free I'm returning your future. Your choices. To you. Only you can decide now what action you'll take, and you must be accountable for those actions."

Betty didn't really understand what he meant so she said nothing.

Thane continued, "Call this a magical mystery tour. We're not stopping here, I just wanted to remind you of where I found you." With a long finger he pointed down the dark alleyway beside the bar. "You were right down there, remember? You'd been slapped by a john and fucked for fifty bucks."

She winced, no doubt not wanting to be reminded of her whoring days, especially when he put it like that. It seemed a lifetime ago probably.

"Drive," Thane commanded. Bingham pulled out into the flow of traffic on a hissed curse.

He could all but hear the thumpety-thump of her heartbeat against her ribs. "Where are we going?"

"You'll see." Thane smiled and stroked a languid finger over his top lip.

Freya

This was beyond cruel. He wasn't going to let her go, instead he was toying with her like a cat with a mouse before eating it.

Resting her head back against the headrest, Betty closed her eyes wondering if this was for real. If the whole fucking thing had been a nightmare. And what she'd do next. *Shit.* The words of Luna and Syn drifted into her mind, she tried to remember what they'd said but not all of their words made sentences…mostly she recalled peace and drifting into someplace else. She tried to drift now, to ease the hurting in her back, her core and her heart but her mind stayed planted right there in the car, beside him. Her right hand gave up guarding her purse for a moment and smoothed over her left breast. It was still there; the little folded note that Luna had slipped into her palm earlier was safely encased in her bra. She would read it. Or maybe she'd never get the chance to if he killed her after all. In any case, whatever Luna had wanted her to know was irrelevant now. It didn't mean shit. Luna–if that even was her name, which Betty doubted–chose to stay. What could she possibly have to say that would mean anything to Betty?

When they'd pulled up alongside the alleyway she'd stupidly believed that maybe she had hope, that Thane would do the right thing finally. Then he'd had the driver pull away and all hope bled out of her heart in a sticky pool of despair. She sank back against the warm cream leather and sighed out a held breath like it was her last, her life force leaving her body.

She knew this neighborhood. He was taking a route she'd walked most nights. Many of the curbs were familiar working ground for Betty, not that she relished the reminder especially not with Thane. Apparently he really did want her to suffer before doing whatever he planned to do. The streets rolled by, taking Betty deeper into her home territory if she could call it home. There was the store where Cody had thieved a pack of Marlboro and a Snickers bar for her fifteenth birthday. The small scratchy patch of grass they'd made their own for hazy summer picnics where they'd sprawled side by side and laughed louder than the traffic noise around them. Where he'd first kissed her in a way that a brother shouldn't kiss his sister. Betty screwed her eyes shut on the memory, then she opened them.

Her mom's street?

"What are you doing?" Betty craned her neck to look as she saw her mom's neighbor, Old Man Tyler, going about his business.

"Be patient, Freya." Thane threw a tight smile but he looked nervous, shifty as he slapped his hand on the back of the driver's seat. "Stop here."

Betty made an O with her mouth. They were stopping at her mom's? Was he making sure she had a place to go? Everything that she thought she knew about this monster–such dark and sinister perceptions–nothing seemed to fit right now. She was so fucking confused; part of her wanted to run from the car screaming for the cops, another part of her mind said to let it go. She was alive when she didn't think that she would be. But he was delivering her from one hell to another, wasn't he? He couldn't know that this was the one place in the world he could bring her to where she'd feel as lost as at the compound. She was free and she was still trapped.

Thane reached between them unclipping her seatbelt and his own. Throwing open his door, he unpeeled his huge frame onto the sidewalk and stepped around to her. The lock popped up, the door opened. Betty hesitated before accepting his hand. He pulled her up from the car, her legs trembling. Holding her hand tight, he led her two doors up to the familiar brownstone, the gate still hanging off its hinges. At the window to the right and up two storeys hung the same yellow floral drapes that had once been white until her mom's cigarette smoke colored them ochre.

"This is where I leave you, Freya," said Thane, cupping

her face. “What you do now is up to you.” Reaching around to the back pocket of his pants, Thane produced a cell phone and laid it in her palm, curling her fingers around it. “My number is programmed in,” he told her. “This is how you reach me if you want to come home.”

Home. Where was home? Not here. Not there. Not anywhere.

Betty nodded and chewed her lip. Her hands were shaking so bad, she wasn’t sure if she could breathe let alone hold the phone. Her head was fucked.

“Oh wait, I have something else for you.”

She watched as Thane walked to the back of the car and popped the trunk. Reaching in, he pulled out two tatty grab bags. She hadn’t dared ask him where the rest of her things were, though it had killed her to think that she’d lost them. The last she’d seen of the tatty sacks of photos, clothes and whatnot was the day he’d taken her, whenever that was. He carried them now as far as the brownstone and set them down, walking back to her with a dour face. Betty was more grateful to him for this final gesture than he would ever know. Her brother’s sweater that still smelt of sandalwood and sweat and soccer was buried in there together with the only family photograph she’d ever seen. Precious garbage. Worthless treasure. She began to cry.

Taking a measured look down at her, Thane’s face creased in a bittersweet smile. He smudged a tear from her cheek with his thumb and told her, “I love you Freya. It’s just–”

Her brows pinched together. He was so fucking confusing, showing this side of him, a part of him that genuinely seemed to care about her. When he was a bastard she could slap that label on him, knew where to channel her hate. This, this was somehow worse. He'd broken her and it was as if he loved her broken pieces more than the whole.

Thane let his head fall back as he took both of her hands in his. His eyes seemed to fix on the patchwork of clouds that stitched together a heavy sky. "I've never made the choice to say goodbye before." His chin dropped, eyes brewing a storm as they pinned her in place. "I never thought I'd find you, you see. Never dared hope. And now, I'm giving you up and it's killing me. I don't know how I'll survive without you and that's the truth of it."

"You're doing the right thing," she whispered, ignoring the part of her that wondered if this was true. The world seemed suddenly more scary, bigger, loud, so loud. Her future uncertain, her freedom beckoning while her subconscious screamed not to make her return to whoring, to not *feeling*.

"Goodbye my love."

More tears channelled down her cheeks. Pain, relief… something else.

Betty looked down at his hands as his strong fingers unfurled. Her palms slid over his until they were joined by only their fingertips. As the final connection broke, Thane gasped. His eyes were glassy as they slid away from hers on a pivot of his heels. And he was gone.

She watched the broad sweep of his back as he walked away, shoulders stooped, arms hanging limp at his sides as though he were broken too. Her eyes lifted up to the same sky that moments before he had been lost to. A small bird cartwheeled from a tree. The sun bled out from the clouds, swollen and pulsing in time with her heartbeat.

What the hell had just happened? Where had innocent little Lacey Porter gone?

Incessant ringing. Thumb on bell. Intercom crackled.

"Who is it?"

"Mom…it's me. I've come home. Open the door."

"Lacey?"

"Yeah, it's me mom."

"Whatdy'a want? I don't have no money."

"Please. I need you. Let me in."

"Did you bring bourbon?"

The Confines of Freedom

Thanatos

His fist clenched so tightly that his knuckles blanched–nails unclipped, untouched–sank into the fleshy bed of his palm. When the fist connected with Boy's jaw it was a sickly crack of bone that shocked Thane more than Luna's scream.

"What have you done?" Syn's voice rang shrill.

Luna continued to scream over the boy's limp body that now lay supine, his left leg twisted through the bars of the cage at a precarious angle.

"What have you done?"

Thane's vision cleared of the red fog enough to look

down at Syn and he realized that he'd never before seen her beautiful face so twisted in anger. Not even when he'd crouched low, crushing an enviable display of dahlias and watched her inside the neat little house on a perfect street with hedges manicured to within an inch of their lives. Not even as, through the sparkling crystal glass of a newly polished window, he'd seen Norman Mansen crack a beer bottle on his wife's head and break her ribs with the toe of his yard boot. Even then her face remained composed, accepting. Now. Now Syn looked utterly terrified of Thane.

She repeated her question, quieter this time, her hands shaking as they gripped his powerful biceps. "What. Have. You. Done?"

"I don't know. I–"

"Wake up!" Luna lifted the boy's bleeding head into her lap, stroking the sandy mop of hair from eyes that were unseeing. "My God. I think you've killed him," she whispered.

Thane turned his head from Syn to look down on Boy and saw that his chest was rising and falling, albeit shallow. "He's alive."

"Why? Why would you do this to him?" Luna's face streaked with tears.

Thane tipped his head at Luna and stepped away from Syn, from Luna and Boy and from the carnage at his feet. It had been true all along; he was cursed with his mother's sickness. The times that he'd dodged out of the way of her blows now made sense to him. It wasn't that he'd been bad. Or maybe he had, but not so bad as to justify the beatings he took. She'd had the mist too…the mist that blinded and enraged, reaching into one's mind, strangling all sense of reason, clawing away at one's soul. They shared a cancer of the mind. Now his father's fear of her before he'd died became less of a weakness, more about self-preservation. The clarity of these thoughts rendered him speechless and numb.

"Thane! Look at me." Syn shook him ever-so gently and rose up onto her tiptoes to meet his vacant stare. "Thane. The boy needs to go to a hospital, he's bleeding. Please, let me call a cab. I'll go with him, you can stay right here."

"Hospital?"

"Yes. Let me take him." Her voice became more urgent, her grip on him a little tighter. "If you love him, you'll let him go," she implored.

"Is he going to die?"

"No, Thane, he'll be okay please God, but he needs help."

"Go. Take him."

"Thank you." Syn hurried past the empty cage, away into the belly of the compound.

"I didn't mean–" He ran his bruised hand over his own jaw. "It's just…I saw red. After Bingham's call. I don't remember what happened then."

"Bingham Suffolk?" Luna looked up at him and wiped her nose on her sleeve. "What did he say? What triggered this for heaven's sake?"

"My mother died. He said my mother died this morning."

Freya

* * *

"I don't have enough money. Take these off." With a sweep of her hand, Betty divided the groceries into essentials and non-essentials, the checkout assistant shaking her head with a pointed sigh. Betty narrowed her eyes, heat radiating over her cheeks. So fucking embarrassing. Someone in the line behind her tutted. "You have a problem?" she quipped over her shoulder. The line behind her looked away in unison. Tossing the last of her cash down she grabbed the milk, bread and potato chips and got the hell out of the store wishing the ground would swallow her the hell up.

It was the furthest that Betty had ventured since…since *him*. She was going stir crazy at the apartment; how she hadn't lost it with her mom was a mystery. Most days Betty ran errands, usually to the liquor store, sometimes to the park where she'd sit awhile with a ghost and talk about old times like none of the bad shit really happened. Today was grocery day and she'd meant to use the cash Mom gave her for healthy food, honestly she had. It was just that when she'd passed a homeless kid she'd been unable to resist giving her twenty bucks. She'd been there, where that girl was. What if she didn't give her the money? Betty couldn't live with her conscience if something had then happened to the kid who was maybe thirteen. If she too had been forced into a life working the streets. No fucker had helped Betty, she wanted to be different, you know? So that was where the grocery money had gone. Now all she had was the makings of a potato chip sandwich but then her mom would be too drunk to care.

Stalking His Prey

Freya

Weeks passed and they made do. Thing is, if you lock up nice and tight and don't think about the bad shit, you can almost convince yourself that everything's okay, that you're in control and shit isn't so bad. You have to make yourself real numb real quick or it's like a quicksand that'll suck you down inch by inch until you're done for.

They had a routine. Nanette Porter needed her daughter even if she never would show it. Truth was, Betty needed her Mom too. It wasn't love–not the conventional kind anyway–but it was a mutual acceptance of their roles that seemed to work.

Until today. Today her mom was getting on her last nerve and Betty felt like the poky apartment was closing in plus she felt like seven shades of crap.

"Lacey. You in the bathroom again?"

"I'll be right out, Mom."

"I need ta pee, or dy'a want that I pee right here on your Aunt Mabel's rug. Seems kind of a shame since she carried it all the way from Persia an' all."

Betty gripped the porcelain basin and breathed through a wave of nausea, then called out, "The same rug Aunt Mabel stole from Old Missus Beardy when she fired her thieving ass?"

There was a pause and then: "Well, Old Missus Beardy, as you call her, had a Persian fancy man. In any case, it don't matter who carried the darn rug, I'll still pee right on it if you don't open the damn door."

"So pee on the rug."

"I'm doin' it–"

"Jesus Christ, Mom!" Shoving off the basin, Betty threw the door open and glared at her mother, a steady stream of urine was trickling in a cloudy orange path down her nobbly legs, soaking into the thread-bare rug. She was pissing pure bourbon. And, wherever Persia was, it evidently had a Walmart - the label may be tatty but it was still attached. "You're disgusting."

"I'm out'a liquor. Be a good girl and run to the store."

"Why don't you suck your piss off the rug seeing as it's neat liquor?"

Nan puckered her mouth into a scowl and wagged a bird-bone finger. "No rer-spect. I should'a never had kids, more fool me. Could'a been one of them ballet-reenas if I hadn't a' been knocked up. Course it's your brother's fault too."

Betty sucked in a breath to calm her temper. "You can't blame Cody for world famine, Mom. Look closer to home. Look in the mirror and see who's to blame for screwing up our lives."

Nanette looked away. They'd never been able to talk about Cody without fighting about him. It was so sad that his memory was reduced to this. There'd been good times, happy times, times that were hard to bring to the forefront now, what with the shadow of his passing darkening everything in their minds and in their wolds. He was just a fucked-up boy who didn't know how to love right. Betty could see so much of him in herself.

Her voice softened as she took in the small damaged woman in front of her. "We need food, Mom, and I'm broke."

"Well don't look at me. I gave you my last thirty bucks yesterday. You bled me dry ya leech."

"That was Tuesday. You sent me for a quart of Jim Beam. You drank it already?"

"Oh stop bitchin' at me, it's Friday now. You kept the damn change."

"Two bucks. And it's Thursday."

"Thursday, Friday, I don't give a rat's cootie what the day is. Six damn weeks you've been here, now ya know what ya need to do so get to it an' earn us some cash best way you know how."

Betty gaped at Nan Porter and tried to remember when Nanette, her mother, became so vile. "Just wow. No wonder Dad left you."

"What'd you say?"

This woman who'd carried her for nine months, given

birth to her and wiped her nose, had just ordered her back on the street. "You heard me. I'm so out of here."

"Good! Get out'a here and when the little 'un comes, don't come cryin' at my door again."

"What did you say?"

Her mother nodded at Betty's stomach. "Think I can't hear ya spewing every darn day?"

"I'm sick." Betty struggled for air. Why couldn't she breathe? Mom was wrong, it had to be a stomach bug.

"Sure y'are."

She watched her mom shuffle into the bathroom, then stared at the closed door for the longest time. Betty looked down at her stomach, running a hand over her tank top to the waistband of her jeans. *Oh. My. God. I can't be pregnant.*

With no cash to buy a testing kit, or even food, Betty had no choice but to work that night. Tugging on her old red tube dress and a slick of lip gloss, she turned this way and that in the mirror, cursing the soft swell of her belly, sucking it in on a deep inhale. Why hadn't she noticed? How could she not know? It was certainly possible that Thane had knocked her up but, of all the guys in the world that she'd screwed, he would be the last person she'd choose to father her child. Or would he? This was the story of her rotten life: one catastrophe after another. She wouldn't cry. Hell, she wouldn't even think about it until tomorrow. It was awful enough that she had to go back on the street without her mind being chewed up with thoughts of what-ifs about a kid. If she thought about it–and she wouldn't–she'd get angry. Angry about what that man had done to her…what he'd continue to do to her if she was pregnant by him. Angry at herself for keeping her promise not to tell the cops. No, she wouldn't think about it at all. She'd get rid of it, end of.

His breath was rank, other than that he was a passable guy: at least a six, maybe even a seven out of ten. Why she'd always scored her tricks she had no idea but it had become a habit of hers, with most reaching highs of only four or five and many more scoring lows in the minus numbers. Oftentimes she'd make up a backstory for them too. This fella, the one with his face plunged between her thighs eating like a starving man, was a used car salesman - flashy with a hint of trashy. He wore a neat white button-down and suit pants rather than jeans but not the expensive kind. Betty noticed detail like that. His hair, into which she wove her fingers as she faked a moan, was a little heavily gelled, leaving a sticky residue on her palms. As she writhed and bucked her hips and begged for more, she supposed that he had a wife back home some place nice. Couple of kids maybe. Kids. She wouldn't think about it.

"Baby you're an animal," she purred as she slipped the hundred bucks into her purse. She'd have accepted fifty but he tipped her for the extras.

"I'd like to see you again next week," he smirked, buttoning his fly. "Same time, same place?"

"Whatever you want, sugar. Why don't you reserve the same room right away so I know where to find you?"

"Oh, okay. That's a great idea, it's a nice place and convenient too."

"Nicest place I've ever been," she said with a forced smile. Casting a cursory glance around the room, it actually was a whole lot better than some of the dives she'd been taken to, having a bed was a bonus. The closet and desk could be considered to be retro; the counterpane no doubt was the color of sunshine when new and the stains wouldn't have been as apparent then as they were now what with it being faded. The carpet was a circus of patterns, criss-crossing in a frenzy that had Betty's head swimming just looking at it. She slipped her feet into silver stripper-heels and pressed a kiss to the trick's cheek. "See ya, big boy." She downgraded him to janitor and with a wink she was gone.

Outside in the parking lot Betty sucked in a deep breath and swallowed bile; the taste of spunk lingered on her tongue. Rule number one of her game was to pack a toothbrush in her purse, big fat thumbs down for Betty for forgetting. Not wishing to be hanging around when Rank Breath appeared through the door, she tottered onto the sidewalk and resumed her position. Ever mindful of patrolling cop cars, she was careful to scrutinize any that slowed down and not to look too obvious. Swinging her purse, chest forward, shoulders back, Betty waited for her next pay check. She shuffled, foot-to-foot. And waited. She bit her nails to the quick and glanced at the neon pink Casio on her wrist. One am. Stifling a yawn, Betty turned as she heard a car slow to a halt beside her. A Jaguar…

Thanatos

Even as he'd watched her enter the motel room…as he'd driven around and around for what seemed like an eternity while some prick stuck his dick inside his precious Freya, even then he'd known in his gut that it was wrong to be there. He'd set her free in the hope that she'd return to him but the gods had betrayed him in the most abysmal manner.

How long should he wait for her? It had been six long weeks, forty-two days, one thousand and eight hours since they'd parted. Over sixty thousand torturous minutes and every single damn one of them spent out of his mind. The pain was intolerable. It was do or die. And so he'd gone there–her mother's apartment–and given the bitch five thousand dollars in exchange for Freya. Everyone had their price; her mother would have sold her daughter's soul for the price of two fingers of whiskey but he felt obligated towards her in some way. Five grand was all the money he had right then. He'd have gone to Bingham, had him make a fire sale of his Quincy real estate, but it would have taken time. His mother's estate had yet to be finalized, most of her assets had been liquidated anyway, to meet her medical fees. So, while his girl was spreading her fucking legs like a worthless piece of trash, he had *again* taken matters into his own hands to try and secure a better future for her. She was his. She would always be his.

He'd known, of course, that one way or another she'd end up right back in the gutter where he'd first taken her from. Life was cruel. She was a fighter; Thane knew it wasn't her fault that she was in there doing what she was doing. She was doing what it took to survive only she didn't need to do it anymore. He'd been too lenient, tried to do the right thing, he could see now plain as day that he'd been wrong.

Thane did not have time. The clock was ticking. Tick tock. The sound of time counting down in a spiral towards his own implosion. That was honestly how it felt. He'd only stepped off the incline to see her one last time and there she was. Beautifully illicit. His Freya…woman of the night. Whore. That's when he'd realized what he needed to do and just how lost she was. When he'd driven like a man crazed, to see her mother. Now, here he was again - using the last vestige of control to prevent himself from storming into the motel room, beating the fucking prick to a pulp, pushing his thumbs into the corpse's eye sockets until his eyeballs popped. He held back. What he didn't know was how long he could rein in the fire before it consumed them both. His finger depressed the window lock. Down it slid.

"Get in the car." His hands curled around the steering wheel. He stared right up into her startled blue eyes. "I. Said. Get. In."

Betty seemed lost for words. Most likely would bolt at any second and make a fucking scene.

"Don't make me say it again. Next time I won't ask so nicely."

"Get away from me." Her head was darting left to right.

"You're a hooker, who's going to save you? You have until the count of three. One."

He could smell the fear emanating from her: pungent, sweet elixir that intoxicated Thane as his flared nostrils sucked in her scent. "Two."

"You promised me."

Thane looked down at her tight little balled fists and narrowed his eyes. "Do I strike you as a man who keeps his word?"

"I believed you!" Ah, she was crying. Hard. And

shaking, whether with rage or straight terror, he wasn't sure, most likely both. In any case, her tears belonged to him.

"You swore you'd let me go," she sobbed. "I kept my promise…I never went to the cops and I could've. I wanted to but I didn't. Damn it! Damn you, Thane!"

His face entirely devoid of emotion, Thane reached over and threw open the passenger door, his eyes sliding to hers.

Betty stamped her foot, pivoted, and strode off down the sidewalk. With a hissed cuss, Thane stretched across to slam the door, put the car in drive and pulled away from the curb. The sleek black Jaguar cast a long shadow that kept pace with the girl–menacing, hanging back just a pace or two. Every couple of strides, the girl would glance over her shoulder and quicken her step. Thane squeezed the gas to keep up. So the game of cat and mouse continued for a block and a half until a cop stepped from the door of a diner and watched the car and Betty.

Pressing the gas, Thane passed his girl. In the mirror he could see the cop talking to her. He wondered if the cop was more concerned with keeping a hooker off his patch or the potential threat that Thane undoubtedly posed. Slamming his palm on the wheel, Thane threw his head back and purged his simmering anger via a deep guttural roar. Not this time, but soon. Soon he'd claim her again and this time there would be no release. If he was doomed, he was taking her with him for an eternity of fiery damnation. His soul needed hers just as his body needed oxygen. It really was that simple.

Promises be damned.

Thane

Pay Momma

Freya

She couldn't breathe.

"Miss? That fella bothering you?"

"What fella?"

The officer tipped his head, nudged his cap back and scowled. "The one in the car. The one following you."

Betty was aware of Thane passing her. The fine hairs on her nape rose. She could feel him, smell him, taste her own fear. She focused on the police officer. "I wasn't aware of anyone following me." Markedly, she turned to throw a disinterested glance as the car's tail lights disappeared. "Oh, that car?" She could tell him, right there and then. Tell him about the kidnapping, the rape, the seed of a monster growing in her belly. She could. Just say the words.

"Hmm. You have a reason to be out here at this time, Miss?"

Betty ran her tongue over her chapped lips. "I need a reason? It's a free country last time I checked."

The two locked eyes, tension palpable.

Say it. Tell him. He'd broken his promise first. He deserved to rot in jail. But then, as he'd said, who would believe a hooker? And was she really any better than Thane? The things she'd done, terrible things. She'd screwed her own brother. She'd fucked with Cody's head until he'd had no choice but to slip it inside a noose and step off a chair. She'd let strangers violate her body in too many ways to recall. She was a bad, bad person. And now, now she had no right to inflict herself on a new human being when she could scarcely take care of herself or her mom.

What would Cody want her to do? He'd want her to take care of the baby, if there was a baby. If she kept it. Get a place of her own, a nest, a safe place to be loved unconditionally and love in return.

"Miss? You do know it's a violation to be soliciting, don't you?"

Betty's attention snapped back to the officer. "Excuse me?"

"You know what I'm saying."

"Fuck you."

The cop arched a brow, his hand coming to rest on his firearm, thumb toying with the stud of its holster. "I'll tell you how this is gonna play out," he said in an even tone.

"I'm gonna give you ten seconds to disappear and head home. I catch you on my watch again, I'll take you in. How does that sound?"

"Very fair," she whispered. She couldn't tell him, don't judge okay? She needed space to think, to really think and to get her life in order for once in her miserable life, without anyone else controlling those decisions for her.

The officer nodded. "One. Two."

What was it with men and fucking counting? "I'm going, jeez!"

Tucking her purse under her arm and with an indignant jut of her chin, Betty walked away as fast as her precarious heels would allow. This was her highest earning block and she needed money fast if she was to fund her own place. She could have earned at least three hundred bucks that night, then snuck back into her mom's apartment to collect her stuff. At this rate she'd end up as a hobo, still that was preferable to staying with her mom another second. No way in hell would she bring a kid into that environment of whiskey and hatred and ghosts.

Having walked a couple of blocks, Betty's eyes scanning the passing cars both for business and for Thane, finally she accepted that she was done for the night. With a heavy heart, Betty trudged back to the familiar brownstone. It took three quarters of an hour; by the time she reached her destination her heels were rubbed raw. Hobbling up the steps Betty fished in her purse for her door key, cursing when it dropped onto the stoop. Her dress rode up her thighs as she bent to retrieve the key. As she grasped it in her fist and made to straighten up, Betty became acutely aware of a presence behind her. Her eyes widened. Inhaling, she slowly turned, already feeling him even before the first scent of his musk triggered an immediate reaction in her; heart clattering against her ribs, mouth dry. "Thane."

Their eyes drew level, Betty standing on the top step, Thane on the sidewalk just a single pace away from her. Neither spoke. Now that he was up close she could really see him, the change in him. Honestly, he looked like shit; dark circles ringed his eyes, the dusting of stubble over his jaw almost a full beard. His head, no longer smoothly shaven, had a gentle fuzz of black hair that would have softened his previous look if it weren't for the menacing wildness that narrowed his eyes and set his mouth in a scowl. It was as if he was puncturing her soul with the sharpness of his pointed stare.

Betty hesitated, considering her options. The key weighed heavily in her palm, safety lay beyond the old green door. If she turned her back on him, he could snatch her before she even knew that he was upon her. What was the alternative? She licked her lips and tugged down the hem of her dress, his gaze still fixed on hers. "You and I have nothing to say to each other so fuck off."

"You know that we do."

Summoning a little of the sass of the girl she'd once been, Betty quirked the corner of her mouth into a smirk. "You do know that stalking just makes you look desperate, right? I can give you the number of a friend of mine. She'd show you a good time, get laid for the price of a hot meal."

"Freya." His voice was laced with warning.

"What? I just thought it would help what with you being so uptight and all." Oh, she was poking the bear. "Mind you, you may want to lose the whole cage thing.

And the goat-killing thing, not cool."

Thane snarled.

Betty glanced at his car, the engine still running, lights blazing. This was not good. Not fucking good at all. Making a split second decision, Betty spun around and slipped the key into the lock, turning her wrist until the door opened with a groan. Throwing herself over the threshold, she shoved back against the door but the damn thing wouldn't shut. She looked down and saw the toe of a black brogue wedged between the door and frame. A fist pounded against the wood with a jolt that made her neck jar. She made a run for the stairs, dropping her purse. *Fuck it!* Upwards she climbed, not daring to look behind her. The top steps were on a forty-five degree return. Gripping the handrail, Betty scrambled around the bend, taking the last five stairs with gasped breaths. She couldn't tell if the pounding in her ears was her own heartbeat or Thane's heavy footfall. A hand grabbed her ankle. She felt it twist. Betty stumbled to the right, her shoulder slamming against the bannister, the fist tightened and pulled sharply back. She was powerless to stop her fall. Falling. His strong arms caught her and righted her on the top step. Her cheek was pressed to the rock that was his chest.

"Time to say goodbye to your mother, Freya."

"No…," she gasped, shoved him back and clutched her stomach. "You'll never have me. Never again."

Betty's eyes grew large as Thane produced her purse, opened the clasp, shoved his giant fist inside and took out the apartment key.

"You should keep both keys on the same ring," he said, dangling it with a smirk.

"Give it to me."

"Of course." Thane shoved the key towards her, his face straightening. "Unlock the door."

She took it, hand shaking. "Please. Please just go away," she whispered, tears coursing over her cheeks.

He shook his head and folded his arms, the breadth of him immense, biceps popping and straining against the confines of his black long sleeved tee. His tree-like legs were planted in a wide stance. Thane waited. He looked feral, dangerous. Predatory.

Her only remaining hope was her mom. What a fucking joke. Betty unlocked the door and walked into the apartment. Knowing it was futile to try to lock him out, still she slammed the door into him and made straight for the phone, her cell being in the purse Thane still had a hold of. No dial tone.

"Darn thing's dead as a dodo."

Betty snapped around to the voice. "Mom. Call…call the cops." Wildly gesturing toward the man who now towered above her, Betty barked, "The cops Mom!"

"They cut it off. Said I owed too much on the line," Nanette slurred.

Betty replaced the handset with a stoop of her shoulders, her heart a heavy stone rattling against her ribcage. She'd always been a fighter but fighting him was a battle she was sure to lose. Something inside of her though, the smallest flame, more of a spark, burned deep and hot. She couldn't give in when it wasn't just her she had to think of. There was a life in there, she knew it - a tiny little pip but still a life and none of this was the baby's fault, it couldn't help its parentage.

As she sucked in a deep breath, Betty looked at her

mom sprawled on the couch, empty bourbon bottle beside her, and up at Thane. Then she told him, "You're both unreal. I'm going to my room. You lay one finger on me, or follow me in there and I'll scream this fucking building down to the ground, I swear." Right there and then she knew that she would never tell this monster about his child. A child that she was sure was inside her belly, made from rape not love. Never!

Thane

He admired her tenacity and fortitude. In other circumstances–another life perhaps–he'd have applauded her brilliant performance. As it was, he was beyond pissed at her, not because of her defiance, but because she'd chosen this life over the life he'd offered her. It was a fucking shit hole. It actually broke him a little to think that this drunk bitch, her mother, was the only person his girl had to turn to. Until him. Thane knew beyond all doubt now what he had to do. Turning to the girl's mother for the second time that night, he curved his mouth in the most enigmatic smile that he could muster. "I congratulate you on baring such a spirited and beautiful creature as…," he wanted to say Freya but instead said, "Lacey. She's a credit to you." That she'd been dragged up was evident; that she'd blossomed into such a flower was not testament to Nanette's mothering skills.

Evidently not accustomed to compliments, the woman smirked and replied with wide eyes that were a dull version of Betty's cornflower blue, and tucked a lank yellow curl behind her ear. "That's awful nice of ya to say so. You the fella that knocked her up? That what the money was for–ease ya conscience?"

What? What. The. Fuck? If a fist had slammed into his gut he couldn't have been more winded than he was right then. "Knocked her up? She's…she's pregnant?"

His eyes slid to Betty where she had stopped dead in her tracks, her back to him in the doorway of a small gloomy bedroom to his left. "Freya, you're pregnant?" The girl didn't reply. A heavy silence hung in the air. *"Freya!"*

When she turned to face him he saw it in her eyes. The truth. A naked truth that was wonderful and terrifying, miraculous and as natural as breathing. He was pissed at Nanette, that she hadn't told him earlier; it was laughable though really that she was too wasted to have used the knowledge of the baby to barter a higher price. And Freya. Would she not have told him? The certainty that she would not was a more painful blow.

"I don't know," she said. "But wait, money?" Betty looked from Thane to her mom. "What money?"

It was Nanette who replied. "Don't matter none, it's mine anyhow."

"What money?" Betty hissed through her teeth.

Thane stalked toward her.

"The big fella there came an' paid me for ya. A thousand dollars, that's what you're worth." Her mom chuckled.

"Five thousand," Thane corrected, eyes locked on Betty's, "and your worth is beyond measure but that was all the cash that I had to hand at the time."

Betty blinked and shook her head. "Excuse me? You bought me? You actually thought you could fucking *buy* me?" A shrill laugh rang out but it was hollow, without humor.

"Mouth!"

"Fuck. You. This…this is beyond crazy. I'm gone." Shoving past Thane, Betty snatched her purse from his fist. At the door she turned to her mom. "Of all the shitty things you've ever done in my life, Mom, this has fucking killed me. I hate you. I wish it was you, not my brother, who was dead."

As he drew himself up to his full height, every muscle taught, he nodded curtly to Nanette. "You will never see her again. I give you my word that she'll be cared for."

The woman shrugged and closed her eyes as Thane left. With a low growl he set off after Betty.

Reclamation

Freya

He knew. *He knew!*

She had to put as much distance between them as she could. A cool wind whipped the ends of her hair as Betty hurried up the sidewalk in search of a cab. He was coming after her, without a shadow of doubt.

She ran then. Ran hard and fast, sobs choking in a throat that was too tight to let them pass.

Her heel caught. She pitched forward, falling heavily onto her knees and hands with a shriek. It was so tempting to give up…for a fleeting few seconds she wanted to, to just to stay there, give in, roll into the gutter and let a truck have at her. But dammit, she was a fighter, she dug deeper than ever before and, tears streaming down her face now, heart pounding, Betty kicked off her heels and ran again. The pain from her grazed, bleeding skin was nothing compared to the pain she would face at the hands of Thane if he caught her. And as she ran, so a clarity of mind dawned like the sun burning off a fog. If she really was pregnant–she knew it deep inside–she would do everything in her power to protect the new life. That was why she ran, she realized. Instinct ruled her actions, and it didn't matter that the kid wasn't made from love because she would love it. She ran not because her life depended on it but because this new life depended on it.

With every pounding footfall on the sidewalk a darker thought crept in…his arms around her like a cocoon. Safe. Conflicting, stupid damn notions of family. It was beyond her grasp. Wrong man, wrong time, wrong fucking circumstances. Nothing ever came easily for her, not like for every other fucker in the world. And all around her, everything was watching her in the darkness; black asphalt, tall railings, looming shadows. Deep penetrative eyes of the unseeing, judging her, goading her.

Behind her a car approached then quietened. Raising her hand to hail what she thought was a cab, she turned into the path of Thane as he stepped from the Jag.

Head bowed, he glared at her from beneath the weight of his brow. His palms toward her, he stepped forward. Betty matched each step with a pace back.

"Freya. Is it true?" His voice a growl.

"Get away from me."

"A child. Is it true?"

"No! Mom was drunk, damnit."

"A baby. My baby."

"There is no baby."

"You're lying. Do not lie to me!"

"Go to hell!"

He was closing the distance between them. One, two, three cars zipped by, none stopped.

He sucked in a breath, fists clenching, voice quieter now. "Get in the car, Freya. I'm not having you out here on the streets where it's not safe."

Betty laughed. "Are you fucking kidding me? It's safe with you but not on the streets?"

She saw his jaw tic. "Get in the car."

"No! And for your information, mister, the only time I've ever been raped was by you. So don't you preach at me about being safe on these streets." She was out of control, she knew it. Her index finger stabbed the air between them. "All the guys I've fucked, not one, *not one* has done to me what you did. Never! So, you think I'd want your kid? If I was knocked up I'd goddamned end it, you hear me? I'd end it!" No she wouldn't. Couldn't.

Betty could see the darkening of his eyes even by the light of the streetlamp and passing headlights. She could see, too, his hand slip into the pocket of his jeans…the small syringe clutched in his fist as he brought it to his mouth and removed a cap with his teeth and a snarl. The tiniest volume of fluid in the barrel, her life flashed before her–saw everything clearly but in slow motion. Her foot drew back to take a step, it struck something hard, a wall. Though her head shook 'no,' it wouldn't travel to her lips, parted as they were in a silent scream.

"Get in the car or I'll make you get in the fucking car."

Her eyes slid left to right, left to right. No passers by. No salvation.

"You wouldn't–," she managed.

"Oh, but I would."

And he did.

Cody pressed the dime in the palm of her hand and beamed his usual lopsided grin, his dimple creasing his cheek in that cute way that reminded her so much of good times when they were small. The smile that he used knowing full well she could never say no to him when he flashed it at her.

Now here he was, not a boy and not yet a young man although with the interest in her body that was all man. All wrong. But she didn't mind too much since it was a means to an end.

"Fine but just one peek." As quick as she could, Lacey pulled up the hem of her skirt, tucking it into the waistband. Checking that Mom wasn't coming, she pulled on the seam of her panties as Cody peered down. "Get a good look?" With a sneer, she covered herself up, the dime safe in her fist.

That night they'd snuck out after lights-out and ducked over to Aaron's place where she'd earned nearly two bucks letting Aaron cop a feel of her chest and between her legs. She'd felt so dirty but the money was owed to the class bully or she'd get a black eye…maybe she wouldn't go to school tomorrow again, just keep the cash and buy some gum.

Dad was looking at Cody weird. Why were they fighting, and why was Mom crying and drinking and hollering?

If Lacey covered her ears with her hands and stayed in the closet until she was a hundred years old, then they'd find her one day, and she'd be a skeleton and they'd be sorry. They'd put her in the ground, throw a handful of dirt on her and chat about how they'd wondered where she'd been all this time, that they'd missed her. Her mom would buy a new black dress and cry real sad tears.

Swatting him away. "We've talked about this…no it's not right. Cody, no." His breath hot on her face, the weight of his body pressing down between her thighs and it hurt so much. Stop! Blood. Crying. Shame, oh the shame of it. No had meant no.

Dirty dirty dirty girl.

He changed then. Wouldn't look at her and she couldn't look at him. Mom asking did they fight? His moods, silences, tears. She'd never seen her brother cry before, she wanted to comfort him and not hate him as bad as she did. Home from school…running upstairs… opening the door. His face. That beautiful face–chalky white, lips blue.

No, no, no!

Cody!

Mom running upstairs.

A scream: Mom's or Lacey's or both.

Tugging at his legs while Dad cut him down.

Gone. That word…a little word that tore her chest open until her heart fell out and died at her feet where her brother's body fell in a pile of bones and betrayal.

"Wake up! Freya, wake up."

A voice that wasn't Cody's but still familiar. Her eyes peeled apart, wet with tears. Bright light. Throwing her arm over her eyes, Betty groaned, a sob ripping through her. She hadn't had that dream for so long. Her brother's face dissolved, the preacher's chiding fizzled away. Silence. She blinked. Two big eyes blinked back, the color of treacle, molasses, with fine threads of gold. Beautiful, dangerous eyes looking right into her soul. Would they find one? Could they see her shame as crisp and clear as if she wore it on the outside of her body? Because she could see it when she looked in the mirror.

Every. Day.

She blinked again and the molasses eyes blinked back. This time they creased at the corners; maybe they weren't looking into her soul but instead saw right through her and out the back of her head. Betty's tongue swept over her dry lips. She lifted her cheek, it was damp. With a grunt she turned her head away from the eyes, unable to bear his scrutiny any longer. She felt disorientated, lost, like walking through sand towards an oasis that wasn't real. The grief for her brother was real though, an ache deep inside of her, crushing and raw.

"Freya."

The voice was deeper than her father's. It was the kind of rumble that vibrated through you, nice–soothing.

"It's me. Thane."

Thane? She watched his mouth, full-lipped and pouty. Narrowing her eyes, Betty mimicked the curve of a smile that twitched at the corners of the pouty mouth. "Thane?"

She would have liked to have stroked her palm over the sharp edges of that jaw, feel the prickles of stubble that peppered his rich mocha skin. Something made her draw her hand tightly beneath her chin, her legs curling up until she was a foetus in her momma's womb. Thumpety-thump, thumpety-thump–Momma's heartbeat. Or her own. Or her daddy's heels as he bore the weight of the casket; rhythmic punctuated steps in time with the organ.

Blowing out a soft breath, Betty closed her eyes so he couldn't see her any more and let herself float away over skeleton trees, over the cemetery with the crowing blackbirds.

Thanatos

As much as he'd like to blame Syn, or Luna, the boy could hardly be blamed this time incapacitated as he'd been, Thane knew that he alone was to blame for his girl's condition. Mostly he was careful, diligent, but whatever had transpired to cause the error, the fact was that the dosage had been incorrect.

Thane's long graceful fingers drummed on the stone floor. His knees ached to the bone as he stayed in place at eye level with her. That they were connected on a spiritual level had never been more evident than at that moment; his seed embedded in her womb forming the bond that he'd all but given up hope of. He'd need to be careful, more attentive, as his priorities had shifted with a tilt to his world axis. He was going to be a father. Scarcely could he have known that his mother's death had proceeded his Freya's impregnation. One light snuffed, another illuminated to guide his path. One door closed, another opened. The gods had bestowed on him the greatest gift of all, one that he'd fight to the death to protect.

Tipping up his head, Thane looked up to the lattice of overhead tracks and pulleys and beyond those, through the roof to where he imagined the gods to be. 'Thank you' was so unsubstantial a statement as to be insulting. He would show them. Today. Or perhaps tomorrow, but show them he would.

"Thane?"

Pivoting his head on his thick neck, Thane levelled his gaze on Boy as the young man crouched a pace in front of him. "Yes?"

The boy paused a while. He'd been slow of late, since Thane had unleashed his demons with the full force of his fist. Outwardly he bore no trace of the event that had transpired shortly after he'd set the girl free and his mother had passed. Inside the boy's head, however, Thane suspected there lay a brain that was damaged, a bruised peach–fleshy and sweet but of little use. The boy parted his lips on a statement that he struggled to say.

"What is it?" There was certainly an edge of impatience to his voice no matter the allowances he tried to make. Again: "What is it?"

A single finger pointed through the bars of the cage.

"Freya?"

Boy nodded.

He knew. Even without Boy saying so, Thane knew that Boy was worried. Softening his face into a semblance of a smile, he nodded and muttered, "She'll be okay," then added as an afterthought, "I won't hurt her."

Boy's eyes searched his as if looking for the truth but not quite finding it there. Brow furrowed, Boy shuffled closer to the cage, reached out a hand and stroked the girl's hair. It was actually rather touching and earned the boy a wider smile from Thane.

Don't misunderstand, Thane regretted his transgression deeply–not that he'd shown remorse within the compound, he wouldn't show weakness–but he'd wept secretly; hot, bitter tears borne of failure, and resentment at his condition that had historically led him to lash out and lose control. It was rare, but it happened. He wasn't medicated, you see, unlike his mother who had been, for the most part, a gibbering imbecile, although he'd loved her beyond reason. Thane preferred the art of self control and risk aversion. Removing himself from the compound during a full moon, for example, usually removed the risk he posed to those he protected there. Usually. Not always. The evidence of such transgressions sat crouched in front of him.

"She's sleeping," Thane told Boy.

Boy rose to his feet, stretched up his arms and tried to make himself as tall as the finial atop the new cage. When he rocked up onto tiptoes, he still fell short of the tip by a head and shoulders.

"You like the new cage, Boy?"

The boy looked down at Thane and nodded, no doubt pondering the reasons for his master to be on hands and knees still.

"Would you like to go inside?"

Again, Boy nodded.

"I need to use the bathroom and to eat," said Thane as he stood too and rubbed life back into his knees. "You may sit awhile with Freya and give her a little water if she wakes." With that, Thane took a key from the pocket of his loose silk pants and slipped it into the lock's chamber. With one creak and a clang, the door to the giant gilded bird cage swung open.

Eyes wide with apparent delight, Boy ducked his gangly frame and stepped inside the cage. Once inside, he sat beside Betty and folded his legs underneath him. Clearly marvelling at how close he finally was to the girl, he beamed a toothy grin up at Thane.

The final words from master to the young man were, "Don't touch her."

Oftentimes, the most simple of instruction is the

hardest to comply with.

About a Boy

Freya

Soft strokes, like a gentle breeze over her buttocks, the lightest whisper on skin–it was enough to wake her with a lazy smile.

"Mmm, so nice–"

The breeze whipped up into a firmer touch, parting her thighs. Betty blinked. Her focus was blurry, dirty beads of gunk stuck her eyelids together; she could see tiny spider legs–eyelashes. Balling her fists, Betty scrubbed at her eyelids until she could see. Where was she? Lines, lots of lines. Not lines. Bars. *Bars?* Instinctively, her thoughts refocused on pressure from hands kneading her ass. She was curled in a ball on her side. Her head craned to the right and there she saw him bent over her.

Boy?

No, no, no! This couldn't be happening. Think Lacey. You were at Mom's then…what then? Working. You were working. The car. *Him.* Thane.

A full on panic attack rising, she drew up her knees to her chest, pushed up with her left arm and sat on her bottom, back pressed against the bars of the cage she was apparently inside of. "Get the fuck away from me."

The boy snatched his hands back, tilted his head and chewed his lip, watching her.

"Get me out."

Boy frowned.

"Get. Me. Out."

Boy shook his head. Why was he acting so weird?

Anxiety was surging through her, fuelling her with an adrenalin rush. "Please. I thought we were friends? Please let me out of here."

As he drew his eyes to meet hers, Betty saw in them a wildness that she'd not noticed before. Always so timid… so subservient when last she was entombed in this hell hole, the way he was looking at her startled her. She'd trusted him before. Now? Now he looked as much the villain as Thane himself.

Betty was sufficiently awake that any semblance of peace seeped from her body into the soft silk on which she sat, replaced by a coldness that crept through her buttocks into her very core. She shivered. Keeping half an eye on Boy, Betty looked quickly at her environment. It was a cage, but a different cage than before. This one was bigger–almost as tall as Thane, she guessed. Circular, it seemed to be constructed of a dull gold metal; bars all around swept upwards to a point high above her head. She lifted up her face and squinted then slid her eyes back to the boy's. He was still watching her intently, head tipped to one side as if he was deciding what to do. She seized the opportunity to again plead with him; he'd cared about her before, why was he so offish with her now and what was with the touching? Jesus. "Where is the key?"

The boy lifted his hand and pointed a long angular finger at the room beyond the bars.

"Out there?"

Boy nodded.

"Can you reach it?" she asked.

He shook his head.

"Does Thane have the key?"

This time he nodded.

"Great. Where is he?"

Her question was met with a nonchalant shrug.

"Oh for–" Betty massaged her temples, a headache thrumming in her temples. "I don't know whose head is more screwed, yours or mine." Shifting around, she faced up to the boy and narrowed her eyes. "Say something. Before, you were mister talkative, now the cat got your tongue?"

"I…want." Boy chewed around the words, his gaze fixed on Betty's chest.

Her hand instinctively rose to cover her breasts. She was naked. Why did this surprize her? Rolling her eyes, a new sense of unease crept in; she had no recollection of getting there, of being undressed, of anyone touching her before now. "Did you touch my ass?"

The boy nodded, his lips tugging up into a smile.

"Don't touch me again or I swear I'll shove your hand up your own asshole." With one arm draped across her breasts, her other hand rubbed over her stomach. Somewhere deep inside of her was a tiny life, or at least she believed there to be. Without having done a test she couldn't be a hundred percent sure, but she sensed it in there. A sudden wave of nausea confirmed her suspicions. She was going to throw up. Looking around the base of the cage, all Betty could see was a pottery bowl and matching clay jug of water, not dissimilar to her Grandma's set on her dresser as a kid. Lunging forward, Betty slid the bowl towards her and crouched on all fours like a dog, head hung over the bowl, hair twisted in her fist. She didn't give a fuck about her bare ass now shoved upwards towards the boy as a tide of puke retched out. Thankfully, having eaten nothing for, well forever, there was very little to spew up. Wiping the back of her hand over her mouth, Betty rocked back onto her heels and brought the jug to her lips, savoring the cleansing water in slow gulps. Setting it back down, she turned to Boy whose eyes looked faraway and vacant. "Sorry," she said, "I feel like shit, I've got to get out of here. Please."

He sat impassive, reflective, making no move to help her.

Threading her fingers through her matted hair, Betty tugged at the roots in total exasperation. She was on the edge of a precipice, holding on tight with a slipping grasp. When next she spoke, it was with a near hysterical voice. "I can't do this. Gotta get out…get me the fucking key!" Every breath became labored, fingertips prickling as an overwhelming sense of panic gripped her. Feeling trapped, scared, her tongue coated in an acrid bitterness that sparked another wave of nausea. There had to be a way out.

Using the bars for leverage, Betty staggered to her feet and held on tightly as her head swam.

To Boy: "What is *wrong* with you?"

He said nothing, just smiled like he was her best friend and this was the most natural thing in the world.

Sucking in a lungful of air she waited and focused on controlling her breathing. As she did so, the lightheadedness ebbed, thoughts cleared and her balance was restored. Curling her fingers around the bars of the cage door she rattled it but it did not give way. She reached her hand through in search of an external handle, finding nothing but an empty lock chamber. It was hopeless. There was no escape. Again she was a darn pawn at Thane's behest. Moving around the circular cage, Betty rattled every bar, finding all of them to be sound and strong but still she moved around and around until, finally, she sank down onto her knees beside Boy. The hysteria bit home then–guttural, belly wrenching, throat scraping sobs that actually produced few tears.

Warm arms slipped around her waist and Betty found herself pulled into a tight embrace against the boy's hollow chest. Throwing her arms around him, she welcomed his soothing hushes, savoring a connection that was as bizarre as it was cathartic. Several minutes passed until her bawling dissipated into a sniffle. Trying to pull away to wipe her nose, Boy tightened his grip of her, the warmth of a palm stroked down over her buttocks. She tried to bring up her arms to shove him back but his grip was strong. The hand dipped between her thighs, a fingertip grazing over her slit. Boy's chin was pressing down on her shoulder as he reached beneath her, entering with his fingers and as he did so, his chest vibrating on a throaty growl.

Betty shook her head no, wriggling and cussing but still he held her firm. No. Not again. *It's not Cody, it's not him, it's not.* And yet it felt as wrong and as forbidden, violating, sickening.

"What are you doing?" Thane's voice cut through the air and struck the boy with enough surprize that he fell back off her.

"Sorry," he whispered.

Seizing the opportunity, Betty shrank backwards against the bars, bringing her knees to her chest, burying her face in her hands as she cried in earnest. She honestly wished she could die. Would this shitty life ever end?

Thanatos

At first he believed the boy to be comforting Freya as a good and caring companion should do. Thane didn't doubt that the girl was bereft at finding herself again captured, but it was for the greater good and in time she'd see that. After all, it wasn't as though she had anyone else to turn to, to care for and cherish her, to keep her safe, certainly not her own mother. No, her home was here now, her family was here.

As he'd approached the cage, however, Thane's eyes had widened with the realization that, in fact, Boy was not comforting but fucking groping his girl. Although he fought the ensuing anger, even blinking away a red mist that settled over his eyes, it was futile for it was beyond his control as it always was.

He repeated his question as he took the key from his pocket and slid it into the lock. It disengaged with a clank. "What are you doing, Boy?" he hissed. Contorting his great frame, Thane was able to pass the narrow doorway and enter the cage, his body filling the space, his hot panting breath loading the air with tension.

The boy shrugged and nibbled on a fingernail that had only moments before been thrust inside Betty's channel. If he was fearful, the boy hid it behind an unreadable face.

Thane's eyes snapped to the girl who was huddled in a compact ball, crying. Her tears were his and his alone, not Boy's, not even her own. He looked down at Boy and this time cracked his knuckles with a sharp snap. The boy jumped.

"Come," commanded Thane as he crouched over once more and backed out of the confined space. The boy had lost his fucking mind.

Boy did as Thane ordered, albeit with a reticence that tested the last shred of his master's patience. No doubt fearing the inevitable reprisal that his indiscretion would yield, still he followed Thane out of the cave-like room into the heart of the compound. Stopping beside the pool, Thane planted his meaty hands on his hips and peered at the boy from beneath a heavy-set scowl. There were a hundred ways in which Thane could destroy the boy; that he had touched, assaulted, his Freya–the one who was carrying his child–was so abhorrent to him as to make almost any punishment inadequate for the crime. He tapped the bare sole of his foot on the cool tile and snarled through his parted teeth. The boy stood shaking not a pace away from him. Thane's right arm rose, his hand contracted into a fist but, before he could plant a punch, his forearm was grabbed by Syn who appeared from behind him.

"Thane! Don't do this. Not again, you'll end him."

Thane spun around and as he did so, freed his arm from her grip. Flattening his palm to slap her face, he stopped an inch from her cheek. The expression on Syn's porcelain face was foreign to him. Worse even than the shock and bitter disappointment that masked her features after last he struck Boy, he now saw in her eyes…hatred? Hatred and fear. *Fuck! What's become of me? Where has the love and respect gone that she first showed me? Is this how it is now, how we are?* The wild thoughts racing through his mind flitted from anger to sorrow to incredulity. That she would have taken the punch on behalf of the boy didn't surprize him, that she looked so utterly contemptuous did.

Thane lowered his hand and tipped his head up to the glass dome above them. Somewhere up there, the gods were mocking him. They had gifted him an heir but were to steal his mind in return–a fair trade, some might say and one he'd gladly make if it weren't for the fact that he was, in turn, sacrificing everyone else's wellbeing. This was unacceptable. As he watched clouds above form moving faces and sheep and demons, an idea came to him. Lowering his face, Thane's mouth curved into a smile.

Syn's eyes widened. "I know that look, Thane," she whispered. "What's going on in that mind of yours?"

Thane replied simply, "I'm going out, I'll deal with the boy later. While I'm away from the compound, you are in sole charge."

"Where are you going?"

The smile morphed into a smirk. "It's time I took someone new, I think. Someone at whom I can direct this fire inside of me."

Syn pressed her palms to his chest and shook her head, her eyes beseeching his. "No. Thane, please don't do this. Enough…you have us."

Thane regarded her and chewed over her words. She meant well, he was sure, but her counsel was borne from her own insecurity; he would never replace any in his compound whom he loved more than life itself. A new girl would, in fact, protect the sanctity of their bond. This one would be selected for her masochistic nature. Upon her Thane could purge his anger and this new propensity for violence would at least have an outlet that wouldn't impact those he loved so deeply. This was the only way - the only way that he wouldn't hurt Syn or Luna or Boy or, God forbid, his Freya. "Do as I ask. I'm trusting everything I possess in your hands, Syn. Do not let me down."

Could he trust her? He had to. At least that's what he told himself as he slipped out of the door to the compound and blended in with a perfectly normal crowd going about their perfectly normal lives.

Softer Petals

Thanatos

The thrum of music, the incessant pulse of a beat, matched in perfect tempo with the sway of the girl's fulsome hips. Reaching out his hand, Thane slipped another twenty dollar bill into her thong and slumped back against the buttoned red leather chair, stroking a finger over his lips. Cheap perfume wafted into his flared nostrils: sickly musk, vanilla and something he couldn't fathom though it took him right back to his Grandmother's hugs–mothballs perhaps. It could be that unwelcome memory, the fact that he couldn't get Betty out of his mind, or the fact that he bitterly resented the dancer's chosen career pathway, but whatever the cause, his cock lay flaccid in his suit pants. Even when she bent over with great provocation and touched her toes so that her slit parted either side of the scant lace, still nothing stirred south of his waistband yet she was a sensual black beauty. His resolve, however, hardened to the point that he wanted to snatch her right then and there. It took all of his self-control to suck it up and wait for her shift to end.

They'd already agreed a price–too fucking cheap; he'd upped her price by a hundred bucks which doubled her original quotation for a quick fuck in his car. As he sat there and watched her, it wasn't the first time that he'd felt incredulous at how a woman could sell herself at all, but to mark herself down to the price of a meal out at a mid-range restaurant? Absurd. The issue was that, while there were pricks who would take advantage of such women, so hookers and escorts and lap dancers would offer a service to them. Needs must. Bellies needed to be fed, kids provided for…he knew this but it broke his heart, to be honest. If he could take them all to his compound and keep them from this life he would do so. As it was, he did what he could. It wasn't much. It wasn't what his great, great grandfather, Nathaniel, would have settled for. An enslaved then freed advocate of equal rights, he'd have fought harder that these waifs be free of the constraints of the sex trade. Would he have approved of the compound? Thane shoved the question to the furthest corner of his dark mind, just as he'd done a thousand times before. Those he took were content, protected, their servitude to him was borne not through mistreatment but from a love of their master. Still the conflict raged deep in his psyche.

They were not slaves. They were not slaves.

A small gaggle of dancers were watching him, each throwing back shots, wearing skirts that were barely belts, too made-up, whores who danced. Whores and lap dancers - same difference to Thane. The redhead nudged the blond who smirked at the big black man from under long lashes. He glared and slid his eyes back to his personal dancer. With his ripped physique, his dark exotic look and dangerous aura, Thane was used to attracting attention from women. Men too. It had always been that way since he reached puberty and began to look different, taller, stronger and chiselled. While Thane was not adverse to using his looks to draw the moth to the flame when needed, it was irritating him tonight. Shoving to his feet, Thane growled in the girl's ear, "I'll wait for you outside. Remember our arrangement and don't mess me around, clear?"

With a sly wink the girl sashayed over to the others and slugged a shot back. "I'll be there, sugar," she called as he exited through to the main bar.

Checking his wristwatch again, Thane kicked at a small rock in the car lot that sat behind The Glory Hole Private Dancers Club. The Lincoln was his car of choice that evening rather than the Jag, luxurious and expansive but not so classy as to make the girl feel out of place; he leaned against it as he waited for her shift to end. It was almost three am before a painted blue door opened and she stepped out. Thane slipped a hand in his pocket, fingers curling around the syringe in readiness. His other hand raised in a wave that was as genial as the wide smile that he forced over his lips. *Remember why you're doing this,* he chided when his thoughts turned to Syn's parting words.

"Payton? Over here."

The girl turned and caught sight of the large bear of a man and tottered on impossible heels towards him.

"Hi, sexy," she purred before puckering her fuchsia lips in anticipation of a kiss which Thane delivered on a sharp inhale. "I wasn't sure you'd wait for me. My bastard manager had me wipe down most all the goddamn place 'cos he's tighter than Scrooge at Christmas. I told him, 'Eugene,' I said, 'y'all don't hire us girls as janitors. We're dancers is what we are, not scrubbers, but would he listen? Would he hell, he went right on and…oh!"

Hissing out a curse, Thane re-sheathed the needle and shoved it in his pocket whilst supporting the woman's dead weight against his body. This was not how he'd wanted this to play out but she would not shut the fuck up. He'd had no choice but to silence her incessant banal chatter with the sedative, it was that or slam his fist into her face and he had never punched a woman in all of his life. Until he'd met this girl. He'd been tempted. He made a mental note to apply a ball gag before the girl woke.

After a quick scan of the parking lot, Thane opened the rear door and heaved the woman onto the back seat before securing her with a seatbelt, ever conscious of safety. The roads are dangerous places, Thane could recite road death statistics if you asked him, hence why he preferred to walk rather than drive wherever possible. Taking someone was not such a time. He slipped behind the wheel and fired up the engine, taking one last look over his shoulder at the ebony beauty that lay supine in a peaceful slumber. She would do very well. Very well indeed.

Freya

"Wow. You're sure?"

With a doleful nod, Betty whispered, "yes."

"You've done a test and everything?"

She shook her head and handed the washcloth back to Luna although she still felt as dirty as before she'd climbed into the bath. "I feel it though, inside of me and I'm throwing up." Betty rubbed a palm over her belly then hugged her knees to her chest, her gaze fixed on Luna's wide enquiring eyes.

"Holy shit."

"I know."

"Does Thane know?"

Betty nodded.

"It had to be you, didn't it."

Betty tipped her head up and frowned. "What do you mean?"

Luna sat down on the edge of the bath and traced a circle with her hand in the water beside Betty's thigh. "He said you were special…that you'd produce an heir, that's why he called you Freya. You knew that, right?"

She thought she did but her mind was so foggy, everything a blur.

"The goddess of fertility, of new life or something. He knew right away that it'd be you. He'd never planned that for me." Luna furrowed her brow and looked for all the world like she might cry before a flicker of something darker flashed over her eyes making Betty shiver.

Are you shitting me? You're jealous?

"You do realize that if you thought he was a control freak before, he'll be unbearable now?" said Luna, a sharper edge to her words.

Betty noticed how Luna's expression had hardened, it made it difficult to know if she could trust her or not. Whose side was she on? There was only one way to know for sure. "That's why I need to get out of here. Will you help me, Luna?"

"Help you? I don't think I can. Do you want his child?"

"I don't know. I mean, I've never had anyone love me and I've never had to care about anyone like I will with my own kid. Does that make sense?"

Luna thought about it and nodded, her eyes softening in a far-away stare that seemed to fix on Betty without seeing her.

"You didn't answer my question," she said as if to herself.

"How can I want his child?" Betty asked simply. "I don't know him other than as the guy who kidnapped me…who raped me and has probably gotten me pregnant. How is it possible to want his child? What if I have a monster growing inside of me?"

Luna's eyes cleared, her expression deadly serious. "You haven't seen the true man that he is. His heart. You haven't heard him sobbing, seen him clawing at his own skin as if to tear the demon out of his soul, ravaged by the same curse as his mom, God rest her soul. You think you're so much better than the rest of us?" she scoffed. "You're a hooker, plain and simple."

Ouch, that hurt.

Luna continued, "But you know what? He saw past that. He saw into your heart and wanted more for you–for all of us–that's who Thane is. Yes, he's messed up in the head but always his intentions are to protect us and love us. A deeper love than you, or I or Syn or Boy, have ever known. A pure love. Why wouldn't you want his child? You're the blessed one." The crease between her brows deepened.

It made no sense to Betty that the violent acts that she'd witnessed and been a party to could be built on a foundation of love and care. This wasn't how the world worked, how love worked. But then, what the heck did she know about love? And so she must base her decisions on fact, not emotion, and the fact was that she was held here against her will and the first thing she should do was to get out, to have space to think of the next step in her life. "I can't stay here, Luna. I want you to help me get away. If not for me then for the baby."

"You have to stay here," she replied in a small voice. "He'll never let you go now, don't you see? You've signed up for the long haul. That kid ties you to him forever. Until you die." Opening her palm, she slid it down between Betty's breasts, pushed away her knees and placed it gently on Betty's stomach as a single tear tumbled over her cheek. Her voice small, "I wish it was me."

"Oh my God. You really do love him, don't you?"

With a shrill laugh, Luna thrust her hand lower until her fingertips grazed Betty's clitoris then cupped her apex. "This. This is all I'm good for. I've never been more than a cunt to any man and that's all I'll ever be. Do I wish it was different? Do I wish that he'd chosen me instead of you? Hell yeah, but it is what it is. I see the man he is and what he's done for me, but I'm evidently not as good as you." Her voice quietened. "That's a reflection on me, not him."

Shocked, Betty's first reaction was to push the girl's hand away but the pain that radiated from Luna was akin to her own; kindred spirits perhaps, albeit with different motivators behind their pain, they were both suffering. She covered Luna's hand with her own, the two sharing an unspoken moment of unity.

It was Betty who broke the silence. "I'm sorry."

Luna closed her eyes for a second and then smiled through her tears. "I'm sorry too." She hesitated for a second or two longer before withdrawing her hand and rising to her feet. With a little tug on white ribbon bows at each shoulder that held up a simple snow-white gauze dress, it floated over her slim frame in a white cloud that settled at her feet. Flickering amber light from the delicate tea lights at the end of the bath cast a golden warmth to the girl's otherwise pallid skin–from chalk to honey.

"Can I join you?" asked Luna. "It's been so long since anyone just held me like my momma used to."

"Okay." Betty's gaze drifted over Luna's breasts to the soft thatch of dark hair at the juncture of her thighs.

With a smile lifting the corners of her lips, Luna stepped over the edge of the bath and lowered herself into the warm water so that the two women faced each other. Opening her arms, Betty beckoned Luna to her as much through her own need for comfort as to comfort Luna. Water sloshing over the lip of the bath, Luna positioned her ass between Betty's legs and rested back against the woman's soft breasts and closed her eyes as two arms enfolded her in a silent embrace.

For the longest time they lay there in the candlelight, neither moving, both absorbing from the other a stoic strength that only a woman can impart to another. When the water turned so cold as to make them shiver, the women climbed out and tenderly dried each other's body. Taking Betty's hand in hers, Luna led them from the bathroom, both wrapped in towels, walking past the pool looking for all the world like two grecian goddesses under the towering height of pillars and ferns. Instead of returning to the cage room, from which Luna had led Betty shortly after Thane's departure, she instead took her to her own bedroom where she closed the door and guided Betty to join her beneath a plump white duvet. There Luna tangled their legs together and lay her head on Betty's chest.

"Your heartbeat is so soothing," Luna said, her fingertips tracing slow circles over Betty's stomach.

Feeling more at peace than she could remember, Betty smiled and stroked the damp threads of Luna's hair that tickled over her own breast. Whether it was the drug that Thane had injected that was still in her system, or just plain exhaustion, Betty could feel her eyes grow heavy; the softness of the bed and closeness of Luna soon lulled her into a deep and dreamless sleep.

Betty moaned as a gentle flicking of her left nipple stirred her into a state of half-sleep-half-wakefulness. *Where am I?* It took a while to remember that she was in Luna's bed. Her hand reached up toward the breast that was now warm and moist, pleasure striking her core as the girl nibbled and suckled on her nipple. This was wrong, so wrong, and yet there was something innocent and earthy about about a woman's sensual touch. Betty had fucked women before, in the course of her career, if you will. Then, though, it was forced and manufactured to please whatever trick was paying for her time. This was so very different…arousing yet sweet, comforting. Betty squirmed and pushed the duvet away, her skin now coated in a fine sheen of perspiration.

Luna shifted on the bed and parted Betty's thighs, settling between them as she pressed her lips to Betty's stomach. Betty's fingers threaded Luna's hair and she wanted so badly to force the girl's head lower to ease the aching need that pulsed through her core. Gentle kisses were peppered around Betty's belly button. Folding an arm behind her head, she gazed down to meet Luna's heated stare through hooded lids. The fire that she saw in the girl's eyes reflected her own, neither breaking the stare until, finally, Luna's eyes closed as her head dipped lower. Betty, too, closed her eyes, both hands reaching now for the velvety softness of Luna's head as it continued to dip between Betty's thighs.

With a gasp of pleasure, Betty thrust up her hips as she felt her labia parted and a soft coarseness as Luna's tongue lapped lazily over her nub. She moaned with unashamed desire as a finger, then two, were inserted deep inside of her, stroking over her front wall with gentle pressure on her sensitive spot. With perfect synchronicity, her erect bud was sucked and lapped and nibbled while her gee was circled and stroked. Betty's hips rose off the bed as she ground against the girl's mouth while twisting handfuls of hair in her fists as her climax began to build. As the pace was increased, so waves of pleasure surged through her body in a mighty crescendo from which there was no going back. Arching her back, Betty tipped over the edge with a breathless cry that had her now tearing at the sheet and barely able to control herself.

When finally Betty's senses returned to her, Luna had risen and lay beside her where the two women softly kissed, the salty-sweet taste of her juices shared between their mouths. So lost were they to the moment that neither noticed Thane watching them from the doorway.

Scrabble Hill

Thanatos

Inherently possessive, Thane's instinct was to bark out a chastisement, an irrational feeling of jealousy tainting the erotic scene before him. He was not insensitive to their needs however, and swallowed back the harsh words forming. It was Luna who first became aware of his presence with a startled gasp.

"Thane, I didn't hear you return."

With furrowed brow, Thane toyed with an iron key in his hand and nodded. "You were both otherwise occupied," he said without sarcasm. "It's no wonder you were unaware of anything at all except her."

It was at Betty that he smiled tightly, extending the hand without the key to her. "Come," he said. "I don't recall giving you permission to leave the cage and, besides, there's someone I want you to meet." Thane even surprized himself at the calmness in his voice which he attributed to the presence of his Freya. A smile curved his lips as he observed the pouting frown of Luna. It was fortunate for her that his chosen one softened his mood or Luna would be in trouble indeed for contravening his simple instructions to keep the girl caged. That they were enjoying each other in secret didn't anger him as much as it aroused him, evidenced by the heavy weight of his erection tenting his pants right now. *Fuck!*

With apparent trepidation, Betty slipped from the bed, pulling a sheet around her as she placed her small hand in Thane's, her eyes lowered. He noted how her fingers trembled against his palm. "Don't be scared little one." He felt more nervous than he should be at the thought of her meeting his new arrival. Thane did not want his girl to feel that she was being replaced or that he would be in any way sexually involved with Payton who was here for one reason alone: to meet his need to channel his aggression in a safe and controlled way. That was all. His cock belonged to his Freya, only her.

The cage room was, as usual, lit only by wall sconces that flickered with convincingly realistic artificial flames. The vast bird cage stood empty, the door ajar. Beside it, tucked into the furthest corner of the small stone room sat the cage that had once been home to Betty in the earliest days of her arrival to the compound. Before he'd set her free. Inside the cage, curled in a ball, was the girl he'd taken from the dancing club.

"Freya, I'd like you to meet Payton." Thane swept his hand toward the cage as Betty stepped forward.

"You...you've taken another?" Betty's eyes grew wide, alarmed. "Why? Why have you done this?"

Thane's brow furrowed, his lips pursed. "Do not question me, Freya. Go and look at her, after all, I took her for you."

Betty's hand rose to her throat, her jaw slack in shock. "For me? What do you mean, you took her for me? Are you insane?"

Shoving his shoulders back, Thane shot a reproachful glare at his insolent muse and said, "Be careful, Freya. Pregnant or not, I can and will punish you. Do as I ask and take a look at her." Could she not keep her sass in check even just this once?

Clutching the sheet tightly around her, Betty knelt at the side of the cage and peered through the bars at the sleeping girl. "She's young," said Betty, head tilting up to Thane. "You have to let her go, don't you see how fucking wrong this is?"

Thane inhaled, fists clenching at his sides. "That's not for you to decide, is it?"

"You said you took her for me. What part of your fucked up mind thinks that I'd want you to put another girl through what you've done to me?" Betty stood up and took the two paces to Thane, chin jutting up in defiance as her eyes burned into his. "Are you going to rape her too?"

"What? No! Why would you think that of me?" Was that how she saw him–a lowly rapist? A despicable monster? That everyone seemed to be forgetting the ethos behind his actions was clear to Thane. The lack of respect too was frankly astounding. It was time to remind them just who their master was. To revisit the core premise of the compound and he would do this one by one, starting with Boy as he was most in need of a stark reminder.

Turning away from Betty, Thane strode towards the passage that would lead him back to the heart of the compound. "Syn!" he bellowed.

On a subtle breeze, Syn appeared. "Yes Thane?"

"Did you purchase what I asked?"

"Yes. It's in your bathroom, I…I wasn't sure where to put it."

"That's fine. Thank you, Syn."

"Of course." Syn fidgeted.

"There's a new girl called Payton, I've yet to decide her new name. I want you to watch her and ensure she's hydrated when she wakes."

Syn chewed her lip and nodded, brow furrowed. "I see. And Freya?"

"She's to be locked back in her cage until my return. Do not allow Luna near either Payton or Freya; that girl is out of sorts and I don't trust her judgements right now."

"Luna's fine, Thane."

Thane stepped closer and growled, "Don't push me today, Syn. I'm not in the best of moods."

"No Sir. I'll see to it that your wishes are carried out."

"I hope so though it'll be a miracle these days. Where's the boy?"

Syn tossed her head towards the door ahead of Thane, her rich red tresses like a fiery Medusa. "In his room I believe. He's not himself, Thane. I'm worried about him–" She let the statement hang in the air.

With a sharp nod, Thane replied. "It's time I reminded

him of all that I've done for him. Go and fetch him. Tell him to dress for outside the compound."

"Okay." Head lowered, Syn left the room.

Thane turned back to Betty and met her insolent glower with an icy stare. "It seems that none of you are grateful for what I do. Perhaps you'd all like to be back on the fucking streets, back in your abusive relationships or scoring the next hit."

"What the–"

"Silence! Get. In. The. Cage." Thane's hand rose to point at the cage. If his Freya knew what was good for her, she'd put up no more fight and do as she was damn well told for once. With a momentary hesitation, the girl stepped inside. *Wise move!* Swinging the gate shut with a mighty clatter, Thane locked the cage and tucked the key into his pant pocket. She was going nowhere until he decided she could. His attention returned to Payton who was still fast asleep. It was possible he'd administered too high a dose of the sedative again. Frankly his mind was a jumble; he couldn't be certain of his actions any more. This was not good.

"Thane!"

Thane's head snapped to the right as Syn called his name on a breathless cry. "What is it? Where's the boy?"

"Gone."

"Gone? Well, go and find him."

"No, I mean he's gone. I've searched the compound and when I retraced my steps, the main door was ajar. Did you lock it Thane?"

Had he locked it? It was operated by a security code punched into an electronic keypad. He changed the code every week but honestly couldn't recall when last he'd done so, or if he'd even closed the door properly on his return. He'd become complacent. He'd given them all too much freedom to come and go as they wished because they would never leave him. Needed him. Until now.

"Watch them," said Thane, indicating to Betty and Payton as he strode from the room, an uneasy feeling gnawing at his gut. It was ridiculous. The boy had to be here, where the hell could he hide? The compound was minimalistic, clutter free. The idiosyncrasy and self-indulgence of personal paraphernalia had never been indulged there. All left their superficial crap behind them when they came, their belongings being only what Thane himself gave them and each having provenance and meaning such as the silver hairbrushes that each muse owned that once were brought from Africa on a boat from distant shores by women with modest wealth and high hopes. Everything had meaning. Nothing had meaning. Boy was gone.

Freya

She decided that, for once, she would do as he said. Thane's mood was clearly dark, his eyes had that scary shit going on, his voice growly. When he clanged the door to the cage shut and locked her in, it took all of her resolve not to scream and fight and hiss and spit but that would make him more pissed. Instead, she screwed up tight into a ball in the center of her prison and screamed silently inside of her until the last of her energy and much of her anger was purged into the staleness of the air around her.

Thane was roaring and yelling and cursing. The only way that she could block out the fear this temper of his instilled in her was to cover her ears with her hands so she did so. She found herself humming a tune that she vaguely remembered her mom singing to her way back when, or perhaps her mom had never sung it, in any case it came to her and she hummed it to herself and then the words of the tune came to her and so she sang them.

There was a maid on Scrabble Hill,
And, if not dead, she lives there still.
She grew so tall, she reached the sky,
And on the moon hung clothes to dry.

"Freya."

"She grew so tall, she reached the sky, and on the moon hung clothes to dry."

"Freya. Stop."

"There was a maid, held in a cage…"

"Hey now, look at me. Freya."

"And, if not dead, she lives there still." Betty's arms hugged her knees as she gently rocked to and fro, this way and that, to the beat of the tune.

"Freya!"

"Momma?"

"It's me, it's just Luna. Look at me please. Look. At. Me."

Betty did as she was told. Seeing that the woman really was Luna and not her mom, she blew out a sigh of relief until the memory of where she was slammed into her head on a gasp. Her lip trembled. "I want to go home." Pinching her eyes shut, she stemmed her hot tears.

Luna reached her hands out to grip the bars of the cage, moving so that her eyes fixed on Betty's, her voice soft. "I know you do, sweetie. If I could get you out of here I would. It's all a goddamn mess. Boy's run away and Thane's sent Syn after him." The girl sank back onto her heels and rested her forehead against the bars. Luna's teardrops dripped onto her white muslin slip. "I didn't see…how bad he'd gotten. I thought he loved us all. That he wanted to protect us. Now, I'm not so sure any more about anything."

Coming back to the moment, Betty shifted and wrapped her fingers around Luna's, her face close to her ally's between the bars. "And now? Now you see?"

Luna nodded. "Trouble is, I love him."

Sighing out a shallow breath, Betty nodded. "I know you do and maybe–in his own fucked up way–he loves you too. All of us. But this isn't right, what he's doing. We've got to get out of here before someone dies." Truth of it was, Betty felt something deep inside of her for the man that had taken them all. It was all kinds of messed up but it was hard to push those feelings aside and focus on hate, on the need to run. Likely it was because he was the first person to really want her, to go to extremes to get her. Whatever this was, it was wrong and it was twisted and it had to stop.

At her words, Luna's eyes widened as they trained on Betty's. "Dies?"

"Yes," Betty nodded. "One's already dead and now Boy…me, you, Syn…it could be any of us. All of us. He's out of control and the scariest part is, he doesn't see it. He honestly thinks he's doing us all some kind of favor, I swear he does." The realization brought clarity to

Betty's mind.

"I'm so confused," sighed Luna.

"I know, me too. I'm so scared," said Betty in a small voice.

The heavy grinding of disengaging locks made both women turn to face the door as it swung open. There stood Thane, a towering, simmering slab of dark, heated flesh. Devoid of a shirt, black silk pants slung low on his hips and muscles perfectly sculpted, he looked for all the world like a bull about to charge a matador.

"Luna. Leave us."

The girl stayed put, eyes wide as Thane stalked towards her with a predatory snarl.

"I said. Leave us."

Evidently torn between her loyalty to him, and empathy for Betty, she chose the path that would best protect herself and scurried away like a mouse into the deep belly of the compound.

Betty glanced at Payton. The woman was rousing to the sound of Thane's booming voice. She looked back at Thane, his legs at eye level, his stance wide and stoic.

"Freya. Come with me." Taking the key from his pocket, Thane unlocked the cage and reached in his meaty hand from which Betty recoiled, scampering back to the far side of the cage.

"Do not make me come inside and drag you out," he warned.

Panic welled. She was trapped and her action, or inaction, had poked the bear more than ever. With fingers trembling, Betty held out her hand, withdrawing it sharply as their fingertips touched, an electric current fizzing beneath her nail beds from the contact. "No."

"Very well." His vast frame appeared to fill the small space between the entrance to the cage and where she crouched. It caused the man some considerable effort to struggle through the doorway but he did so and now he consumed the entire cage and sucked the air from her lungs.

Craning her neck, Betty looked up at Thane's face which was staring down at her, his jaw–every part of him–taut and solid. Sweet, acrid testosterone invaded her senses; she could smell him, taste him, hear his heart clackedy-clack. He was inside of her and all around her. There was no escape.

Truth Time

Thanatos

His fingers tightened around Betty's narrow wrist, her skin cool to the touch. Clammy. Maintaining his grasp of her, he reversed and manipulated his body as though he were some great contortionist, his frame twisting until he was free of the cage. It was regrettable that his girl needed to be dragged by her arm–he abhorred inflicting pain on his Freya unless it was pain that was succeeded by pleasure. His or hers, it mattered not.

"Help me…" Payton was waking up. This was good, very good.

"Quiet, little one," said Thane. "All is well. Rest, and

Syn will attend to you on her return."

Payton whimpered.

With Betty now at his feet on the cold stone floor, Thane bent low and scooped her into his arms, supporting her beneath her thighs and her shoulders. Her head rested against his chest which was slick with sweat from his toils. Her eyes were screwed tightly shut, lips pursed until they blanched. The girl looked terrified. If only she knew how her fear of him hurt his heart. All he wanted was to care for her and prove that he was worthy of her love and devotion…her and his child. It was time to divulge the truth. To see if she was in fact also worthy of this love and devotion that he was about to smother her in.

Carrying his girl with great care, Thane traversed the compound until he exhausted the network of passages and reached his own quarters. There, in the expansive room, with sunlight flooding through the open drapes, he stood a while and looked down upon her. He'd never seen a sight more beautiful than Betty: naked, golden, his. There was only one thing that would complete him–aside from her damned acquiescence of course, and less of her interminable sass–and he was about to ascertain whether the gods loved him or were playing some sick joke with his mind. It was either trickery or reward. Thane carried Betty through to his private bathroom and placed her carefully on her feet by the toilet. Turning to lock the door, he then proceeded to unwrap a small package that lay on the white porcelain basin.

When Thane looked at his Betty, he noted that she was staring intently at the small stick that he held in his right hand.

"A fucking pregnancy test?"

Thane nodded and inhaled. She was really trying his patience with her filthy mouth. Reaching behind her, he put down the seat. His hand on her chest, he gently eased Betty down onto the toilet then knelt his enormous body, parting her thighs as he settled between them, thankful he hadn't let her wear panties, he wasn't in the mood to complicate this any more than it was. Their eyes locked–anxiety flickering over both sets of irises in unison.

"I want you to pee," said Thane, as he thrust the white stick into the toilet bowl between her thighs and held it still.

"I can't." Betty shook her head, her tongue sweeping over her bottom lip that was cracked and dry he noted.

"You're thirsty." The stick in his right hand, Thane flicked on the faucet with his left and formed a cup with his palm, capturing a modest amount of water which he put to Betty's lips. "Drink."

Clearly parched, the girl lapped at the water while keeping her gaze steady on his. Much of the water seeped between his fingers to run in rivulets over her breast. It was an erotic sight, the effects of which were not lost on Thane as his manhood twitched and lengthened inside his pants until his crown nudged the low-slung waistband. He let out a soft moan. "Oh what you do to me, my love." As the girl's tongue licked over his palm, his sack drew tight, the muscles in his thighs and buttocks clenching. "Fuck. Pee now or I won't be responsible for my actions," he warned.

"I can't piss in front of you."

"You can and you will."

"Leave me in here and I'll do it," Betty said with a frown.

"Pee. Now."

"Why? Why can't I do it alone, you freak?"

Thane tapped the juncture of her thighs with the stick and cupped her face with his wet hand. "This is too important to me. I want to see for myself every second from when you pee to when you push my child out into this godforsaken world. Do it. Now."

"I fucking hate you."

If her words cut him deep he didn't show signs of it, for as she spat her curse at him, so a wet warmth began to trickle onto his hand. Thane's eyes remained firmly on the girl's as he waited for her urine to adequately coat the small probe. As the stream ran dry, he removed the stick and rocked back onto his heels, removing his hand to his lap. They sat in silence. And waited.

Freya

Betty held her breath so long that she thought she might pass out and it would be a blessing if she did, honestly. She needed to know if she was pregnant yet was so shit scared of the test result that the fight or flight reaction was already building inside of her. If negative, he'd likely slit her throat right there in the bathroom. If positive, he'd never free her, she'd be bound to him for life and that was as bad as being dead–worse in many ways. Either way she was doomed…caught between a rock and a hard place, wasn't that the saying?

He was watching the little window on the stick as intently as she was. Her eyes darted from that to his face and it was the widening of his eyes and slackness of his jaw that confirmed her condition even before she saw the two faint lines appear. Her fate was sealed.

"Oh my God," she whispered. Her heart beat so fast and so strong that it clattered against her rib cage and threatened to rupture through her breast. The air grew thick and stale.

Thane rose back up to his knees and turned the little wand so that she could see the result as if she didn't already know. "It's positive." His voice was too small for the man and as full of wonder as a boy on Christmas morning unwrapping his first bicycle. "The gods have granted my wish. My mother was wrong. She said…she always told me I'd never be a father because the madness had to stop with me. That evil eventually burns itself out."

Numb, Betty could barely think. The only response that came to her in the moment was, "Oh shit. I'm really pregnant."

With a mighty burst of laughter, the man nodded. Setting the test on the washstand, he closed the space between them, drawing her into a hug that pressed her body to the rock that was him. "Yes. Yes you are, little one. Pregnant with my child. Oh, the gods have served me well, very well indeed."

As Thane pulled back, Betty could see tears spill from his eyes, tumbling over his chiselled face, catching on the black stubble that peppered his jaw. A jumble of words came to her, none of which she spoke. Rape, entrapment, a sudden irrational desire to slit her own wrists…words too terrible, words that, if verbalized, would send her as mad as the man at her feet. So she locked them away in a corner of her mind, the place where she had always tucked her anxieties and fears and anger. Hell, it must be so crammed full of the bullshit that was her life that there could scarcely be room for such torture as this. Guilt lived there too. The guilt of her brother's suicide, of what he'd done to her, of what she didn't say to him that could have stopped him ending his life. All the anger that she'd wanted to direct at her mother, at the school bully…at Thane; a cacophony of pain stirred into a thick soup of misery that sloshed around in that dark place inside her head.

"Don't cry," he said, wiping tears from her cheeks that she hadn't felt leak. "This is the greatest day of our lives, don't you see? Now you're mine in the truest sense, Freya. My Freya. My savior."

With a sharp breath in, Betty stood, not caring that pee trickled down her inner thigh. Thane stood too and opened the door. Taking her hand in his, he led her into his bedroom and there they both stood, neither speaking.

"You have to let me go now."

Thane furrowed his brow, the light that had illuminated his features now dimmed. "Never."

"Please. If not for me, then for the baby." Placing her hand over her bare stomach Betty pleaded with him, knowing it was futile.

"Why do you loathe me so?"

Not wishing to antagonize him further, Betty shook her head and said, "I don't hate you. I don't understand you, and I'm scared shitless, but I don't loathe you. Fuck knows I should…"

"Watch your mouth," he warned, eyes flashing with something dark and menacing.

Her mouth snapped shut. Thane took a step closer,

Betty took a step back.

"Perhaps you should," he conceded as he continued to walk her back towards the bed. "Or perhaps you should remember that your life wasn't so fucking perfect before I brought you here. Was it?"

Anger spiked through her body, ending with the fine hairs at her nape. "You're unreal," she hissed. "At least I was free. I wasn't kept in a mother-fucking cage like a damn canary. I could come and go as I wanted. It was my life. My choices. My decision who I screwed and when I ate and when I peed. *My* life and you stole it from me. Now you've knocked me up and you honestly think we'll play happy families in this goddamn prison?"

A smirk tugged at the corners of Thane's lips as he wiped a hand over his shaved head. "You're delusional. I saw how you lived. You forget I watched you for some time before I chose you. Do you think I didn't see through your ballsy veneer to the little girl lost inside you?"

Betty's breath caught in her throat as, in one fluid movement, Thane tugged free the tie of his pants and let them drop to the floor. He watched as her eyes tracked down his stomach following the path his pants just took.

"Do you think, for one minute that I didn't see the pain you suffered? That I didn't pace and fret and worry as I watched fucker after fucker treat you like the cheap whore you pretended to be?"

"Leave me alone. If anyone's made me a whore, it's you."

"No, not me. Circumstances. Your parents. Your guilt and shame," he countered.

As he leant his body down over her, Betty had no place to go but backwards onto the bed. Crawling away from him, Thane grabbed her ankles and pulled her beneath him as he covered her body with his. Nostrils flaring as he glowered down at his muse, all the fight left Betty's body. As it did so, her shoulders relaxed into the soft down comforter, her eyes closed. Whatever he would do, he would do. She was bone tired.

Thane continued, his weight supported on his bulging arms. Her gaze drifted up to his dark lashed eyes searching, needing to see his true feelings whatever they may be and what she saw was such raw emotion that it floored her. Damn him. A part of her hoped to only see the asshole that she'd conditioned herself to hate. Instead she really did see reflected in his honey eyes a truth, emotion that she'd never witnessed except for in Cody.

Thane sighed and slid his gaze away from hers. "And you perceive me to be a tyrant when all I want is to protect you. That's all I've ever wanted–for any of you. To offer you something better than you'd ever known. I've sacrificed…the life my father and his father built, none of it matters to me, don't you see? Because what I want and need is right here." Placing his hand between them he stroked her stomach. "You. Our child. My chance for contrition, for righting the wrongs. Is that insane?"

Her face contorted in a sob, Betty couldn't look at him. She couldn't believe what he said to her because nothing made sense any more. Everyone lied to and used her, how could this man be any different? It was a contradiction too far, the words he said versus the manner in which he took her–kept her. How could a man love her and treat her like an animal? And she yearned to reach into her chest with her own fist and snatch out the pain from her heart, to let it pour from her lips even knowing that once she allowed it to leak from her, it would be a tsunami of emotion that would make her so light that she'd undoubtedly float away into the ether–to Cody, her brother–fly high on a cloud freer than a bird. A bird in a cage. Her eyes snapped open as his mouth crashed to hers in a possessive, tangled, aggressive kiss that she fought. A battle of tongues, lashing, sucking, biting, her legs wrapping around his torso drawing him inside of her as her inner self screamed out, demanding to know what the fuck she thought she was doing.

He was on her, he was in her. Thane was the taste, the sound, the touch…smothering, possessing, controlling, filling her until her insides stretched and yielded to the point of rupture and still she drew him in. His flesh seared with white hot heat that transcended the kiss until she swallowed his spit that scorched her throat and clenched her core. Again and again his beautiful, velvet soft, iron hard, punishing cock struck and drove and pierced until pain melded with pleasure so intense she cried and bit and took everything that he gave to her.

Lost and bereft, found and claimed, Betty's orgasm tore through her as Thane's growl rumbled from his chest, vibrating through her tightened nipples, directly to her heart. He held her as she shook, she held him as he buried his face in the crook of her neck and told her that he loved her and, somehow, she knew that he did. Fucked up and twisted, he loved her. A love so wrong, yet a love that was raw and as base as life itself. She was suffocating from the weight of the dawning of this truth, just as she could breathe again…he had killed her and given her life. She was doomed and she was liberated. Could she be Freya?

Do or Die

Thanatos

He was blinded. His heart thundered inside his chest; surely it would give out for no mere human organ could sustain such brutal torture as this. Collapsing onto his back, Thane blinked at the ceiling until the mist dissipated and he could see again. Beside him lay his world, his reason to be and he knew that she had felt it too–the connection, the outpouring of his love for her, but he feared that his love would never be enough for her. If she left him, he would die. This was not dramatics, but a simple fact. That he also loved Syn, Luna and Boy was undeniable but the love he felt for them was mere adoration in comparison to these feelings that he had for his Freya. He'd never doubted his capacity to love another, for he'd loved many in his lifetime: his mother, father, grandfather, even his lawyer was held in high esteem, but this...this was different. The ferocity of love he felt for this girl was an achilles heel, a weakness that was likely to end him, to fell the beast that he was. The beast inside him–could it ever be quietened by the softness of her whisper? Was it possible that the purity of her spirit could bleach out the stain of evil that marred his own soul?

Turning onto his side, Thane traced his fingertips around Betty's belly button, her stomach rising and falling with each labored breath that she took. Her skin was the paleness of buttermilk, sticky with traces of their juices. He walked a path with his fingers over the small swelling that was apparent as she lay supine and still. His son. His heir. His future. Deep inside of her, he was there. Thane felt him. The gods, creators of this new life, were watching and Thane knew that they were smiling.

Behind him, a sharp tapping on the door startled Thane. Lunging forward, he slipped from the bed and strode to the door where he threw it wide and glared at Syn. "What is it?" He'd been negligent, lost as he was in a temporary respite with his girl. Boy was still missing.

"Thane, forgive me. You need to come quickly."

Her chest heaving, it was apparent that Syn had run. Over her corseted dress, she'd wrapped a conservative overcoat that now she clutched tight about her.

"What's happened? Did you find him?"

Syn nodded and grabbed his forearm, her eyes beseeching him. "I remembered where you took him from," she panted. "The place where the bastard was abusing him..."

"What? He went there?" Impossible. Boy would never go back there even if he had the wits about him to actually get himself there.

"Yes. He's locked himself in but I could see through the window and he's not well, Thane. He's unconscious I think...please come. Now."

As Thane rubbed a knot at the back of his neck, he looked over at Betty. There was no way in hell that he was letting her out of his sight but he needed to go to Boy. He could leave her under the close supervision of Syn–he didn't trust Luna's mind right then–but even that didn't sit right with Thane. Turning back to Syn he barked his instructions. "You stay here and take care of Payton. I'll take Freya with me."

"No, please. Let me come with you."

"Syn. Do not defy me." To Betty he snapped, "Get up and go with Syn. She'll find you some clothes suitable for outside. I want you dressed and ready in five minutes."

Both women looked incredulous but hurried off to do his bidding without a word.

The brief walk to the underground parking lot had been a challenge. Unsure as to whether the girl would bolt, he'd kept a tight arm around her waist and a syringe in his pocket. He was taking no chances; it was risk enough that she was outside of the compound.

Thankfully she had neither run nor screamed for help. Fear, or whatever, had rendered her compliant, at least for now. Shoving Betty into the passenger seat of the Lincoln, Thane screeched out of the lot and traversed the highway to where he knew Boy to be. It had been so long since he'd been to the shit hole but his memory served him well.

Rarely did he forget a single fact, name or place and within thirty minutes he pulled up alongside a row of garbage cans adjacent the gray stone house.

"Wait here." Not giving Betty the chance to object, Thane exited the car, locked the doors and took the half dozen steps down to the basement apartment. Peering through a dirty pane of glass, he could see the boy lying on a littered floor, his clothes soiled, no movement detected. Although he knew the door to be locked, he tried the handle nonetheless. As he thought, the door held fast. Stepping back, Thane charged at the door, ramming his broad shoulder against the rotting wood. Three shoves more and the wood splintered. He reached in his hand and disengaged the lock, kicking open the broken remains of the door. Rushing over to Boy he felt for a carotid pulse then a radial one and found both to be thready and weak. This had been his fault; if he hadn't punched the boy and inflicted God knows what damage to the boy's brain, he'd be safely home at the compound. Of all the terrible things that Thane had done, striking Boy had haunted him since that fateful day. The day Thane's mother died. No excuses. He would die if Thane didn't take action and fast.

Boy weighed next to nothing in his arms. When did he lose so much weight? Thane's lips pursed with realisation that he'd neglected to oversee the boy's welfare for quite some time. There was a great deal pressing down on Thane's shoulders, the weight of his wrongdoings was a cross that he would bear and willingly so. There would always come a time of reckoning, he'd been under no illusion and he felt that time approaching like the Grim Reaper sharpening his scythe. Thane knew what he should do.

Heaving the boy onto the back seat as Betty gasped and wriggled from the front to the rear of the car, Thane told her to watch him, to ensure his airway was unrestricted while he himself jumped into the car and pulled out into the traffic.

It was a warm, hazy afternoon in Boston, with traffic lighter than usual and Thane was thankful for that. He'd asked the gods for so much and they'd granted him most every wish but–for the first time–a small crack appeared in his precious road to salvation, in his beliefs. With each mile that ticked by on route to his destination, so the crack branched and deepened into a wide canyon, with the gods firing arrows of scorn on the small man that he'd become on the dusty floor below. Were they mocking him? Was every golden chalice filled with poison? Were...were the gods even real? If not, then the foundations on which he'd built his life was nothing more than a symptom of his madness and his mother was right. The doctors were right. And all this. This world he'd created. Was wrong. He felt his confidence slide for the first time since establishing the compound way back when. If he really was sick, then this sickness inherent in him had infected those around him. They'd fucking suffered enough and he'd only meant to help them, to give them shelter, a better life. Oh, sweet irony.

The wheel gripped tight in his fists, Thane pulled into the parking lot of the hospital emergency room. There would be no holding back, the time had come for him to face the music no matter the consequences.

Tense Times

Freya

Boy's breathing was shallow, his poor face pallid. Fighting a wave of nausea, Betty stroked the boy's hair, his head nestled in her lap, a little spit trickled from the corner of his mouth onto the ill-fitting blue denim jeans that Syn had dressed her in.

Thane was quiet, Betty assumed it was because he knew that, once inside the hospital, she'd betray his ass to the authorities. She'd been surprized to see him indicating when the hospital sign had loomed large at the roadside. The man was a jumble of contradictions, after all, he'd done this to Boy and now here he was most likely dumping him outside the emergency room in the hope that the young man would receive the care he needed–with no insurance most likely–and that Boy wouldn't speak of the compound or of Thane because he was so fucking loyal to him. That Thane was seeking help for Boy was at least one redeeming quality in the monster.

When Thane slammed on the breaks, Betty fell heavily against the seat. Vomit was a single motion away, she swallowed it down and waited for her captor to drag the boy from the car and put him somewhere. Instead, Thane took the boy from her, gently cradling him in his arms like a baby. Genuine concern shaped his features into a sorrowful frown.

"Come with me," said Thane.

Silently, she did as instructed and climbed from the car, closing the door and following Thane. She could run. Betty's eyes darted around the lot at cars, an ambulance, people hurrying about their business oblivious to her plight. To Boy's plight.

Intuitively, Thane turned when he reached the automatic doors that were sliding open to reveal a bustling department within. "Freya." Thane inhaled as their eyes met. "You must do what your heart tells you to do."

That was it. That was all he said but those words said everything to Betty. He was acknowledging that she held the power: at that moment she could tear apart his world and the compound, and Betty was completely floored.

"Sir–what do we have here?" Asked a nurse in scrubs as she looked over the young man in Thane's arms.

Tell them the truth. The room stood still. Betty struggled against a fresh wave of sickness.

Thane nodded to Betty as if reading her mind and told

the nurse, "Head injury. I'm afraid that I hit him several weeks ago." *Jesus! He really said that?*

The nurse's eyes narrowed. A gurney arrived onto which Thane laid Boy.

"He's not been right since and I think I damaged his brain."

Betty exhaled and closed her eyes. *Finally, you did the right thing.*

"I see," said the nurse. "You'll need to talk with the police but right now my priority is getting this young man the help that he needs. Is he on any medication? Does he have any underlying medical condition? Sir?"

"No…not that I'm aware of."

"His name and date of birth?"

"Boy. His name is Boy. I don't know his date of birth but his birthday is November second and he's the sweetest, kindest boy you'll ever have the privilege to meet. And I love him, I'm sorry Boy. I'm so fucking sorry…" His voice tailed off into a whisper, his colossal hand stroking the young man's hair.

Betty looked on aghast. That he loved Boy was not a revelation, but that he was clearly so tortured inside showed a vulnerability and sensitivity that punched the wind from her lungs. Without hesitation, Betty reached out to Thane and stroked her hand down his back. Her need to comfort that great bear of a man was as natural and un-orchestrated as it was shocking to her. He was weeping.

"Come with us please mister."

Both Thane and Betty turned in unison to face the surly faces of two security guards. Seemingly torn as Boy was wheeled away and rapidly surrounded by a team of medics as he was pushed through a set of doors, Thane's head tore right to left from the guards to Betty. Deer in the headlights.

Stepping forward, Betty gripped both of his arms and rose up onto the balls of her feet so that she could meet his eyes. "Thane, listen to me," she said sternly. "He'll be okay but right now we need to go with these men and do the right thing."

"No. I need to be with Boy…to tell the doctors what I've done…that I'll pay for his care, I want the best treatment money can fucking buy."

"I know you do and we'll make sure he gets it."

Guard one pulled Betty away, guard two crowded Thane and guided him through the department with Betty following on his heel.

"Where are you taking us?" she asked.

"Cops are on their way," replied guard one. "They'll likely have some questions."

It was a small and soulless room in which they found themselves. Devoid of windows, it was lit by a flickering overhead strip-light that cast an orange tinge over the yellow plastic chairs and grey table in the center. An hour passed, then another, and still Betty had kept her mouth shut. This was huge. Life changing. There would be no going back.

Neither wanted to sit, Thane paced while Betty leant against the wall and focused on her breathing to quell the ongoing nausea.

Oh, little baby, you're already causing trouble for your momma… but Momma doesn't mind. I think I'm going to love everything about you, no matter what you do to me because you're mine. And perhaps…your daddy will love you too, very much. Your daddy—your fucked up father–you'll visit him in jail. How can I do that to you? I should run away, tell no-one and go now, but he'll never let us go. Payton, what about her? This isn't just about you and I, little cookie, this is about her too. I have to tell. A sudden thought rocked her. *What if they take you away from me? I'm a whore. A dirty broken whore.*

The door opened, a physician in scrubs walked in and took a seat. "Please, sit," he said to Thane.

With a deep breath in, Betty pushed off the wall and wiped her clammy hands over her stomach. *Do it now. Tell him.*

Thane pulled out the remaining chair and sat down. "Is he?"

"He's alive, yes."

Betty blew out a held breath and felt her body relax. Her eyes rested on Thane's stooped form as he spoke.

"I didn't mean to hurt him. My mother had died and I lost it with him."

"Sir, whilst I don't condone violence in any shape or form, the punch you allegedly threw was not what caused the young man's loss of consciousness."

"It wasn't?" Thane tilted his head and scrubbed a hand over his face. "What do you mean? It had to be, he's not been himself since."

"We carried out a cat scan and found a tumour on his temporal lobe."

"A tumour?"

Betty gasped.

"Yes, Mister…err"

"Call me John."

"Well, John, you did the boy a great service bringing him in here when you did. Another few hours and I'm not so sure he'd have made it. You saved the boy's life, it's fair to say."

"I saved him? But I struck him…the fall he took…"

"Wasn't what caused this. The scan showed no evidence of swelling or contusion. He's a very fortunate young man that you took the action you did in bringing him here and, I have to say, I'm impressed that you were man enough to own up to what you did. Most wouldn't have."

"Will he live? Can you operate on this tumour?" Thane lifted his head and looked at the doctor with hope.

The doctor nodded. "He has every chance. He's being prepped for surgery now, you can't see him until after and I think the police will want to take a statement." Turning his attention to Betty, he asked, "Are you related to the patient?"

Thane shifted in the seat and looked at Betty. Two sets of eyes, plus the guards, all awaiting her reply. It was her chance to be free. Tears leaked from her eyes as she looked back at all the men before setting her gaze on Thane. He smiled at her and nodded but behind the smile she could see his pain, and she knew. She knew that inside of the beast beat a heart, a good heart. There were so many unanswered questions and concerns–fears, dark thoughts–but this man loved her in a way no other had ever done. Inside of her was his child, their child, and yes, he was one fucked up father, but what was she? What life could she offer the baby and yet the thought of an abortion was abhorrent to her. She wanted this baby more than she'd ever wanted anything in her life, it was as if a light had been switched on inside her darkest corners. She had no family–her mom was dead to her, betrayed her own daughter, Dad was gone, her brother dead too in the most literal sense.

Looking back at Thane, Betty replied. "No, I'm not related to Boy but he's like a brother to me."

The brother she lost. How life comes full circle, she reflected, the boy was virtually a stranger and yet he was a kindred spirit, a lost boy searching for love and acceptance, just as she had for so much of her life.

There was a knock on the door. The guard opened it and a police officer entered the room. He questioned Thane, who recounted the same tale he'd told the doctor–the truth, or part of it. The officer turned to Betty. "Your name is?"

Betty looked at the cop and pursed her lips.

"Miss? Your name."

"Her name is Freya." Thane looked at the officer and then at Betty.

"Freya what?"

"Just Freya."

Betty's eyes widened and locked with Thane's in a silent stand-off, a challenge to defy him.

"You'll need to tell me your full name, lady, I'll need a statement from both of you."

"My real name…is Lacey Porter." There. It was out. Figuring her mom was more likely to have filed a missing liquor report than a missing person report, it made little difference him knowing her name. That knowledge wouldn't save her. "Will Thane be arrested?" she asked, wondering if she should have called him John.

"Not at this time. The boy didn't report the alleged attack at the time. Unless, if and when he recovers from surgery, he files a complaint, there's no case here."

Betty chewed her lip. She should just come out and say it: 'This man took me and he took others.' They were just words, why couldn't she say them? What kind of masochistic monster was she?

The cop folded his arms. "So, what's your story - you two married?"

"No," said Thane. "We're not married legally, but…," his eyes met hers as a smile shaped his mouth, "our bond is deeper than any licence."

"Spare me the poetry," the cop scoffed.

"It's true," Thane said with a hint of a snarl.

Betty tugged at the hem of her tee. She was going to puke, a fresh wave of sickness causing a sheen of perspiration over her forehead and top lip. She swallowed back not only bile but her chance to speak out, the cop ambled to the door.

He'd be right back, he said, right after he called into the precinct and ran a few background checks. The guards and doctor followed the officer out, leaving Thane and Betty alone.

"Freya," Thane sighed as he rose to his feet and stalked towards her.

"Thane. No." Her hands rose to fend him off as she shook her head. She disgusted herself with her weakness and inability to do the right thing.

He closed the distance and planted his hands on the wall either side of her, pinning her in place beneath him. Resting his forehead to hers, he exhaled. "I need you, Freya. Please…give me a chance. Fuck knows I'm insane and I'll make your life hell, but please don't leave me. You could have told him, but you didn't. You couldn't, could you? You feel it too."

Free As A Bird

Thanatos

"You're delusional," she hissed. "What about Payton?"

"I'll set her free," Thane replied simply. "I'll give her a property I own in Quincy, it's worth a tidy sum. She'll be free to dispose of it, the proceeds will set her up for life."

"You don't think she'd go to the police?" Betty laughed, probably at the irony. She hadn't even done so herself. Yet.

Thane nodded. "If she does, then I'll face the consequences."

"And Luna, Syn…Boy? What about them?"

"It will be their choice. If they want to stay, they can. I

hope that they do, but I won't coerce them."

Her voice rose an octave. "You promise me?"

"You have my word, for what it's worth."

"I'm being fucking sarcastic," she quipped.

Leaning into her, his eyes drilling into hers were molten lava scorching her retinas but she held firm, didn't look away.

"Thane, you need help. Professional help."

With a sigh, he acquiesced. "Then I'll seek it, for us."

"For you, Thane. Do it for you."

At that very moment, slicing through the tension in the air, the door opened. Thane and Betty turned in unison and locked eyes with a young nurse who blinked up at Thane's towering stance from beneath copper bangs.

"You are?" he boomed.

"Marie."

With a sharp inhalation, Thane stepped closer, his voice a throaty growl. "Come here, little one." His fingers curled into a fist. "You have news of the boy?"

"Yes," she whispered, eyes wide. "No…I mean, he's gone for surgery." The nurse hesitated and looked over at Betty. "Can I bring you a cup of coffee?"

Betty felt for the girl for she knew only too well how intimidating Thane's snarly voice and moody glare could be. Tugging up the corners of her mouth in a tight smile, she said, "No thank you." Even the smell of coffee would likely make her puke. Glancing at Thane who was still staring intently at the nurse, she asked, "Will the cop be back soon? I need to talk to him."

"Let me go see if he's around."

Thane drew back his shoulders and folded his arms and the nurse's eyes widened at the soccer ball biceps that popped and strained.

"Thank you," said Betty and the nurse left.

The atmosphere in the small room fizzed with a frisson of tension.

"Think very carefully, my love." Thane stalked closer, his hand slipping inside his pocket to withdraw a syringe.

Sucking in a deep breath, Betty's hand moved without hesitation to cover her belly. "You wouldn't."

"You really doubt that I would?" He huffed a caustic laugh.

Her eyes narrowed, lips pursed. "The baby…," she whispered.

Closer he came until his ragged breath and stormy eyes were upon her like a tornado whipping her spirit and resolve into his vortex until the only outcome could be her destruction, the scattering of the pieces of her about the earth that was forever cruel. But then, the storm dissipated and the air calmed. He took a pace back. He could take her, he could stick her with the needle and remove her from the hospital before they were even missed yet that look in her eyes was one that crushed him; an expression of pure resignation–acceptance of her fate–and he couldn't do it. Everything was different now. Thrusting the syringe back in his pocket, he expelled all the air from his lungs, his vast frame deflating too, until he was sure he'd completely fold into himself and wished that he would.

The girl was watching him. Freya. So small and vulnerable, and yet in her palms was the power to destroy him, his world, his future and he welcomed the destruction because to rid the world of his madness was surely a kindness to Mother Earth. He'd procreated, he'd live on through his seed. His insanity would live on. He hadn't thought about that before.

"Thane."

He shook his head and rested back against the wall, chin on chest, hands loosely at his sides. "Do it," he snarled. "Tell them and put an end to me."

Silence.

The thrumming of his pulse became amplified in his head. The silence between them rose to a crescendo that was deafening to Thane. His breathing shallow, he could hear the quickened inhalations and exhalations of his girl. The soft sound of her chewing on her lip brought a sad smile to play over his own lips as the thought of tugging that lip free and kissing it floated into his dark mind. Another noise, louder, as the door flew open. Heavy footsteps. He lifted his head and nodded to the police officer. "Do what you must do, Freya," he said quietly.

"Ma'am?"

Thane's head tipped to the left and he smiled at the girl then sucked in a deep breath at the sight of her torment, tears threading over her freckles. Like a frightened rabbit she looked from Thane to the officer then stroked her little bump.

"Officer," she said.

"Nurse said you wanted to talk to me." The cop set a file down on the table and took a pen from his top pocket before taking a seat. Indicating for Betty to sit, Thane merely watched as a bystander as the two others in the room decided his fate.

"I…I did."

"Take a seat ma'am." To Thane: "Care to give us a few minutes alone?"

With a dour nod Thane left the room. As he closed the door he was met by the two guards.

Freya

She took a seat opposite the cop and chewed on a thumb nail. He was watching her with that same look of judgement–of utter disdain–that she'd become familiar with over the years. Trailer trash. It still fucking hurt. With Thane out of earshot she'd expected the words to come freely to her, instead his aura lingered in the room, hanging about her like a cloying fog. His scent was in her nostrils, his presence had settled inside of her…a tiny heartbeat deep in her core reminding her that she would never be free of him even if he was in jail.

"When you're ready." The cop's fingers drummed a steady rhythm on the table. He gave a weary sigh.

"I wanted to talk to you about Thane. John."

He arched a brow. "Are you in danger?" he asked simply.

Was she in danger? He loved her, or did he love the idea of her? The kid…Jesus Christ, the poor kid was going to have two fucked up parents and here she was about to have its father incarcerated for who knew how long.

Say the words, Lacey. Tell him about the compound. About Payton. About being drugged, raped, taken from the street. Taken from a life of prostitution so that he could love you…tell him. Tell him.

"No." She gasped. The small word didn't come from her lips, but from the baby in her belly. "No, I'm not in danger."

The cop furrowed his brow, lowered his eyes and wrote on a piece of paper that he'd taken from the file. "You sure about that ma'am? You seem kinda scared to me." His head rose until his accusing stare met her wide blue orbs.

Betty shrugged. "I umm…I'm sure, but you could give me a ride home?"

The cop chewed the end of his pen then set it down. "Look, oftentimes when a woman is being abused it's hard for her to talk about it, you know? I want you to know we have people–specialist officers–who are trained in this kind of thing."

"I'm not being abused. I just want to go home."

"Hmm." He wrote some more. "Were you a witness when the guy calling himself Thane struck the kid known as…" he glanced down at the file, "Boy. What's his birth name?"

"I don't know. I only know him as Boy, it's what he calls himself."

"When 'Boy' was hit, were you there?"

"No I was not."

"So you don't know anything about any injury…and you're not being abused." He closed the file and pushed up to his feet, his expression unreadable. "Seems like you don't know a whole lot, young lady."

"No Sir I don't, so how about that ride?"

There was a moment, a few seconds, when the two regarded each other and Betty knew that he could read her. He knew. He was also powerless to act on what scant information he had and so he nodded and acquiesced. "Fine. I'll go take a statement from the big fella out there and then I'll give you a ride home. You have family to go to?"

"My mom's house. I can go there."

This seemed to appease him a little. The officer smiled for the first time. "Now you're making me more comfortable. A girl needs her mom. Let me go finish up, then you can tell me all about your mom on the drive over."

Truth was, there was no way in hell that Betty really intended to go to her mom's. Where she'd go, what she'd do, she'd have to work out somehow. Thing is, when you're caught between the proverbial rock and hard place, when you're screwed no matter what, then the thing that takes over is survival instinct pure and simple. She didn't understand why she couldn't tell her story to the cop. All she knew was that she was broken into so many pieces that nothing she inflicted on Thane would help put her back together again. And, even more confusing, was this feeling that the only place she felt a little more whole, a little safer, was in the arms of the one man who she was most scared of.

How fucked up was that?

"Ready?"

"Yeah. Get me out of here."

Momma

Thanatos

Thane paced with the two meat-heads who were currently trying to match his wide stride alongside him and failing miserably. What they expected him to do, he had no idea. What was she saying to the police officer? That the gods could snatch his entire world from him was beyond cruel and he'd never forgive them. Never forgive himself for being such a fucking fool as to believe that his life would ever amount to anything more than that which was promised by his lineage. Destined to lead a rotten existence he'd done all that he could to appease his mother and the gods by doing good. Surely his forefathers would have been proud of his work? Still, here he was, his world about to implode and he was powerless to stop it. This enormous man was as weak as a mouse. He curled his lip on a growl.

When the police officer appeared through the doorway, Thane held out his hands in anticipation of the snap of cuffs. Instead, the officer indicated for him to follow him over to the nurse's station where he slapped down a file, opened it, and took out a form. "I'll need to take a short statement from you, pal, then you're free to go."

And just like that, he knew that his Freya had not betrayed him. She'd been loyal and true…was this possible? Dare he hope that all would be okay?

"The girl?" asked Thane when the statement had been written down and he'd signed his name beneath the words that told only of his altercation with the boy.

With a frown the officer cut him a glare. "She'll be leaving without you and, if you know what's good for you, you'll leave her alone. Understood?"

Thane nodded, suddenly he could breathe easy. She was returning to the compound…she was coming home. "I'll take her home."

"Leave her alone, I said."

"Alone?" Thane stroked a hand over his jaw. "She belongs with me."

"Seems the lady disagrees. I'm taking her some place safe. Too many damn weirdos out there, get my drift?"

Thane did get the man's drift. He was referring to him. "Did Freya say she was leaving me?"

"That's not for me to say, pal. All I know is you'll be going your way and she hers. Now, if you'll excuse me I'll be off. We'll be in touch when the kid's awake and, be warned, if he presses charges you and I will be seeing a whole lot of each other so don't go too far buddy."

As Thane watched the officer reappear from the room with his Freya, he inhaled and gripped tight to the lip of the nurses' desk as he fought the urge to snatch her back. His eyes burned into her but she didn't turn and look at him. Head down, she walked beside the cop, out of the doors. Out of his life.

I'll never let you go, my love. You can run but you can't hide from me.

"Bingham. It's John."

"John, all okay?"

"No. I need you to do something for me."

"Of course. What do you need?"

Freya

As it turned out, the cop was one of those old school types who sees a job through to the bitter end. Long serving, battle weary kind who'd seen it all, heard it all but who was ultimately a good guy. He had kind smiley eyes and a creased face that had frowned a lot, laughed a lot, lived a lot. He reminded Betty a lot of her dad, actually.

She hated lying to him.

The journey had mostly passed in silence with Betty giving little away about her home life. Thane had to be going out of his mind right now. She knew this wasn't over by a long way. He'd never let her go so easily. That's why Betty needed to run far and run fast. Chances were, her mom would still have his cash. If she could grab that, she could take a bus to New York, lose herself in the city, make a new start even. She'd call the hospital and check on Boy, maybe even send him a couple hundred bucks to see him okay when he got out. If. Hey, she could even find work, send for Luna and Boy, they could share an apartment, live together.

"Thanks for the ride. See ya." Betty smiled at the cop who had gotten out of the squad car instead of driving off, dammit. There they both stood outside the brownstone, Betty shuffling foot to foot. She never thought she'd see her mom again, truth be told, but here she was outside of her home.

"I'll see you inside."

"Oh, that's not necessary," Betty countered. "Besides, Mom's kinda funny about cops. She'll think I'm in trouble, you know?" With a wink and roll of her eyes, Betty fished around in the back pocket of those stupid baggy jeans. "I've got my key so I'll just let myself in. Thank you though. For everything." She smiled her cutest smile, the one she used to use on her dad as a kid to get her own way.

The officer hesitated, his gaze taking in the tall, paint-chipped house then Betty's freckled smile. "Okay. You take care of yourself, you hear?"

"I'll do that, I promise." Rocking up onto her toes, Betty planted a small kiss on the officer's whiskered cheek. His hand reached up to touch where her lips had pressed, a warm smile over his face. "You take care too, Mr. Officer Sir." With a sharp salute and a grin, Betty turned and walked up the path without looking back. She heard him chuckle softly then the car engine fire up, the sound of it pulling away from the curb while she faked turning a key in the door lock.

Maybe the neighbor still had the spare key her Mom had given him for all those times she was so drunk she could barely remember her name let alone a door key. Drawing back her shoulders, Betty stood on the stoop and pressed the buzzer.

After a short wait the old guy appeared the other side of the door and squinted through the glass. "Who is it? Lacey, that you?"

"Hi there, can you let me in?"

With a frown Betty noticed the shake of his hands, she'd seen Parkinsons' before and it was a shame if he had it. She'd always liked the old man, he'd been kind to her. The door held wide, he moved aside to let her into the communal entryway. "Not seen much of you around here," he said with a black-toothed smile. "Your ma okay? Not seen too much of her but then I been sleeping more often than not."

Her fingers tucked into the back pockets of her jeans, Betty shrugged. "I think so, I've been…working away for a while."

He frowned. "You should take care of your ma, she's not as young as she used to be, none of us is. A child needs to look out for its parent, old age is a bitch ya know."

With a small smile Betty nodded. "Yeah well a parent's meant to take care of its kid too."

"Touché," he chuckled. "Well go on up and tell Nan if she needs anything, she should holler."

"I'll tell her. Oh, do you have Mom's key?"

With a shake of his head he disappeared into his apartment then returned and placed a small silver key into

Betty's palm. "Forgetful just like Nan."

"Guess it runs in the family. Thanks, see you around."

"Sure." Turning from her, he closed his door and Betty was alone in the tatty entryway.

Why Betty still felt a need to walk in to her mom's arms, to have her hold her tight to her breast and stroke her hair, to tell her everything would be okay, she honestly didn't know. Nothing made sense to her anymore. Her mother had sold her own daughter for five grand and the tragic thing was, even knowing that, she was still the only family that Betty had. Inhaling, she locked the hurt away and reminded herself that she'd just take the money and leave. It was the one last thing she'd ever take from her mom, the last time she'd see her. *Be strong, Lacey, you have this.* Betty climbed the stairs.

The key turned in the lock, the door swung open…and she knew. The air was pungent, sweetly cloying, the light poor. Ahead of her was the old stained rug–rancid with piss and stains–her mom's pride and joy. Gingerly, Betty walked up the small hallway toward the living room. Tiny hairs on her nape and arms prickled and rose. A bluebottle fly buzzed around her face, she swatted it away. Her heart clattered against her chest wall and tears leaked over her cheeks. She was shaking. Couldn't draw her eyes from the rug underfoot as she drew to a still and struggled to breathe. The stench made her stomach roll. Slowly her gaze lifted to meet her mom's where she sat in her peach floral armchair beside the part closed drapes. Glassy eyes looked back at her from a white-grey face that was barely recognizable and yet was most definitely her mother's.

"Mom?"

She knew.

"Momma? It's Lacey…I've come home, Momma."

All was hushed and her momma didn't stir. The woman was gone.

"No, no, no! Mom don't do this." Betty fell to her knees at her mother's slippered feet and reached out to grip the woman's shoulders which were clad in pink chiffon and were hard and cold and unyielding. "Mom! Momma, wake up…it's me, wake up!"

Folding over into her momma's lap, her cheek resting on the woman's knees, Betty sobbed and sobbed and begged her momma not to leave her. Her heart broke, she felt it, shattering into splinters of pain that radiated through her entire being until her mouth formed a silent scream and her hot tears soaked her mother's nightie.

"I need you," she gasped. "Don't you fucking dare leave me alone." Betty's hands scrunched into tight fists as she drew herself up and rained blows on Nanette's corpse. "I hate you! I fucking hate you, how could you fucking do this to me when I need you most? You useless piece of shit, you're gonna be a grandma…I'm all alone." Sinking to her knees. "Oh God. *Please* Momma. Please don't go. Don't go don't go don't go. I'll be good, I swear."

From behind her, someone grabbed her fists. "I have you." She was being pulled to her feet then lifted and she turned to bury her face in the stranger's chest. A strong, solid wall against which she shook her head and beat her fists some more as she was carried from that godforsaken room. Carried away from the only family she had left and who had left her too, just like Cody…same as they all did eventually.

"Shh, my love. I have you and I'm never. Ever.

Leaving you."

The Sanctuary

Thanatos

He hadn't been fast enough to tail the police car but the officer had told him all that he needed to know. She was going back to a safe place - her mother was all she had which was pretty shitty. It hurt his heart that the girl would consider that hell hole safe. That she would choose a drunk, the woman who treated her worse than dirt on her shoe, above he who loved her so. He had to make her see the depth of his feelings for her, she was his life. His light. His reason to breathe. Plus, he wasn't about to let her walk out of his life with his son. Oh no. Over his dead fucking body.

Pulling into the street as the cop car disappeared into the traffic ahead, Thane had wasted no time in rushing inside after Betty, thankful that the door was ajar, but cursing the girl's complete lack of security awareness. Taking the stairs three at a time, he'd reached the apartment in no time at all. He'd heard her then, her screams, her wailing, and he'd guessed.

Now here she was in his arms, cradled against him like a lost child as he carried her upstairs to Bingham's office, thankful that his lawyer's staff had left for the day. Traffic had been light, Betty had cried herself out as the car lulled her.

"What the devil is going on, John?"

"I told you not to ask any damn questions, Bingham, and I meant it." Thane shot a warning to Bingham Suffolk who rang out his hands, eyes wide and fearful. "You'll get me disbarred."

"I don't give a rat's ass. Get some brandy."

"Damn you," replied the man as he did as instructed and handed a crystal glass of brandy to Thane.

The girl was snivelling, shaking, as he lay her on a cream leather couch and wedged a cushion under her head. Bringing the glass to her lips, he forced a little of the liquor down her throat. With a cough and a curse, his girl sparked back to life, the ever-present fire not yet re-ignited in her eyes that were red and puffy, cloudy as puddles.

Looking over at his lawyer and confidante, Thane asked, "Is my mother's Cape Cod house habitable?"

Bingham Suffolk looked shocked. "I'd imagine so. You've been paying a housekeeper for the best part of six years. Are you thinking of taking a vacation? What the heck's going on?" His beetle eyes slid to Betty then back to Thane. "What's happened to her?"

There was an edge of accusation lacing Bingham's question that Thane didn't like. "Her mother passed. Make some calls. I want the house aired, clean and stocked with food. Then, I want you to drive Freya up there tonight and stay with her until I arrive with Luna and Syn."

"What? I can't just take off, I've a practice to run here…clients to see tomorrow."

"You're refusing to do as I ask?" Thane asked, each word punctuated with an undertone of malice.

"Jesus. Fine, I'll do it." The lawyer paced and loosened his tie. "You'll be the death of me, John. The death of me."

"Then at least you'll die a rich man."

"Money's no good to me if I'm six foot under. What of the boy?"

"The boy will be provided for. See to it that his medical bills are settled and I'll be keeping a close eye on him. When he's well enough, I'll bring him to the Cape house."

"How long are you planning on being up there?"

"Until my child is born." Thane's hand cupped Betty's swollen stomach as he smiled down at her. She didn't smile back. Her face was blotched, red, utterly broken. She looked so lost, so despondent, honestly it shredded him to see her this way. He drew his hand back and ran it over his jaw then looked over at his lawyer to gauge his reaction.

"Your child? You mean…?"

"I'm finally going to be a father. Now's my chance to

do something right, Bingham. And I intend to see to it that Freya wants for nothing, that she's safe." It was a gamble. Just how loyal was the man in front of him? How far could he be pushed before some moral standpoint won out over what was being asked asked of him? It was a risk, Thane was all out of options though.

"Okay, now it makes sense. I had no idea that you–" Bingham turned to face the window then, after a beat,–" I'll make sure she gets there safely."

Blowing out a held breath, Thane stood and walked over to Bingham, extending his hand which the lawyer gripped tightly. "Thank you, my friend. Thank you."

"I don't condone this, John, not at all. I want you to know that."

"I'm not seeking your endorsement, but I am expecting your help."

"You have it, as always."

Striding towards the door, Thane stopped and turned back to face Bingham. "Oh, one last favor."

Bingham rolled his eyes. "What?"

"There's a girl called Payton. I want you to transfer the deeds of my Quincy real estate over to her, but I want a contract that ensures her…discretion."

Bingham blew out a breath and shook his head. "What have you done this time that needs a gag clause?"

"Just do it please. She's to be under no illusion that talking to the authorities will have serious consequences for her. One word against me and the asset reverts to me, am I clear?"

"Perfectly."

"Very good. I'll see you at Cape Cod later tonight. Drive safely and ensure she eats." Thane dropped a kiss on Betty's hair and set off for the compound. Time was of the essence.

Freya

"Where are you taking me?" It was a dumb question, Betty couldn't care less where they were headed. She felt detached, melancholic, shut down inside. Numb. It was as if nothing really mattered anymore, the fight had left her body and all Betty could do was rest back against the soft leather and watch the world fly by the car window. She was no longer a part of the universe, she was void. Cancelled out. Never been born. The guy driving–Bingham he'd said his name was–could take her to Timbuktu for all she cared, it really didn't matter any more. That's the thing about being an orphan…you lose your reference point and your identity. Life should be a compass set to home. She'd been a sister and a daughter and now she was neither. She was Betty and she was Lacey and she was Freya, but mostly she was nobody at all.

"Here we are." The man cut the engine, climbed from the car and opened her door. "I'd prefer you didn't mention this to John, I've taken a detour. There's something I think you need to see."

John. Such a proper name, she thought. A distinguished and biblical name. *John.* She rolled it over her tongue and wondered when John became Thane. When man became beast. And yet, he'd seemed so caring at the office. She'd seen it in his eyes, that look of love almost? Pfft, she was delusional. Unlovable. He wasn't even capable of love, he simply took what he wanted - a psycho kidnapper. She'd seen it though, there'd been no disguising the way his anguish seemed to match hers and that wasn't the reaction of a monster, was it? The more the miles had ticked by until this point when they'd stopped wherever, the more her head grew cluttered with conflict and sadness and hope and despair and, oh God, how she wanted out. To hide away. To be loved. To be held and never let go of.

"This way please." Bingham took her arm, Betty allowing him to lead her. There were steps…two or three…and a tall brown door on which was a small, neat sign made of brass. She read the engraved words: *The Sanctuary.*

The man pressed a buzzer in the entryway, the door opened automatically as a camera's eye winked above their heads.

"Mister Suffolk, well ain't this a nice surprize!" A rotund African-American woman, with impressive décolletage and a happy face, clutched his hands in her own and beamed a genuine smile. "And who's this lil' lady?"

"Dulcie, good to see you," said Bingham Suffolk as he covered the woman's hands with his own and shook them. "I'd like you to meet Freya, she's a friend of John's."

"Any friend of John's is a friend of The Sanctuary. Sugar you look beat. Come have some coffee and a slice of my key lime pie."

"Freya's had a rather nasty shock today and I'm certain that your key lime pie will cheer her up." Bingham and Dulcie walked on ahead, neither checking to see if the girl was following them. She wasn't. Instead she made herself very small by stooping her shoulders, folding her arms about herself and shuffling into a corner of the expansive entryway. Tucking herself behind a wooden umbrella stand, she became all but invisible.

"Hey."

A small redheaded white girl, maybe seven or eight or so watched Betty with a frown. She had the cutest button nose and a dusting of freckles over the apples of her cheeks that were similar to Betty's.

"Hey," Betty whispered.

"I'm Lexi, what's your name?"

"Get lost kid."

"That's a weird name."

"It's not my name."

"Then, what's your name?"

Betty narrowed her eyes. "Lacey. Where's your momma?" Fresh tears stung her sore eyes as she said 'momma.'

"I'm her ma." Replied a slim woman in a simple green dress that matched sparkling emerald eyes.

Dulce appeared from a doorway up ahead. Looking from one woman to the other, she smiled. "Em, why don't y'all show Freya your room and meet out back for pie?"

The woman nodded and held out a hand to Betty. "I'm Emma. Thought you said your name was Lacey, Freya."

Betty shrugged, ignoring the hand.

To the little girl the woman said, "Lexi honey, why don't you go see Ma Dulcie while I take Freya here, for a tour."

"Okay." Off she skipped.

"Don't be scared," said the woman in a strange accent that Betty couldn't place. "We're all friends here. Come see my room…I have a bottle of whiskey hidden away, how about we have a sneaky shot? You look like you need a drink, so you do."

It didn't matter to Betty what the woman said, or even where she took her, but her curiosity was a tiny bit piqued. The aroma of baking at least went part way to erasing the sickly sweet scent of death that still hung in her nostrils and throat. All about her was an aura of tranquility and calm that was as foreign to Betty as if she'd been teleported to another planet. The walls along the hallway were papered in flowers and birds and butterflies. She caught sight of a small deer chewing grass, an apricot pelican, resplendent, elegant. Onwards they walked to a doorway that was mostly covered in crude paintings that Betty supposed were the work of Lexi. Involuntarily her lips pulled up in a smile.

"Welcome to my safe space," said the woman as they both stepped inside the big room. "Take a seat on the bed. I had a chair but Lexi rocked on it 'till the back broke."

Gingerly, Betty sat down on a snow-white lace comforter. The bed was soft and gave under her weight. She had a sudden urge to lay back and spread out her arms and legs like a snow angel.

"What is this place?"

"Hmm?" The woman slid open the bottom drawer of a powder blue dresser and took out a bottle of bourbon. Pouring generous measures into two china teacups, she handed one to Betty.

"This place," whispered Betty. "What is it?"

"It's a safe harbor in a stormy world, is what it is. Drink up."

Scrunching up her nose, Betty took a tentative sip of

the liquor. She'd never been much of a drinker having seen how it wrecked her mom…how it likely ended her mom. Her hand stroked over her tummy before she placed the cup down on a nightstand that matched the dresser. The color of cornflowers.

"Rough day, hmm? Lay down and let me tell you a story," said Emma having drained her own cup.

With a sigh of resignation, Betty lay back against a stack of pillows that were as soft as clouds. She closed her eyes, exhausted, defeated.

"Once upon a time there was a girl from Dublin, Ireland. She travelled on an adventure with her ma and pa and arrived in a land called America. Emma was the girl's name and Emma was a wild one, ta be sure. Soon, Emma was old enough to leave home and so she came to a place called Boston. Here she met a boy called…let's call him Thomas. Thomas was the most handsome prince she ever did see and she loved him with all her heart. He treated her like a queen until one day he hit her. Out of the blue, so to speak, she'd done nothin' wrong. Emma had a baby borne of love and hope but soon Thomas would take out his anger on the little tot, so he would. Emma spent her nights screaming and crying like a banshee until one day a big man called John followed her and asked her why her eyes were black and purple and no bigger than little slits. They hurt too bad to cry but she told him about Thomas and the big man called John got a fury on him, the likes of which Emma hadn't seen before. For once though it wasn't directed at her, but at the man who had used her as a punchbag for near on five years."

A tear slid over Betty's temple. She turned her head and looked at Emma. The pain in those emerald pools was a mirrored reflection of her own.

"He said he had a place where she'd be safe but that the little'n couldn't go there. Emma refused to leave without her…without my Lexi. He promised to help us and later that night a swanky car pulled up and we were taken from the hell that was our home, and brought here. 'Course back then, three years ago, this place was quieter. It wasn't called The Sanctuary then, it was just Dulcie's home. She'd been taking in lodgers who rarely paid their rent. John bought the building and gave it to Dulcie to keep forever so long as she offered a home to women such as Emma. Me. Women with kiddies. Women who've been mistreated. And so, you see, the story has a happy-ever-after where we all live safely and take care of each other. The end."

Emma's smile was infectious. Reaching out her hand, Betty lay it gently on Emma's arm. "Thank you," she said simply.

"For what?" asked Emma.

"For showing me that kindness still exists in this fucking rotten world."

"Oh, it's not so bad. There's still good in the world. John's a good man. Without him, there'd be dozens like me who might not be here today. There are other places, you see, just like this. He sets them up and Mister Suffolk mostly oversees them, but every now and then, John shows up and checks on us all. You'd never think that a bear of a man such as he would have a heart of pure gold."

"John did all this?" Betty's eyes widened.

"Sure he did," Emma affirmed. "Pays for the kiddies' education and they all call him Uncle John Bear." She chuckled, great affection for the man was quite apparent in her face.

Thane did this? The man who raped and imprisoned her? So he really was trying to take her from the street and, in his fucked up way, keep her safe. Could it be true?

Key lime pie and freshly brewed coffee set them up for their journey as Betty hugged Dulcie, Emma and little Lexi goodbye. Somehow they'd lifted her spirits just a little bit, shown her that–no matter how bad life seems or how tragic–there were little pieces of good in the world if you sought them out and held them dear.

As the car traversed interstate ninety-three towards who-knew-where, Betty closed her eyes and let a fitful sleep claim her. Dreams of Cody, her mom and dad and a small girl who had no name. In her sleep she was lifted in the strong arms of a man called Thane who looked down upon her and said, "You are Freya. You are mine." Anointed by his words, she became a person for the very first time. Her family faded into the ether as the car jolted and purred and took her onwards.

The Beach House

Thanatos

"We're leaving. Go and pack your things. You may take one small suitcase, which I have provided for you."

Syn blinked up at him. "Leaving? Whatever do you mean, Thane?"

"Don't question me, Syn. You have ten minutes."

"But…Boy? What about him?"

Rolling his neck, Thane glared down at the woman, his patience was being tested and she would pay a heavy price if she wasn't careful. "Boy is being taken care of. I've already told you, he's in surgery and in the hands of the g…in the hands of the surgeons. He'll join us when he's well enough."

"I want to be close to him. Please let me stay."

"No."

"And Payton?"

"I'll deal with the girl."

"Will she come with us?"

Thane glowered at flame-haired Syn, jaw ticking. "No. Now, enough of these incessant questions. If you're not packed, then you'll take nothing with you. No clothes or belongings. It's really that simple."

Syn's mouth pinched in a scowl. She looked for all the world as if about to launch a tirade against him, thought better of it and turned on her heel, leaving Thane's room. Luna had been less difficult, eagerly scurrying off to pack her meagre belongings into the suitcase that had appeared in her room. It shouldn't fuck Thane off that she wanted to please him so damn hard, but for some reason today it did. There was something about Luna–he couldn't put his finger on it–he no longer trusted her and his instincts were never wrong. With furrowed brow, Thane set about throwing essential items into a neat brown suitcase of his own, strewing superfluous paraphernalia across his bed. With clothing packed, Thane took a small wooden box from beneath his bed and tucked it alongside his pants. The array of syringes and ampules would hopefully not be required but one could never be too sure.

Inside the innermost sanctum of the compound, within her cage, curled up tight, lay Payton. Lowering his body into a crouch, Thane reached through the bars and stroked the girl's hair. She looked so peaceful and innocent that, for a moment, Thane contemplated keeping her for she'd surely break in the cruel outside world. He'd made a decision though, and more than that, a promise. He'd sworn to his Freya that he'd release Payton and this was what he intended to do.

"Little one, it's I, Thane."

"Leave. Me. Alone."

With a sad smile he brushed his knuckles along her cheek bone.

"Don't fucking touch me..." Payton recoiled against the bars.

Drawing back his hand, Thane frowned. "I know you're feeling scared and dejected and, in part, I blame myself for neglecting you. For that, I'm sorry. However, tomorrow you'll be free to leave."

"Free?" Her eyes peeled open, she rose up onto her arms and searched his dark eyes for the truth behind his words. "You're letting me go?"

"If free is the word, then yes. You'll be driven to a place called The Sanctuary by a man named Bingham. Once there, you will be under the mentorship of a dear friend of mine called Dulcie. In a week or two you'll become the owner of a piece of real estate that will make you an exceedingly wealthy young woman, but take heed...if you are mindful to go to the police, or anyone else at all, then you'll be stripped of your asset. Furthermore, you and I will meet again and it won't be such an amicable joining should such an occasion arise. Are you with me so far, little one?"

Payton considered his warning and gulped. "I...I think so."

"That's good," he said, "very good. Now, I see you have food and water and a toilet bucket. Use them sparingly because you'll be alone here until my man Bingham arrives at first light." He left the girl then without further dialogue, he'd said his piece. If she was wise, she'd comply with his directive. If not…he hoped she'd comply.

Thane glanced at his watch for the hundredth time. He needed to get back to his girl. He knew the pain of losing a mother and, no matter how inherently twisted and fractured the maternal bond, still the wound left was raw and deep.

"Luna. Syn. We're leaving."

With a flurry of skirts and lowered eyes, the two women clutched their cases and waited by the main door to the compound. Neither spoke initially, their body language was enough of a message for Thane. They were anxious and skittish.

"The car's outside. Do you have everything you need?"

Both women nodded in unison. "Yes, Thane."

"Where are we going?" asked Luna finally.

Picking up his own case, Thane punched in the door code. With a soft whirring of the mechanism, the door slid open; harsh yellow street lighting flooded over the tile floor of the entryway. "To the beach."

"The beach? You mean like a vacation?"

"A vacation, yes."

The women exchanged glances. Luna opened her mouth to speak, Syn shook her head.

Having engaged the alarm system Thane punched the code into the keypad. The door slid shut with a final clatter and he wondered fleetingly if he would ever set foot inside the compound again.

Freya

With the rhythmic rocking of the car replaced by a bumpy crunch beneath her, Betty stirred from sleep, rubbing the remnants of the fitful nap away with balled fists.

Either side of the car rose towering columns illuminated by blue floodlights that rendered the stonework a luminous violet. Connected to each column hung a tall gate of intricate ironwork, each topped by silver spears. Sharp. A stark warning to keep out…or stay in. The gates had almost fully swung open as Bingham set the car in motion once again. Betty sat forward in the back seat so that she could peer over the driver's shoulder at the view. A vast house lay sprawled ahead, nestled on a dark emerald blanket of lawn, the hushed whirr of sprinklers barely audible. As with the gate pillars, so the house was illuminated too, this time in a rainbow of color from cerise through gold; a long line of colored spotlights were carefully seated along a grassy boundary, each bathed in light a point of interest on the façade of the building. It had a Grecian grandeur to it, not dissimilar to the pool area of the compound. Betty rubbed at her arms to abate a sudden chill.

The car came to a standstill beside a portico entrance, the place had to be worth a king's ransom.

"Holy shit!"

"Impressive isn't it?" As they exited the car, Bingham held back to allow Betty time to marvel at the detail of the house. "I've not been out here for quite some time, I'd forgotten just how grand it was."

"He owns this joint?"

With a wry chuckle Bingham nodded. "He does now his mother's passed. It's belonged to his family for decades, though why he never uses it, beats me. Too many ghosts maybe."

"Wow," she sighed. "Where is this place?" All about them trees stood to attention like soldiers, waving bony arms against an ink-black sky. Vast, swaying, marching on the spot to the beating of the ocean's drum.

Bingham creased his eyes in a warm smile. It was the first sign she'd seen that, in some small way, he empathized with her, or maybe he pitied her. She wondered if he knew. If he knew that his client kidnapped people. And, if he did know, why he was so loyal to him. But then, she reflected, the man she knew as Thane was to him simply John: a man who saved whores and victims and gave of himself and his wealth. It was almost like the giant was two people, the good and the bad. She rested a hand on her belly, her thoughts drifting to her mom. Betty was glad when Bingham spoke before her mind slipped her further into its dark abyss.

"Welcome to Wychmere Harbors," he said, like she'd know where that was. "Out back there's a jetty. I recommend you take a walk in the morning, the view of Nantucket Sound is to die for."

"I'll do that, thank you," she replied with a roll of her eyes. "Right after I have a pedicure at the spa and check out the room service menu."

Bingham Suffolk chuckled to himself. A comfortable silence hung between them for a moment or two. "Talking of food, come on, let's get you inside and see if we can't find something for you to eat. God forbid he arrives to find you a bag of bones."

With the gentle constant of lapping waves emanating from somewhere beyond the house, Betty took a deep cleansing breath of salt, of peace, and followed the lawyer inside. The vestibule was welcoming, she could only imagine how it would look with daylight flooding through the vast windows that framed the space ahead. As Betty gently trod over a polished hardwood floor, her head tilted to the left as she caught sight of an impressive study. To the right, a formal dining area with ornate oval ceiling. Ahead of them was a circular grand room with oversized fireplace flanked by double sets of french doors accessing the outside but she couldn't see what lay beyond; the lighting to the front was not replicated at the rear of the house. She imagined the ocean stretched out there in the blackness.

Bypassing the grand room, Bingham led Betty through to a kitchen. It was the kind of space that a girl could only dream of: a true focal point, a place to entertain. With a vast array of cabinets, huge island and a breakfast area with one wall entirely of windows, it was an inspiring space. Nothing looked lived in, however. There was no evidence of family, no nicknacks or photographs, no favorite cup or well-used chopping board. It was like a show home. Stark in its luxuriance. The heart of the house was flatlined.

"Here we go," said Bingham. "We have crackers, a cheese plate and fruit." Retrieving the items from the fridge, Bingham set them down on the island. After opening several cabinets, he found two plates and handed one to her. "Thank goodness for the housekeeper," he muttered.

"Does she live here?"

"I believe she lives above the boat house out back," he replied.

Betty and Bingham pulled out stools and sat at the island, both picking at the cheese plate. Betty was more hungry than she'd realized and the cheese was good; for once her sickness was gone.

After a beat, Bingham offered, "The house sits on nearly four acres, the boathouse has a phone connection to the main house. You'll only find a phone in John's office, however. The family were big on cutting themselves off out here. You'll find no television or computers. It was always intended as an escape from real life if I recall."

"I see." Betty furrowed her brow as she snapped a cracker into tiny pieces. "And I'm guessing this whole big place is secure?" She threw him a sideways glance. "Like…no-one can get in. Or out?"

Brushing crumbs from his lap, Bingham considered what she'd asked and shook his head. "It's true that it's gated and the boundaries are secure to the front and sides, but it opens out onto a boardwalk and small beach so, in that regard, it's not closed off from the outside world." He locked eyes on hers and frowned.

Chewing her lip, Betty wondered how far she could trust him, if he'd disclose every question she asked, to Thane. At the end of the day he was a lawyer. He'd have a lot to risk, right? She chanced a statement. "I think he'd stop me if I tried to leave here."

The man looked genuinely affronted. Swivelling on the stool, he pressed his lips together and reached out to take her hands in his. "Young lady. Whatever you think of John, his intentions are, in my experience and for the most part, good. Now, I don't know what goes on inside his private residence, nor do I have a mind to find out, but he's a man who's lived through a difficult past and that he's come out of it and still wants to help others, shows a great deal of fortitude in my humble opinion."

Betty looked down at his hands cupping hers and back up into his eyes framed by greying brows and sighed. "I think he's two different men," she whispered. "I think he's John, and John's a good man…and I think he's Thane, the bad part of him."

Drawing back his hands, Bingham folded them on the counter and nodded. "You may be right. I can tell you that many experts have tried to explore not only John's mind but his mother's too. I'm not privy to the official diagnosis but I know that he went to therapy for a while." He pushed a piece of cheese around his plate with a knife, his expression troubled. "I also know that therapy didn't help his mother in the end."

"Meaning?"

"Meaning she was cared for twenty-four-seven, medicated, and even then she was quite mad."

Betty inhaled the news and let it settle inside of her. "Is it hereditary?" She looked at him.

Avoiding eye contact, Bingham shrugged. "In part, perhaps. I don't know. John never talks about it and I'm only a hired hand. I look after the family affairs but these types of people don't air their laundry in public, you know? I'm only privy to what they've wanted to tell me."

"Ah, come on. You know a shit load more than you're letting on."

With a soft chuckle the man nodded. "This is true. I do find stuff out in my line of work but I'm always discreet. Always."

Slipping from the stool, Betty stood and tugged her fingers through the knotted tangles of her hair. She was dirty, in body and mind. "I don't believe you," she said simply. "You two are close, you know more than you're letting on."

When he rose too, Bingham stood a foot or so taller than Betty but with his shoulders stooped, he appeared smaller suddenly. "There's a reason he does what he does for those women," he stated.

"Which is?"

Bingham let out a deep sigh, she could see conflict darkening his eyes. "He had a sister, a twin. Apple of his eye, they were inseparable." He chuckled to himself. "You know, they used to finish each other's sentences. I recall when they were, oh about eight or nine years old. I was in their father's study going over some papers when the twins blew into the room like a tornado. He was already big for his age, her not so much but they had identical mannerisms; there was no mistaking that they were siblings. Anyhow, in they breezed with that look of pure mischief in their eyes. Announced I was needed in the kitchen." His eyes glittered on a smile. "Course, at the time, I didn't stop to wonder why or to think it odd that they hung back and let me go first. Down came a bucket of water on my head. They'd wedged it over the half opened doorway, the little devils. She started to tell me there was rain forecast, he cut in finishing the sentence while she handed me an umbrella. Off they ran then, leaving me a dripping mess. Ah, yes. I loved them, you know. That's the truth of it."

This was too much. "Oh my God. He had a sister, he's

not talked about her at all to me. Had?"

"Kim. She sort of sparkled, honestly. Beautiful, but inside too, you know? She'd do anything for anyone. She was growing into such a fine young woman."

She could barely take it all in. "What happened to her?"

The lawyer tutted and shook his head as he picked at a fleck of lint on his jacket sleeve. "So sad. She was a bright girl, straight A's until she met a punk with a fast car and a taste for cocaine. Soon, the coke didn't do it for him any more and so he moved up the line to heroine. Got Kim hooked on it then sent her out prostituting to fund what was by then a joint habit."

"Oh." The room began to spin. Betty reached out to steady herself against the counter.

"Of course John saw the changes in her, did all he could, everyone did, but in the end…she was found on their birthday in a motel room. She was beat up, naked. She'd overdosed and choked on her vomit. Coroner never could prove if it was the drug or the beating that killed her, said most likely if it hadn't been one it would've been the other anyhow."

Eyes wide, hand over her mouth, Betty gasped. "Was it the boyfriend? Did they catch him?"

"He ran. Found dead a week later way up in Minnesota. Overdose, so they said."

"Fuck…"

"Indeed. John and his mother took it badly. John in particular was crushed. For a long while he wouldn't talk to anyone at all. Not a single word. When I did have reason to go up to the house, I saw a young man consumed with rage, eaten up by hatred like a cancer.

Little by little he began to talk to me, seemed he trusted me. His mother, though, was swallowing sedatives and antidepressants like candy. Liquor too. We talked about how he could channel his anger into something constructive and, well, that's eventually how The Sanctuary came to be. Opened on their birthday."

She wanted to weep for him but was still so very numb inside. "And the religion thing? What is that about?"

"Ah yes." He narrowed his eyes. "He began to take an interest in Norse and Greek mythology shortly after Kim's passing. I figured it gave him some comfort at the time. Grief does strange things to us all and sometimes it's easy to turn to religion for comfort…to make sense of a loss."

"I see."

Bingham regarded her sadly. "Look, I don't condone what he's become, not at all, and Lord knows I'm up to my eyes in it all too, but deep inside of him is a good heart. I've known John all his life and whatever you think he's done to you, somehow in his mind he's done it for what he sees as the right reasons. That's all I can say."

What else was there to say? The pain that Thane had been through was almost unimaginable. She had judged him so harshly and yet–

Lust and Revelations

Thanatos

Thane knew that his confidante would not let him down. There was no-one else in the world that he'd have entrusted his Freya to but him. And there she was, his girl, curled beneath a crisp white duvet in the center of the master bed. He stood awhile resting against the door frame watching her chest rise and fall, a thread of gold hair curled over her cheek, lips parted and fuck, she looked so peaceful. Angelic. *His.*

Weary from the day's events and the drive to Cape Cod, Thane wanted nothing more than to bury himself deep inside her, to fall asleep with his love in his arms but first he needed to talk to Bingham Suffolk. He'd found his lawyer staring into an empty glass on the verandah out back. Taking a seat next to him, Thane had kicked up his long legs onto the rail and drank straight from the bottle of malt that was still at Bingham's side.

"All okay, Bingham?"

"I guess so, John. I guess so."

The two men listened to the lull of the ocean before Thane finally spoke. "I have something else I need you to do for me tomorrow."

The older man sat forward and rested his elbows on his knees, head hung low. "Haven't I done enough?"

"You're a loyal and true friend to me, I know that and I'm eternally grateful."

"This needs to stop, John."

"It will. Things will be different, I swear to you."

Bingham shook his head and slid his eyes to Thane's. "How?"

Thane explained his plan for Payton and instructed the lawyer to leave at dawn and drive directly to the compound. He was taking a chance, the man had never set foot inside the base before. He would see things, Thane said, that would shock him. He was trusting him to remember his loyalty to the family that had spanned many years, but still, it was a fucking risk.

Once Payton was with Dulcie, Bingham was to have the bird cage transported there to the beach house. He was to pay well and in cash. It was to arrive no later than nightfall tomorrow after which, Bingham would likely not hear from Thane for some months other than to oversee the hospital fees for the boy. Lastly, Thane asked Bingham to take care of matters regarding Betty's mother, to oversee the clearance of Nanette Porter's apartment and the settlement of her estate, if any. It was unlikely that Betty's mother had left any equity, likely just debts, but any proceeds were to be put into a new bank account that he was to set up for her daughter, Lacey. He was to make the arrangements for a simple burial and notify Thane of the details. With no other family that Thane was aware of, he did not foresee any problems.

If Bingham objected, he did not express anything other than a quiet acceptance of all that Thane asked of him. Then he retired to bed, eyes hooded, shoulders stooped as if bearing the weight of the world upon them. He was a good man but all good men had a limit to how far their loyalties could be stretched before they snapped. He just needed to do these last few favors. Just a few more days.

Alone with his thoughts, Thane tipped his head up towards the moon and inhaled the salty breeze as a calmness settled over him for the first time in many weeks. He was regaining control of his life again. It occurred to Thane that he had finally found what he'd been searching for his whole life. Someone to love and to love him in return like no-one had done since, well since Kim albeit that was love in its purest form. A love for one's sibling transcends all the shit that life throws at you, except of course life's shit had ended Kim in the cruelest of ways. It was time to stop mourning her, to stop blaming himself for not protecting her, he knew this. Would he continue to help victims like her? Hell yeah. But, he wouldn't take others. From now on he would do what was right, he'd grow the chain of women's shelters with Bingham's help and the proceeds from the sale of the compound, of his mom's estate. *Mom.* He hadn't called her than since he was a kid, after which time all informalities had been beaten out of him or educated out of him at the very best schools.

Now, he had his Freya. He had Syn and Luna and Boy who he'd always look out for. He was blessed beyond that which he deserved in view of the past. He would not fuck this up.

With a languid stretch, Thane took one last look over the starlit sky and walked inside the house. It was time to go to her. To be what she needed him to be. This was his new start - *their* new start together.

She'd not moved a single finger nor hair since last he'd checked on her. The slow rhythmic rising and falling of her chest decreased the tempo of his own heartbeat to a steady thrum as he slipped into bed behind her. As the bed dipped, she stirred; an arm swatted away whatever it was that his girl was dreaming of. Forming an O with his mouth, Thane blew a warm breath over her nape.

Betty squirmed. Adorable.

He did it again, this time chasing it up with a gentle kiss to her top most vertebrae.

"Momma?"

"No love, it's me."

Betty mumbled incoherently in a state of half-sleep and shifted onto her back, affording him the perfect chance to splay out his long fingers over her stomach. She was naked. He growled as his cock twitched and bucked its approval of the discovery. Unwittingly, Thane felt a dark mist drift over his view of her, fuelled in part by her vulnerability and his own animalistic need to protect her, to claim her. In one swift move of his burning torso he had covered her. One large fist pinned her wrists above her head even before she'd fully woken. And wake she did. With a whimper and a string of cuss words that had him narrowing his eyes, his teeth biting so hard into his bottom lip that he swore he'd drawn blood. Whilst he admired her sass, her filthy mouth would need to be addressed over time.

"Do. Not. Move." One fist held her in place, the other massaged and kneaded her breast, tugging on her hardening nipple before dipping down between her thighs to cup her sex. Betty gasped, her hips arching off the bed as the pad of his thumb rubbed relentlessly over her bud as one then two, three fingers parted her slit and speared her. Fuck, she was dry. Dipping his head, Thane grazed his teeth along her jawline. His tongue lapped a path down her sternum to the sweet valley between her breasts. A little further to the right and his lips found purchase around her areola. The flat warmth of his tongue lapped at her nipple before his teeth nibbled and nipped as his fingers fucked her until her body responded as he desired. Juices coated each of his digits even as she writhed and bucked and thrust her knee between his buttocks, likely aiming for his balls. A low rumble vibrated in his throat.

"Don't fight me," he warned, though in truth he could read her well enough to see the desire flashing over her startled eyes. She wanted him, she just didn't want to want him.

Slipping his fingers from her, he brought them to her lips and fucked her mouth with his hand until she'd sucked him clean. He took himself in hand, fisting his erection until the first beads of pre-cum soaked her folds. He was going to explode if he didn't take her then. His knees shoving apart her thighs, Thane slapped his slick crown against her wet heat, eyes locked on hers in silent warning as he drove inside her.

Throwing her head back, Betty cried out as her walls stretched to take him. He'd never known his cock to be so huge, so fucking painful, as it was right then. Frantic for a release, he rocked his hips and claimed her deeper than ever before. Betty screamed, her fingers raking over his back as she met each thrust with her own. His mouth slammed over hers, teeth clattering, tongues brutally battling. The little minx bit into the flesh of his lip. He roared and deepened the kiss, fucked her harder still - a punishing rhythm that soaked his shaft, each thrust a piston of steel as he chased his orgasm. This could kill them both, his heart pounding in his ears. So be it.

Freya

Oh, the conflict in her mind; what the hell was wrong with her? She ought to hate him with every fiber of her being and yet…shit! He hit her sweet spot again and again until she didn't know whether to fight him or draw him in deeper and use him the same as he was using her. He was making her feel when she didn't want to feel. Making her need him when she needed no fucker. Breathing life into her on a raw and brutal kiss when she thought the world was dead to her.

Never had Betty felt so full, so utterly and completely joined to another human even beyond a physical connection. Every thrust struck her end until she tore her mouth from his, her teeth sinking into the hard slab of his chest.

"Tear my flesh, I don't care," he rasped. "You. Are. Mine."

She tried so hard, really she did, to battle against the waves that rippled from her sex and racked her body. Again and again they struck, clenching every muscle of her vagina, thighs, buttocks and belly as she cried against his slick skin. As Betty's orgasm drenched Thane's cock, he too succumbed with a shattering roar, a pulsing stream of sticky warmth coating them both.

Thane withdrew and fell like a dead weight to the side of her. Both were gasping, neither talking. The air was stale with the scent of lust and testosterone. Her tears leaked in a steady stream. Betty threw her arm over her eyes and gave in to her pain, both physical and emotional. Honestly, she didn't quite know what she was crying for more: the loss of her mom, her own shame in the pleasure she'd derived and her need of her captor–these growing feelings for him,–or the physical pain inside her bruised, torn channel.

"Freya…don't."

She felt him even before she heard his hushed words against her ear. Two powerful arms enveloped her into a tight hug, her tears melding with the beads of sweat on his skin, her face pressed to the crook of his corded neck. There they stayed until she'd cried herself out, the storm blowing itself out until she was limp and his arms never once released her from the locked embrace. Finally, he pulled back and reached over to snap on a lamp on the nightstand. A pale yellow warmth bathed the room as he lay on his side and shuffled down the bed until his eyes were level with hers.

"I'm sorry about your mother," he said, a crease forming between his brows.

It was the first time he'd expressed empathy in this way yet it didn't seem disingenuous. She wondered if he'd thought her outburst was all grief. If he'd had any comprehension at all that everything, all this, that it was just too much for her to cope with. She came over as ballsy, strong, but she wasn't. Truth was she was scared and alone and needed him in a way that was so fucking wrong. And, worse than needing him, she wanted him. How fucked up was that?

Betty chewed her lip and shrugged, sliding her gaze from his. She'd always locked up tight, it had been the only way she'd survived after Cody. When he died it was like a wall built up, impenetrable and true. That's why these endless tears frustrated her so, uncontrollable as they were. Releasing her lip from her teeth, she managed to whisper, "What fucking hurts the most is that she was never once there for me. I needed her and she wasn't there. And I feel so fucking bad for being so selfish because I wasn't there for her either, when she needed me."

With a dour nod, Thane tucked her hair behind her ear. "I understand."

He probably did understand more than anyone. She wanted to ask him about his sister but bit it back. It wasn't her scab to pick.

"Don't forget, little one, I lost my own mother just a few weeks ago. Like you, I felt the pain of rejection over many years and like you, deep down I loved her. We can't always make sense of the conflict in our minds, in our hearts, but we can accept it as a part of us, of who we are."

Frowning, Betty asked, "And do you accept who you are?"

Clearly that struck a chord. Thane furrowed his deep brow and chewed over his carefully considered reply.

"I bear many scars, Freya. Here." He took her hand and placed it over his heart, she felt its strong beat pulse against her palm.

"And here." He touched her fingertips to his temple.

The urge to stroke her palm along the angular roughness of his jaw in comfort was a strong one, an irrational one. Betty quickly pulled her hand away from his.

Thane closed his eyes and sighed. When he opened them, his eyes were pools of liquid honey but behind those amber irises, was a pain that Betty connected with and understood. When he spoke, his voice was was smaller than she'd ever heard. "You and I are the same."

"Excuse me?"

"I know about your brother, what you don't know is that I had a sister. A twin sister, Kim. She died too."

"I know." Betty masked her surprize that he'd opened up to her on this.

"You know?" Thane pulled back a fraction, arching a brow.

Betty nodded. "Bingham told me earlier. I'm so sorry for your loss."

Thane's lip curved in a half-smile as he scoffed. "Never trust a lawyer with a secret."

"Don't be mad at him," said Betty. "I kinda dragged it out of him. So, you know pretty much everything about me, huh?"

His expression hardened. He said simply, "I know everything about you, I've told you this before. You weren't taken at random, Freya. I chose you, remember? I researched you and I followed you. There was no corner of your life that I hadn't explored prior to my decision to claim you as mine."

Betty's eyes widened. "Oh my God. I see what you did. You matched my scars to your own, didn't you?"

"If you wish to put it that way, yes I did. We'd lived parallel lives, albeit mine was somewhat more privileged than yours. Your poor damaged soul, Freya, is a mirror image of mine. Therefore, we can heal each other because we are the other. Only someone who has experienced what we have, who is fractured in the way that we are, can piece together the shards to make a whole. I can heal you, just as you can heal me…our son will heal us both. He's the purity that we both lack, don't you see? The best parts of both of us without the bad parts. He bonds us forever."

"Whoa…this is too much." Pushing up on the bed, Betty hugged her knees then, worried she'd squish the little cookie inside of her, she instead sat back against the pillow stack. "I don't want to talk about this shit with you." He'd hit too close to home. What he said made perfect sense, comforted her and scared the shit out of her in equal measure.

When he moved beside her, it was clearly to resume his power, his control. He crowded her with the breadth of his shoulders sweeping down to an etched V. He was impossible to ignore.

"Talk to me. Tell me about him. You loved him."

Betty cut him a 'don't go there' glare.

"Okay, then tell me about you, as a child."

Drawing the duvet up to her neck, Betty smiled tightly as her mind drifted back to happier times. "I was a pain in the ass and Cody was a bright-eyed, bushy-haired angel. Mom used to say I'd gotten mixed up in the hospital. That he and I were so different that we couldn't be related. I used to believe her too. Once I ran away to find my real mom and dad. I only got so far as the grocery store before Cody found me and told me mom hadn't meant it literally, she was just being mean. He gave me his candy and we went and caught some newts and kept them in a jar. Named them Cody and Lacey." She chuckled at the fond memory.

"When did things change?"

"Between us?"

"Mhm."

Betty drew a thumb nail to her lips and chewed on it. Thane tugged it free, bringing her hand to his lap where he held it tight. Again, so confusing.

"I guess as soon as I started changing. I got all curvy and grew–" She glanced down at her chest. "He started looking at me different. If he caught me talking to a boy at school, he'd get shitty. Possessive. At the time, I put it down to him being a protective bro, you know?"

"And then?"

Her eyes grew fearful. "Don't make me say it."

"Say it."

"I...I can't." She gripped the duvet around her, suddenly cold to her bones as if Cody was in the room with them. *Don't make me go there, it will kill me.*

"Freya. Say it."

Damn you! Her voice rose an octave, her words spilled out of their own accord. "You want me to spell it out to you? Do you? All the sordid detail of how he fucked his sister? Or…or how I was the one who found him hanging by his neck or how he'd shit himself or how Mom was screaming and Dad couldn't find the phone to call 911?" Hysterical now. "Or his eyes…how they were all glassy and they stared right at me when they cut him down and said he was gone? And I hit him like I hit my mom when I found her too, because I was angry, Thane. I wanted to hurt them for hurting me, for leaving me."

As Betty's small fists rained blows against his chest, her eyes vacant–some place other than here, darker than here–his arms caught her once more. She couldn't know Thane's own pain as memories of his sister laid out in her Sunday best at the funeral parlor were wrenched before his eyes and played over and over like a grainy movie reel against his lids.

They held each other.

This beast who had taken her and terrorised her…how could he comfort her? And yet that's precisely what he did. Both utterly broken, the two locked in a silent scream that only the other could hear.

The Bird Cage

Thanatos

There was something cathartic about being there at the beach house. The scent of his mother's perfume still hung in the air, or perhaps in his imagination, in any case he sensed her presence. She was always different out here, just as he was. The madness inherent in them both was somehow blown away on the Atlantic ocean breeze. Of course, he'd never been to Cape Cod during the times of his own madness. When the rages took hold. Instead, he'd elected to lock himself away at the compound or, more recently, to remove himself from civilization and wander aimlessly in quiet places lest he harm those he loved. On reflection, had he instead come to the beach house, perhaps it would have abated those darkest times. He was changing, a new clarity of mind was dawning. As he stood at the picture window of the breakfast room and gazed out towards Nantucket Sound, he was thankful for Freya. For new beginnings and fresh wisdom. For once, he wasn't thankful to any gods, instead he was simply grateful to her. For her.

"May I go outside?"

Snapping his head around to Betty, jolted from his thoughts, Thane smiled at her. "Ah, good afternoon. I'd thought I'd let you sleep in." She was wearing his black tee which reached almost to her knees. She was a sight to behold and his manhood jumped to attention against the soft silk of his low-slung pants. "Not today. I'll be at the hospital and, frankly, you haven't yet given me many reasons to trust that you won't run. I want you safe inside your cage today." He inhaled, waiting for her to argue with him as inevitably as night followed day.

"Cage?"

"Yes, Freya. It arrived not a half hour ago which, I must say, is quite impressive and I must give Bingham a bonus. It arrived barely three hours after his departure this morning."

Betty's jaw grew slack. Thane smiled. "Relax. When Luna and Syn have finished their chores, I'll see to it that they make you comfortable."

"Please, don't. I won't run, I swear. Not the cage."

"No, you won't, little one. Look, it's for your own protection. I'm thinking not just of you, but of the child too. Trust my judgement please."

"So, what? You'll keep me locked up like a damn bird

in a cage until I have the baby? Haven't we moved past this shit?"

The tone of her voice was grating on him but Thane knew that he too must adapt. Learn patience and understanding. "This is not open to negotiation nor discussion. Now, you can either comply with my directive or not. Either way you will go in the cage so I suggest you do so willingly." Pinching his lips together, he cut her a glare.

Betty shook her head. It was apparent to Thane that his sassy girl was going to cause him trouble today. So be it. With a roll of his neck, the towering giant of a man closed the distance between them. Betty held her ground, head tipped up to glare at him but he could see past her anger to the fear beyond, she was so transparent, so easy to read. With one swift movement, Thane had Betty in his arms and set her down in the cage. She beat her petulant little fists against him, though truthfully it was little more than a flutter against his ripped chest. He tolerated her pissy attitude because, frankly, she amused him with her fake bravado and because there was really nothing about her that he didn't find endearing, if a little irritating at times. A rough diamond. His diamond.

The bird cage stood resplendent in the center of the circular grand room; he'd given a great deal of thought as to where it should go but then nothing Thane did was by chance or on a whim except when his temper got the better of common sense. Above the tip of the cage rose the dome of the ceiling, ornately carved to match the fine detail of the cage. The view from the wall of glass was sublime. Betty was very fortunate indeed to enjoy such a fine vista. At times like this Thane was more than grateful for his family's money as it honestly had bought the best lot in the entire county.

With Betty safely locked within the confines of the giant bird cage, he stood back and marvelled at the sight before him. She was sat cross legged on cushions of the rarest silk in hues of crimson, gold and vermillion. With soft curls (albeit knotted like a bird's nest–he'd have Luna sort that out later) and eyes the color of sapphires, his Freya was the most beautiful of all little song birds. A jewel and a prize. The love of his life. Thane would do anything to protect her. Anything.

As he stroked his stubble-peppered jaw and enjoyed the sight, Luna and Syn joined him. Beaming at each of his muses in turn, Thane reached out a hand and asked, "Isn't she a sight to behold?"

"She really is," Syn replied with a tight smile.

"She's a sight, alright," said Luna, narrowing her eyes.

Thane wasn't an unreasonable man. He knew that taking them all from the compound with no warning or explanation would require adjustment and time. He was an empathetic man, as borne out by the work he did with vulnerable women. He knew this but still he couldn't fathom why Luna was being so prickly. He made a mental note to watch her closely; something about her demeanor gnawed away at his gut, had him on edge. She appeared antagonistic toward his chosen one. It needed to stop right now or there would be serious repercussions for Luna, make no mistake.

Clapping his hands together, Thane ordered the women to prepare an early lunch. He was starving.

"I'm going out," he told them over a freshly brewed cup of coffee. "The boy is being woken up today and I want to be there."

"You've heard from the hospital, Thane?"

"Yes Syn. I called at dawn. It seems that his surgery went well, they removed the growth from Boy's brain and scans will hopefully prove clear, that they got it all. He'll need a long period of convalescence which we'll provide for him here."

Both women sighed their relief. Luna asked, "When can he come home?"

"I hope to find that out today when I visit with him. Let's pray for a quick discharge from hospital, we need him here with us, his family."

"Yes sir, we do," they both agreed.

"While I'm gone I want you, Syn, to care for Freya, understood?"

"Of course, it goes without saying that I'll take great care of her."

Thane nodded. "I know you will. Thank you."

"What about me?" asked Luna. She was dishing up a simple meal of lobster bisque and crusty bread.

"You will spend the time in quiet reflection." He shot her a warning glance, eyes narrowed. "You're not to go near Freya. Do you understand?"

"What? Are you serious?" Slamming the plates and bowls down in front of Thane and Syn, Luna planted her hands on her hips, brows pinched together.

Pushing back his chair with a scrape, Thane folded his arms, his pectoral muscles popping were clearly noted by the obsequious Luna. "You're challenging me, Luna?" His eyes darkened as a storm blew across them.

Luna hesitated, she knew that look, she'd be foolish to push him further, and yet that's exactly what she did. "I just don't understand. Why let Syn have all the privileges when I've done nothing wrong?"

"Your tone and your behavior are the reasons why I will not permit you near Freya." Thane shoved to his feet, clenched his fists at his sides, the stool falling back with a clatter. "Come with me."

Luna looked wide eyed at Syn who quickly lowered her gaze to her food and sampled the bisque. Back at Thane. He met her incredulous stare on a sharp exhale. "Fine."

"Fine?"

"I mean yes, sir."

"Better. Come then."

Thane led the girl down to the walkout basement where he extended a finger and pointed to the bare cement floor. Why his parents had never done anything with the space had always confounded him. Now, he was glad of it. "Kneel."

There was a defiance in the girl's eyes that he'd never seen before. It concerned as much as angered him. Feeling the red mist begin to form like crystals over his eyes, Thane drew in a deep breath and snapped his fingers. "I said, kneel."

"Why? I don't understand, Thane. I've always been so loyal and thankful for all you've done for me." The girl was weeping now, her crocodile tears meaning little to Thane.

"You seem to have forgotten your place at my side," he said in a voice that was calmer than the storm inside of him. "I'd be negligent if I didn't take time to revisit the premise of your salvation."

Luna shook her head, making absolutely no move to kneel.

Thane stepped closer until he felt the soft panted breath from her lips blow lightly upon his chest. Reaching out a hand, he gripped her chin in a vice between his thumb and index finger and tilted her face up. "Be under no illusion, Luna, that my wishes will prevail. I can destroy you. You'd do well to remember that."

It was hard for her to speak, her lips pushed together by his unyielding grip. She managed, "Or else?"

Folding over so that his mouth was close to hers he snarled. "Or else you will be taken from here and tossed back into the godforsaken life that you once lived. And that's if I'm feeling fucking lenient, which I can't guarantee."

The girl swallowed and blinked. He was intimidating in the extreme, he knew this, such was the power that he exuded. That he could never harm Luna was not a fact he wished to disclose for to do so would be to show weakness and she would never learn from a weak man. She would never serve a weak man. In any case, right at this moment, Thane wasn't certain that he wouldn't hurt her. She was pushing his fucking buttons.

Releasing Luna's chin, he swept his palm over her cheek until his long fingers threaded her hair. Closing his fist, he twisted her locks into a ponytail which he used as leverage to force her to her knees. "There," he said. "Kneeling as I asked, good girl." As Thane stepped back his mouth quirked up into a smile. "Stay exactly where you are in that position until I return. Your knees will be numb very shortly, then you'll feel the cold of the stone permeate through to the bone. Even then, you do not move. Say 'yes Thane.'

"Yes. Yes, Thane."

"I'll be back late afternoon." With that, he turned and left the girl to dwell on her actions and the repercussions of such.

Alone in the basement, all was not still. With the mighty man gone, a little mouse stirred. The little mouse squeaked before it scurried upstairs and watched from the shadows for the cat to leave.

Freya

She was a goddamn fool to think the man was anything less than the devil. To think he cared. That he had felt what she'd felt. What an idiot she'd been.

Last night, after he'd fucked her, they'd shared secrets that she'd never shared with a living soul before, having felt connected to him in a way that had scared her. Had she imagined that he'd really felt the same way too? Oh God, she'd peeled her skin back and torn open her ribs until her fractured fucking heart was on show for him. *She'd let him in.* How then could he do this to her? To lock her inside a cage as if she was nothing more than a pathetic pet? His kid was growing in her stomach and Betty had no idea if Thane intended to keep her locked away until it was born. Weeks. Months. She'd whither and die here, for sure. And Luna. What the fuck was up with her? Jealousy?

It just went to show what a lousy judge of character she was when she'd first thought of Luna as the one to trust and Syn as her enemy. She'd gotten closer to Luna, intimately. And now? Now she didn't know who to trust, who was really there for her. Syn, at least, seemed compassionate, kind to her now. She'd talk to her, try and talk Syn into letting her go outside and catch some rays on her skin, smell the ocean…Syn would let her, she hoped beyond hope.

From the very edge of the left window, a small sail boat came into view. Watching it dip and drift and bob to and fro on the gentle undulations of the tide, Betty tried to let the scene calm her. In her mind's eye, she was aboard the little rose colored sail boat, her skin warmed by the sun's rays as she steered into foamy froth and let the ocean carry her far far away to paradise. To a golden beach fringed with swaying palms, pelicans and the scent of fried plantain and tropical flowers.

"You. Look at you."

"Excuse me?" Betty's attention was immediately pulled from the window to the angry face of Luna.

"You think you're so fucking special." Luna's face was screwed into a bitter sneer as she circled the cage. "His chosen one." She laughed. "Look at you with his cage and his love and his…his *kid.* You do know you're actually nothing more than a dirty, flea infested whore? No better than any of us. And yet, here you are, perched on a fucking cushion thinking you're the queen bee of the hive. Well let me tell you little missy, once they sting, bees die. Dead and gone. Oh, and did I mention that Thane's not here?"

Why You?

Thanatos

The nurse looked up from her paperwork, a pen slipping from her fingers as she licked her lips at the sight of him. He'd be mildly amused, smile even, if he wasn't so anxious to see Boy and speak to the doctors.

"Are you a relative?"

"I'm all he has, so yes, I'm a relative."

Pursing her lips, the nurse frowned. "He's not supposed to have visitors. He's being brought out of a medically induced coma right now. Take a seat and see if the doc will let you visit with him later."

Shooting her his most charming smile, Thane planted

his palms on the desk so that his biceps swelled and leant forward, eyes fixing on hers. "I understand but I've driven up from the Cape especially to see him and I know he'll be pretty darn scared when he wakes if I'm not there."

Her eyes dropped to his full lips as his smile slipped, tongue flicking over his teeth. Her lips parted, a blush spreading over the apples of her cheeks as she watched him skilfully work his sculpted mouth. "I guess…oh hell, it can't do any harm. Through those double doors, first room on the right."

With a wink, Thane thanked her and set off to find Boy.

"You're welcome," she called.

He was a pitiful sight. Wires, monitors, tubes, surrounded by a medical team, the young man of whom Thane was so fond looked paper white, small and vulnerable as he lay supine and still. A bandage was wrapped around his head, tufts of hair sprouting this way and that.

A doctor glanced at Thane as he entered the room and stood at the foot of the bed. "You are?"

"John, the boy's only relative. How's he doing?"

"You clear it with the nursing staff to be in here?"

"Yes. Yes I did. I wanted to be here when he wakes."

"Well your timing is on point. We've just administered a drug to bring him round. Take a seat. You can hold his hand but don't touch any of the wires or lines."

Thane did as he was told, any qualms about being ordered around vanishing as the boy's eyelids began to flutter. Taking Boy's hand in his, he held it gently and leant forward on a sigh as the young man coughed.

"Breathing tube came out. It's quite normal to cough," the doctor advised.

Thane nodded and chewed on his lip. *Wake up, Boy. Wake up.*

Beneath his hand, the boy's fingers began to flex. A second or two later, his eyes opened albeit just a crack.

"Hi there, it's me. You're awake, sleepy head."

"Thane?"

Thane's laughter cut the tension in the room as he tightened his grip and nodded. Damn, he felt so choked up. "Yes it's me, welcome back. You're going to be just fine." A single tear leaked from Thane's eye, falling with a plop on the sheet covering Boy. "You need to get well and come home."

"Sir, we need to run a few checks so you'll need to step outside now please."

"When can he come home?"

"I can't say yet. Vital signs are good but there's a long road ahead and of course it's all dependent on the test results. If we've got it all."

Thane drew his eyes to the doctor. "What do you mean, 'if you've got it all?'"

The doctor looked away. "We're hopeful."

"Please…do your best for him," said Thane. "He's very precious to me."

"We'll do our best, you have my word."

"Thank you." As Thane stood, he bent down low and brushed a kiss over the boy's forehead. "Soon," he whispered, "soon you'll come home to us and we'll take care of you and love you. One big happy family." He added quietly, "I'm sorry. I'm so sorry, forgive me." His eyes screwed shut as his forehead pressed to that of the boy and the great weight of Thane's actions settled over his own spirit in a dark cloak of remorse.

* * *

He paced a while and then paced some more, an empty paper coffee cup scrunched tight in his fist. Hours passed until day bled into night into day. Thane scrubbed a palm over the new growth of stubble dusting his jaw and looked for the hundredth time at the large white clock above the nurse's desk. "Is this normal?" He was holding on by one last tenuous thread of patience, about to snap.

"Ah, John?" The doctor's voice was gentle, measured, with an edge of something that Thane didn't like.

"Yes, that's me."

"Would you follow me? I'd like a word in private."

The small room in which Thane found himself was austere: clinical, pale lemon walls saturated with the pain of bad news and hopelessness with an underlying stench of disinfectant. "You have news?" He wanted the doctor to hurry the fuck up and just tell him.

The doctor indicated to a small pink chair. Thane shook his head. "John, I believe in being direct." The two men locked eyes.

"Direct is good."

"The fact is that, regrettably, the CAT scan showed a grade four tumor, a glioblastoma and the lab work confirms this. What this means is that the cancer cells are very aggressive, it's unlikely that any chemotherapy or radiotherapy would halt their growth."

His pulse thumped fast and loud in Thane's ears. "Unlikely? What the hell does unlikely mean? There's a chance, correct?"

The doctor shook his head, pursed his lips and looked up at Thane. "There are other complications, I'm so sorry."

"Such as?"

"The blood vessels supplying the tumor. We took what we could but…"

His stomach rolled. Sweat beaded over his top lip and brow. A coldness settled in his bones. "How long?"

"How long does he have?"

Thane nodded, words escaping him.

"It's not an exact science, I'm afraid. I've already set the ball rolling for palliative support. Our main focus will be in keeping him comfortable."

He couldn't see, couldn't breathe. The need to hold his girl was almost overpowering as Thane felt his usual control ebbing, slipping away. How? How could there be nothing that medical science could do for Boy? "There has to be something we can try? I have money, we can take him abroad, try alternative therapies."

"I'm honestly so sorry, no. We'll start corticosteroids immediately to reduce the swelling on his brain."

"I see. I want to take him home," said Thane simply, his voice little more than a croak. "To the beach house."

After a beat, the doctor nodded. "I don't see why not. The ocean would be a restful place for him to be. The air…"

"Would be good for him?" Thane bit out a sardonic laugh. "When can we leave?"

"A few days. I suggest you go home and get some rest. That young man is going to need you to be well and strong to support him through this journey, okay?"

"Very well. I…I'll return tomorrow."

Outside the hospital, as the entire world went about its business like Boy wasn't dying, and birds skittered oblivious across a wide blue sky, Thane snarled low and deep and cursed every fucking god and then himself. For the first time in his life he was as weak as a rag doll, sliding down the wall, head in hands.

Boy was barely a man.

His whole life ahead.

All that he'd been through, for nothing.

Worse still, Thane was powerless to change this for him. Death was stalking Boy and closing in and it was an adversary that even Thane himself couldn't crush.

Freya

"Luna! What are you doing?"

Both Betty and Luna turned their heads to look at Syn in the doorway of the grand room.

"Oh, am I breaking the rules?" she quipped. "Should I go back and kneel for fucking hours until the mighty one decides I'm worthy of his attention?"

"What the *hell* has gotten into you?" asked Syn on a growl.

With a sickly smile over her lips, Luna toyed with a ribbon tied about the waist of her simple blue dress and laughed. "Hell? Oh, that's a good one. We're all in hell, my sweet loving Syn. All of us except Princess here."

"What are you talking about?" Syn hurried closer, putting herself between the cage and Luna. Standing a good foot taller in spiked heels, she formed an impenetrable wall between Betty and Luna.

"What I'm talking about is that Thane never chose me. Why was that do you think? I mean, I could give him babies same as her." Her hand drifted over her midriff as

Luna glowered at Syn. "But it was never me, I was never good enough."

"That's all in your mind," said Syn. "He loves you, just as he loves all of us. He always has or why would he have taken us from our fucked up lives and given us safety?"

Luna threw back her head and laughed. "No. He doesn't, or why wouldn't we have been enough for him? What can she give him that either of us could?"

"That's not for us to question, Luna. Why he chose all of us was for the same reason…why he does everything, is for the same reason. For us. To give us a place of safety. Does he get things wrong sometimes? Hell, yes. Is he insane? Of course, yes he is, but he loves us and he'd protect each of us with his life…including you."

"Lies! It should've been me!" Luna's fingers stroked a circle around the lip of a tall red vase on a table beside her.

Betty shrank back against the bars of the cage and folded her arms protectively over her bump. She felt sick to her stomach as she watched the two do battle with words. "Stop. Just stop."

"It wasn't meant to be you, or it would've been," Syn said quietly, ignoring Betty's plea as she took a step closer to Luna. "Now, come with me and let's go and sit down and really talk over a nice cup of coffee."

Luna shook her head left to right. "No. I. Want. Her. Gone."

"Luna, no. Come with me, come on."

Betty held her breath. She saw Luna's hand close around the narrow rim of the vase. Saw it lifted above her head. Heard the sickly thud as the girl brought it crashing down on Syn's skull. As if she were boneless, Syn crumpled to the floor and lay motionless.

"I. Said. No!" The vase slipped from Luna's hand with a clatter, smashing into tiny shards of red and blue porcelain.

Eyes wide with terror, Betty screamed. And screamed. And scrambled around the cage needing oh so badly to get out, to check on Syn, to get help. Thane. She needed Thane of all people, a notion she didn't think she'd ever feel. Talk about irony!

So long. Why was he taking so long? Shortly after Luna's outburst, Syn had come to at which point Luna had helped her to her feet like she cared a damn and hadn't knocked Syn out. She was clearly disorientated, unstable on her feet; Luna had slipped an arm around her waist and taken her from the grand room. It was just Betty. Alone. It had been that way for ages until the light had faded to little more than a dim glow from light chasing through the house from the driveway. Colored lights, not car lights, no sign of Thane. Betty had peed twice in the bucket and long since drank the water left there for her. There had been no food, not that she could eat anyway. Eventually, curled in a ball, Betty had fallen into a deep sleep where nightmares found her, tormented her, twisted her mind and left her wrung out as shards of sunlight caught dust motes inside of the cage and her whole body ached real bad.

"Good morning, Princess. How are we feeling today?"

"Luna."

The woman barked a caustic laugh. "You look like shit."

"No kidding. How about you and me go visit a spa for

the day?"

Luna tilted her head and chewed her lip. "Oh, Miss Sassy Pants, I think that's a wonderful idea. In fact, why don't we start with a swim?"

It all happened in slow motion. Luna fumbling in her pocket, a key, the gate clanging open, her hair pulled so hard, head slammed against metal and, in spite of how she scratched and hissed and punched and kicked, she was being dragged from the cage. Burning pain in her scalp. Knees scraping over the threshold of a door…scrabbling to get to her feet. Being shoved onwards, forwards. Out through the house, no weapons to grab, moving so fast. Sand beneath her feet, scratching her soles; a splinter in her heel as the sand gave way to the planks of a jetty. The sound of the ocean amplified with the shrill cawing of gulls overhead. Salty wind whipping her hair, blinding her eyes.

All the time, Betty begged and sobbed. "My baby… think of the baby. Luna, please, no–"

"There'll be no baby, don't you see?" Luna stood in front of her, the house splayed out beyond her back.

Betty glanced over her shoulder at the swell of the sea below. Gone was the gentle calm of yesterday's tide, now there were white horses whipping against the framework of the jetty. One hand gripped at her swollen stomach, the other reached out toward the wild-eyed woman in front of her. "Please."

"I'm sorry Princess," said Luna simply. "Time to take that swim."

A shove. Pain in her shoulder. Falling backwards. A splash. Cold, so very cold.

Can't see.

Can't breathe.
Oh, God…

Drowning

Thanatos

The more he thought about it, in a small way Thane felt a weight lift everso slightly. The guilt he had felt over striking the boy had been somewhat assuaged by the knowledge that his actions had not been the precursor to the young man's deterioration. That said, he felt crippled with grief as he walked out of the hospital grounds and located his car. Grief and an underlying frustration that, for once, he was not in control and there was nothing that he could do about it. How could he carry on without Boy when he had been so intrinsic in everything that Thane had done, everything that he was. He hadn't shown it, hadn't told Boy enough what he meant to him and, now that the changes in Boy's behavior of late made perfect sense, it only served to compound Thane's guilt.

Still, he loved him. It's funny how you only realize what someone means to you when you risk losing them, he reflected. They were all more precious than he'd ever really appreciated, every one of them. True, they owed him a debt of thanks for the new lives he'd set them up in but now it was evident that he owed them too in return. He owed them his thanks, his love, his protection yet he had failed in protecting Boy and that was a bitter pill to swallow. It wasn't honestly possible for one man to protect from an entity such as cancer, though. No-one could do that, not even the surgeon or medic and certainly not any god. Life is beautiful and life is a cruel bitch, don't you think?

That the boy had recognized Thane had been more than he had hoped for in the circumstances. He would bring him home soon. It was where he belonged, where he should spend whatever time left - with his family taking good care of him. It was the very least that they could do for Boy. The least that Thane could do for Boy.

The drive back to Cape Cod was a laborious one; he was keen to be home but savored the space and time to gather his thoughts and to make plans. He would set up a bed in the picture window of the grand room where Boy could watch the boats and the ocean and the birds. The haunting notes of Tchaikovsky settled over Thane with a melancholy as the miles ticked by and the traffic thinned.

Thane's cell phone rang. Punching the volume button on his dash, he hit the call accept button. "John speaking." As no-one from home ever called him, he always used his given name when answering calls.

There was crackling on the line.

"Hello?"

"Thane, oh thank God!"

"Syn?"

Fine hairs and goosebumps rose on his arms, his nape. "What is it?"

"Where are you? Please, please, come quickly."

"Freya? Is she okay? What's happened?"

There was a pause on the line.

"Syn?" He swallowed his panic and gripped the wheel, his foot squeezing the gas pedal hard.

"It's Luna. She…she hit me. Thane, she has Freya."

Nostrils flaring, Thane snarled as every muscle in his body tensed. "Has her where?"

"I don't know…outside I think. She had me in your office with a knife all night, rambling on and on and on. Then, when she left to get Freya I managed to get to the phone, to call you. She's gone mad, Thane, I mean seriously fucking loco. I can't reason with her."

"Goddammit!" He needed to stay calm. *Fuck!* His palm slammed against the wheel as he wove around a slow car and floored the gas. "Listen to me. How badly are you hurt?"

"My head."

Thane inhaled. "I want you to hang up and call 911. Open the perimeter gates and unlock the door. Can you do that?"

"Yes, but–"

"Good. Do it. Do it now. I'm on my way."

If anything happens to Freya…I can't think about that right now. Need to get there…

Cutting the call, Thane dialled Bingham Suffolk. Barking his orders to his lawyer, not waiting for the man to respond, he cut the call and drove for all he was worth - as if his life depended on it, which it did. Freya and his unborn child were his life. Right then, Thane didn't give a fuck about the implications of police swarming over the beach house, his own freedom meant nothing to him. His entire world was at the mercy of Luna, the one he had nurtured and cared for. The girl who had taken his love and used it as a knife to plunge into his gut. He would never forgive her. Never.

He would fucking destroy her.

Freya

Breaking through the surface of the water, Betty spluttered and sucked in what little air she could before another wave claimed her. Down she was pulled by the hands of the tide…cruel, clawing hands that tugged her deep then spat her to the surface.

Daylight. Darkness. Daylight. Darkness.

Gasping. Lungs burned.

As she thrashed and fought against the ocean, against the hands that held her firmly beneath the ceiling of water now, her world went dark. In her mind, she called to Cody but he didn't come. A peace settled over her as her consciousness ebbed away, the struggle ending.

On a painful gasp, Betty's face broke through the surface of the water. Fingers clamped tightly around Betty's arms; the same hands that had shoved her into the sea now pulled and dragged her until her knees grazed on course shifting sand, her feet struggling to find purchase, life slamming back into her. As the hands released her, Betty staggered, falling heavily onto her side where she lay retching and coughing and spewing salty bile as a hermit crab raised his pincers and funnelled deep and safe beside her.

Betty blinked repeatedly until her vision cleared. A pair of startled eyes blinked back. Luna.

"I'm sorry." Her voice was small, like a child. "I didn't mean to. I lost it, I'm sorry."

Holding her stomach, Betty vomited. Spitting the last of the puke from her mouth, she hauled up with her arms until she was sat facing Luna. The girl was hugging her knees and sucking her thumb. Still gasping and heaving, eyes stinging like a bitch, questions began to crowd Betty's head. So many questions, the loudest being *why?*

Somewhere a siren drowned out the haw-haw-haw of gulls. Then, out of the corner of her eye, Betty saw Syn flanked by uniformed men, all were hurrying towards her with a gurney that slipped and slid and sank in the sand. It would be comical if Betty had a mind to see the humor in it. She didn't. Her eyes locked on Luna's as she bit out the last thing she thought that she would say: "Go."

Luna tipped her head and drew her thumb from her mouth. She too turned and watched the ascending cops and paramedics. Turning back to Betty, Luna shook her head. "Too late for me and for him. It's all over now."

"No, go. I won't tell." She wouldn't tell because she actually pitied the girl. Luna was no more fucked up than she was, than they all were. Their pasts had collectively set them on a path to destruction, Thane had merely been the vessel that they rode to journey there. Or perhaps he wasn't. Maybe Thane tried to derail their ride to hell unaware that he offered a hell of a different kind but still a hell. Right now though, Betty was alive and her baby was alive, she knew it. A gentle fluttering deep inside of her confirmed this. And there it was. Her future.

Pushing to her feet, Luna swayed, her eyes darting from Betty to the encroaching medics and back. "Sorry," she said simply again. Betty fell back onto the cold sand and stared up the clouds, watched how they slid across the sky. When she crooked her neck to look up at Luna, the girl had gone. Instead there were faces that she didn't know. Syn's face etched with worry. Fussing and lots and lots of talking. Closing her eyes, Betty shut them all out. She could hear Cody whispering to her at last. Could feel his warm breath blow over her cheek, or it was a breeze or it was him. "Thane," she said to herself or out loud. "Thane."

"There we go. Can you see it?"

Squinting up at the monitor, Betty could make out a grey oval joined to another oval and in the center of that, a small, black pulsating hole. That's the heartbeat?"

"Sure is. Beating strong, too. Seems this little one is none the worse for your little swim."

Letting out a held breath, Betty smiled as her tears streamed. "Can you see if it's a boy or girl?"

"It's a little early to tell," said the technician. But I'll take some measurements and print off a picture for you to show the baby daddy.

The baby daddy…

Fifteen minutes later: "Okay, we're all done."

Betty hugged the small image to her chest and closed

her eyes.

"Let's get you back to your room."

Her kindly nurse, Sylvie, was waiting for her. Helping her to step from the wheelchair to the bed, she fussed and cooed over the image of the baby. "He's gonna be over the moon when he sees that you're both fine."

"Who?"

"Your husband. He's right outside, I'll send him in."

"Husband?"

She sensed him even before she saw him, one strong forearm braced on the door frame, filling the space with the breadth of his shoulders. In his other hand, he clasped a single red rose.

"Freya."

"I'll leave you two lovebirds to it. You need me, press the buzzer dear."

With the nurse gone, Thane tentatively walked to Betty's bedside and lowered himself to perch on the edge. His eyes were ringed with dark circles, rims flame red, he'd been crying?

"Luna?"

Carefully Thane placed the rose on Betty's stomach. When he looked back at her, the golden flecks that had once laced his honey eyes were gone. Instead they were lifeless, the fire snuffed out. The urge to reach out and touch him was strong.

"Gone. I trust she stays gone or I won't be accountable for what I'll do to the girl."

"Do you know where? Are the cops looking for her?"

Thane shook his head. "As far as the story goes, it was an intruder. Robbery. Struck Syn, knocked her out. You panicked and ran, then slipped off the jetty." His eyes rose to meet hers. “Plausible, don’t you think?”

Betty looked away. “The cops bought it?”

Thane took a thick ribbon of Betty’s hair in his fist, winding it around his finger absently. “They had questions for me,” he said. “The cage. Our living arrangements. Then they took Syn and questioned her. All I know is that she was given medical treatment and has not said a word against me…at least, not so far as I’m aware. I’m still free, so I think not, but then I do pay my lawyer well.”

As she thought about what he’d said, Betty realized that in a perverse way she was relieved that he was free. Of course, the power now lay in her hands alone. Syn had turned out to be loyal to him in every sense when the shit hit the fan. Luna - well, Luna would stay away if she knew what was good for her. Betty didn’t dare to think what Thane would do to Luna if ever he caught her. Now, Betty alone held the key. A key that could lock this man away for a very long time.

As she took the rose in her hand, she plucked a single petal and held it in her palm. “Take it, Thane.”

He did so and let it rest in the center of his own wide palm - a tiny blot of crimson on a vast sea of darkness.

“Do you feel how fragile it is?” she asked him.

Thane nodded. “I could crush it.”

“Yes you could. But, do you see what a loss that would be–to destroy something so beautiful?”

Silence. Both looked down at his hand.

“What I’m saying is, you’re holding something pure, a little petal that’s only a part of the beautiful flower. If you nurture it, it’ll bloom.”

“I see that.” He thought a while and then said, “And

had the rose not been cut, then it would have become an even more lovely rose bush. It would've blossomed year on year. Once cut down, yes…its beauty is there for the eye to see, but in time it will wilt and die."

"That's right, Thane. You can crush something beautiful or you can nurture and love it…and if you do, then you'll be rewarded a thousand times more."

"When did you get to be so wise, love?" His mouth pulled up into a wide smile that radiated to his eyes, firing up that gold again. *There it is.*

"Not all hookers are fucking retards," she replied on a smirk.

"Mouth."

"Oh, I'm sorry. Kidnapping charges?" She suppressed a grin. Why was she so happy all of a sudden? Crazy but true.

"Freya," Thane growled a warning.

"Lighten up, Thane. I'm not scared of you any more."

"Is that so?" The corner of his lips tugged up in amusement in spite of his eyebrows pinching together.

"That is so," she stated and sniffed the rose.

"Hmm. I see the sass is back." He arched a brow.

"Oh trust me, it never left and you'll be seeing a whole new level of sass," she grinned wide now. "Call it guaranteed sassisfaction."

"Sassisfaction? That's not even a word," he scoffed.

"Whatever."

"You 'whatevered' me?"

"I did."

"Be careful Freya."

Lowering the rose, Betty sat forward until her mouth was close to his. "Shut up and kiss me," she demanded.

"I mean gentle, not all freaky monster style. A real kiss."

"I don't know how to be–" he dropped his gaze "–different to how I am. I could hurt you, hurt you really bad. Fuck you up even more than you are."

Betty replied on a whisper. "But you could try. I mean, my life is so screwed up anyway. I have no-one, just the baby. You. Boy…"

Thane hesitated on a sharp inhale and the hint of a snarl before meeting her lips with his own. Lingering, he kissed her slow and deep. He kissed her like he'd never kissed this way before, almost like he was nervous and with a reverence that Betty had never experienced in her life. And for the first time ever she felt needed, loved, even in his insane fucked up way.

At peace almost.

It was the uniting of the hunter and his prey in an unlikely tryst and, you know what? It could just work or the hunter could eat her alive. Time would tell if the risk paid off.

New Dawn

Three years later
Freya

"Ashes to ashes, dust to dust."

Opening her fist, Betty released the small handful of soil so that it scattered on to the casket nestled in the grave at her feet. Beside her stood Thane and between them both, a small scrap of a girl in a navy wool dress with chocolate curls and a pink rose held fast in a chubby hand.

"Let it go, sweetheart," Betty urged with a sad smile.

"No, I kweep it. It's pwitty."

"Let her keep it." Thane ruffled the child's curls. He was such a push-over when it came to their daughter.

Thane reached out his mighty fist and uncurled his fingers until all of the soil pitter-pattered onto the casket too.

Syn stepped forward with a rustle of black taffeta. "I miss you kiddo." The single pink rose in her gloved hand was tossed into the grave.

At the far side of the graveyard, beneath a bony tree, stood a woman in black. Luna. Betty saw her and raised a palm in a silent wave. The woman hesitated then turned and slipped into shadows. She had loved Boy as dearly as they all had loved him. That he'd clung to life way longer than the doctor's had dared hope was a blessing that in some way lessened the devastation they felt at his loss now. Last week, while Thane had been overseeing his new women's refuge in the city, Luna had visited Boy on the beach to say her own goodbye. It was shortly before his body slowed down and down in a steady decline until finally he'd drifted away in a last sleep under a rug and a prayer and a wide blue sky.

"Okay?" Thane snapped Betty's attention back to the graveside. He'd known that this was especially hard for her. She had grown to love Boy almost as a brother, not like Cody but different.

Betty looked up at his face which was etched with concern. "I've leant," she said, "that it's better to have loved someone even for a short time than never to have known them, even if it breaks your heart to let them go."

Bringing her hand to his lips, Thane brushed a kiss over her knuckles. "So wise, love, so wise."

"I'm grateful to have loved Boy," she whispered.

"And I," he replied.

With a happy squeal, the little girl ran over the sand toward the sea, mommy close behind. With a shriek of delight, the little one jumped into Betty's arms, puckered up and pressed a kiss to her tan cheek.

"Come on, time for your nap." Syn was close behind, always the clucking mother hen. She'd proven to be a loyal friend to Betty, not at all the scary dominant force that she'd first taken her for. Taking the child, Syn smudged the child's button nose and winked at Betty.

Two strong arms folded around Betty's waist. With a contented smile, she covered Thane's hands with her own and leant back into his chest as the two marvelled at their little miracle.

"She has her mother's spirit," quipped Thane.

"And her father's temper."

Thane chuckled. "She's the best of us both."

"Yes she is."

"Vaetta."

"Hope."

"She is our hope. Our light."

"Vaetta Kim. It was the perfect name."

Turning to face Thane, Betty placed her palms on his firm chest and tilted up her face until her lips brushed his. With a small groan Thane's lips parted to give access to her tongue as it swept over his in a deepening, tender kiss. Her body reacted instantly as the two joined in a connection that transcended the ordinary. No-one but her would understand why she didn't betray him. Betty knew. She understood that this man was broken, a lost boy not so very different to herself and maybe she could heal him, or maybe he'd destroy her in the end, but right now she was his. She was Freya.

A note from me to you

I based this book on my earlier novellas, The Muse Keeper series. Using them as a starting point, I rewrote them, changed a great deal of the story and added 20,000 more words where I felt the points of view needed to be fleshed out. It has been a tremendous challenge to write.

I don't condone the violence or non-consensual rape that was portrayed within this story and found it gruelling to write–an often emotional journey for me and one in which I had to overcome my own views and values in order to express those of my story people. However, story-telling is, in my view, an expression of one's imagination. Not all paths taken have been comfortable, but this book has been fun to write.

This story contains triggers and so, if you have been affected by something in the story, please talk to someone and know you're not alone.

Much love,
Janey x

If you enjoyed reading 'Thane,' please share on social media and leave a review. A review is life-blood to an author. Also, why not connect with Janey Rosen on Twitter @JaneyRosen or 'like' her page on Facebook www.facebook.com/janeyrosen Tell Janey what you thought of Thane, of Betty, Syn, Luna or poor Boy. Pick up a copy of her other books including the No.1 bestselling *The Sebastian Trilogy* and sequel, *Penmorrow*.

20575771R00162

Printed in Great Britain
by Amazon